Hitting the Send Button

Anna Goodwin McCarthy

ISBN-10: 0692457100
ISBN-13: 978-0692457108

DEDICATION

For my family, friends and teachers who always supported my dream.

Hitting the Send Button

1 THE BLACK AND WHITE OF MY SOUL

My words were under her coffee cup, a creamer leaking on the black and white of my soul.

I may be exaggerating, but isn't that what all good writers do? We exaggerate the mundane to make life interesting.

As I waited for my usual, a toasted bagel with cream cheese and a hot chocolate at the Pemberley Deli & Bistro, I glanced at my phone and saw the typical messages that collected in my inbox everyday.

Raindrops slid down the window like tiny streams. My focus turned to one as it hung for all its life to the glass before finally plopping onto the sidewalk. When I was a child I would have placed my fingertip on the cool glass and traced the path of the drops, but I refrained from doing that now because I am a 30-year-old woman. There are certain things a 30-year-old woman does not do, and that is one of them.

The woman giggled, coming dangerously close to knocking over her coffee on the newspaper. I wanted to spring up from my table by the window and rescue my article from its inevitable doom, giving it a chance to be in other people's hands before it hit the recycle bin reeking of café mocha.

It was not in my personality to cause a scene. As a matter of fact, I avoided conflict with every ounce of my being. It made me nauseous to my stomach. Ever since my surgery I had taken a new carpe diem approach to life, but assertive aggressiveness was still something I had yet to accomplish.

I placed my ear buds in my ears and began to search for something on my playlist to drown out the noise from the nearby table.

My eyes kept drifting to the couple. They were too happy, too early. This was definitely the beginning of a relationship.

Your heart beats so loudly it echoes in your ears with the promise of a lasting love that is unmarred by reality with its newness perpetuating the seemingly deceptive thought that the feeling will never change or alter with time.

It was similar to how I felt when I walked to the blue newspaper box, inserted a couple of coins and pulled out a paper with my first byline in years.

I had not picked up the pen since I interned at a newspaper during college, returning home and settling into small town life after I accepted a position in public relations with a non-profit organization.

I was contributing to the good of society by aiding the organization in its efforts. However, with the progression of each year, it felt like every day would dissolve into another, my life playing a broken record of routine. Often I found solace in reading novels, escaping my own reality. Although, I was reading other people's words when I wanted to write my own.

When I saw my name in all caps under a headline, it felt as if everything had meaning again. I was on my destined path, and it forced me to consider a new career.

It had been six weeks since I turned in my resignation and began working with the newspaper full-time. The decrease in salary meant moving into the apartment that was over my parents' garage adjacent to their two-story home in the historic district of a picturesque North Carolina coastal town. I made a small flower and herb garden on the stairs and deck that led up to my door. I walked or rode my bike to the newspaper office whenever they needed me to come in, but most of the time I emailed my stories to the editor. It was a refreshing change and a freedom I had not been accustomed to on a daily basis.

My ultimate goal was to write a novel, but the newspaper was a start in getting acclimated to the water before I began swimming in the deep end. It was instant gratification. I did not have to wait through a series of edits and rewrites that often accompanies writing a novel. The product was consumed by the public and discarded each day in the aforementioned recycle bin.

Occasionally, I would cover a city council meeting or the opening of a new business, but it was my features in the lifestyles section that had become my favorite assignments when they crossed my inbox. I covered community events and highlighted the lives of individuals. People invited me into their homes, offices and studios, but sometimes we would chat over the phone. Everyone had a story that was their own personal narrative of life.

The local mailman backpacked in Europe and was a roadie for a famous band before becoming the clean shaven community helper who delivered our mail. Now I recognized that familiar tune he whistled as he waved every afternoon when he made his rounds. It was these conversations that I had with people that helped drive my creative spirit to write.

A perfectly manicured hand moved up and down before my eyes, and I pulled out my ear buds.

"Hey, Lennon. I guess you did not hear me with that blasting in your ears."

"I was trying to deafen the sound of new love."

She ignored my ambiguous statement since I was the only customer now in the café.

"What ya doing this Thursday, Sis?"

This was a loaded question. My older sister by two years, Quinn, was a stay-at-home super mom. I am not being facetious. My sister is truly a remarkable woman making life perfect for her family on a daily basis. Her husband, Jack, is an attorney and had essentially inherited his father's firm. They have two Golden Retrievers, Sally and Sam, and the most adorable child in the universe, Ralph, who stole my heart the day he was born.

If it was just Ralphie she was going to ask me to take care of that would be fine, but Quinn often had another duty that even Mother Teresa would shy away from. Mrs. Olivia Gray, her mother-in-law, lived next door and was a constant source of polite tyranny. Quinn waited on the spoiled woman hand and foot.

"I am sorry. I have a deadline and a doctor's appointment."

"Olivia is on a day trip with her book club. It's only Ralphie you will have to watch Thursday. I will prepare some of my vegetarian lasagna, and you can warm it up in the oven. I know it is your favorite."

Quinn hardly ever allows carbs in her kitchen, so this really must be important for her to break her dietary rules.

"Well, ok. I might be a little late. I never know how long I will have to wait at the doctor's office."

"No problem. Ralph has karate lessons at the gym. Tara will be there with her daughter, and she will watch

4

him until you can pick him up. If you run later than the karate lesson, she will take him home with her and you can pick him up there. I will give you her cell number so you can text her."

I silently prayed my doctor's appointment did not run overtime so I did not have to go to Tara's house to pick up Ralphie. I doubted she would even open the door if she saw me through the peephole on the other side.

Tara's husband, Steve, is a partner at Jack's law firm. We went on a couple of double dates with Quinn and Jack before he started seeing Tara five years ago. The snooze fest of a man-boy kept encouraging me to drink shots "to loosen me up" when I found his jokes and incessant talk about himself and his adult soccer league maddening.

Tara got wind of our meaningless dates from another viper in the social club of wives, and you would think I had an affair with the beer bloated Neanderthal.

"Tara hates me."

"I am truly sorry, but someone had to watch Ralphie at karate practice and she volunteered. She is nice if you just talk to her."

"Yeah, right. I think she put a curse on me during your housewarming party last month. I swear I saw her cross her fingers and blink her eyes at me across the room. The next day my phone would not work, my contact lens tore, I got a cramp on the treadmill and the person I was supposed to interview was a no show."

"Thanks, Lennon. I knew I could count on you. You are the best sister in the world," she said, texting me the evil witch's cell number.

* * * * *

"Lennon Tyler," said a nurse with flower patterned scrubs, holding a clip board in her hand. After a two hour wait in a waiting room full of anxious people, the enthusiasm I displayed at the sound of my name was how I envisioned people acting when bingo was called. I grabbed my handbag and quickly followed the nurse.

"Step on the scales."

She looked down at the paper. "You have lost weight since we last saw you."

"I call it my Cinderella Diet. I eliminated all sodas and no meals after 7 p.m., or I return to my round orange pumpkin status."

"I'll have to try that. You look good."

"Follow me to Room 5. I will take your temperature, blood pressure and ask you a few questions. Then you can get undressed, and he will be right in."

The gown was a sad large piece of faded cloth worn undoubtedly by hundreds of patients before me, but it did have a pleasant floral scent from a strong discount detergent I recognized from the grocery store aisle.

I waited and waited swinging my naked legs back and forth in my XXXL gown as a tiny radio on the counter played classic rock music until there was a knock at the door, and a tall man bustled through in aquamarine scrubs and a white lab coat.

He looked up at me, absentmindedly closing the door on his nurse who was following behind him. She pushed it open with her large arms and continued into the room like a shorter, wider shadow.

He shook his head in disbelief.

"You look...," he glanced down at the computer screen at my photograph.

He gazed back up at me for a few seconds in stunned silence.

I smiled knowing this was truly the first time he had ever seen me when I actually looked attractive and felt well.

"You definitely need a new photo. Tell them to take

another one before you leave."

As if to defend my dreadful appearance in the picture the nurse explained, "She had surgery the week when we took that photo. Of course, she looks better now."

He ignored her comment and leaned against the wall. "How have you been feeling? Any changes in your health?"

"I still have some occasional pain. Although, I have been exercising which helps."

"Exercise is always good."

He moved toward me and instructed, "Lie back. I am going to press down. Let me know if you feel any discomfort."

My face crumpled into a crinkled paper lunch bag of a frown, and I let out a most unattractive curse that I am sure the waiting room full of people could hear echoing down the hall.

"You may feel pain from the scar tissue."

A tear began to fall down my cheek. I immediately swiped it with my hand so he could not see. I felt like showing my pain was a form of weakness that I did not want to share.

"Just breathe."

I reluctantly let my head fall onto the stiff pillow and began the breathing method I practiced in yoga class. I closed my eyes and blindly reached for the sides of the examining table hoping to grasp something to bear down on while he continued the examination.

I felt a hand patting mine, like a grandparent would attempt to comfort and calm a crying child. I thought it was the nurse, but as I turned my head to the side I saw she was on the other side of the room. I lifted my head, and Dr. Kent was patting my hand with an uninhibited compassion that I had not witnessed from other health care professionals.

Seeing my puzzled face, the nurse cleared her throat

getting the doctor's attention.

He stopped patting my hand, and began to review my records on the computer.

"I think the pain will go away in time. Let's make another appointment soon to make sure."

He saw my distraught face and said, "There is nothing to be concerned about right now."

While the nurse began to prepare the room for the next patient, Dr. Kent continued typing on the keyboard to update today's visit, and I sat up and caught a glimpse of my photo which was admittedly pretty scary.

"Dr. Kent, did you receive my phone message I left with your secretary? I write for the newspaper, and I would love to feature you."

His head lifted from the screen and paused.

"I have read your work in the paper. I did not know that L. Tyler was you. You are a journalist?"

Before I could reply he continued.

"I always wanted to write a book. I have this idea for a children's book series with the characters traveling in time and learning about history."

"I can help you write it."

Did I just say those words? I wished I could swallow them back down with one big gulp like the putrid generic cherry cough syrup I always took when I got a cold. He had not asked for my help. I waited for him to laugh and turn down my offer.

But he did not flinch. He proceeded to talk about ideas he had for other books, short stories and characters. His imagination was unyielding and surprising for a man of science.

All I could see were his big brown eyes that danced as he spoke and his long legs stretched out in front of him.

Is this what guys do when women talk about shopping or work? It was like I was hearing his words, but my mind was somewhere else.

His lips kept moving as his long, strong fingers gestured in front of him.

"I am sending your prescription to your pharmacy for an acid blocking medication for an ulcer that may be forming. The aspirin you took for your appendicitis pain may be the culprit. If you do this, the symptoms you are experiencing will eventually be alleviated with time."

How much did I miss while I lost focus in the deep depths of his dark eyes?

"I will see you soon," he said, closing the door behind him.

Was he talking about my next appointment, or were we meeting to write? Who knows?

My brain went into overdrive. What was happening to me? Was this some kind of Knight in Shining Armour Syndrome? Was I attracted to him because he saved my life?

He was tall with an athletic build, intelligent, blond wavy hair, dreamy eyes that I would never say no to and a kind smile. Evidently he liked me, so what if I liked him?

And then I remembered like a punch in the face in the boxing ring with the monstrous green Incredible Hulk of reality....he's married.

2 A SECOND CHANCE TO LIVE

"**H**e's good looking, but he is married with kids," said the emergency room nurse with bleached white highlights on dark black hair that made her look like a skunk. "If you care about that sort of thing."

If I was not suffering immensely in excruciating pain on a bed with wheels and scratchy white sheets while my insides felt like they were being slowly torn from my core, I might have replied sassily with, "When I asked you who the surgeon on call was, I was not looking for a date. I wanted to know what kind of doctor he is since I am clearly dying."

My eyes drifted down at myself taking in a pitiful sight. A pair of comfortable black tennis shoes that had been on my feet were now in a plastic chair by the door, my long hair was scattered over the pillow like a mess of dark black spider webs and not a stitch of makeup remained on my face under thick glasses. My attire consisted of a paisley red and black turtleneck and gray polyester elastic waistband slacks covering legs that had not been shaven in a while. It was an outfit a 70-year-old would refuse to wear much less a 30-year-old who had been told in the past that she could be a model before she had given in to mediocrity and the old maid stereotype.

The expression on the nurse's face as she glanced at me again before leaving the room seemed to say, "This is not an individual that would care about a handsome doctor, and he certainly would not look two seconds at her. No competition here."

She was probably reapplying her lip gloss at that very moment in preparation for the arrival of the medical Adonis.

My parents and I had eaten at a seafood restaurant earlier that night and were watching the Tar Heels slam dunk a win over Duke at their house when I had fallen on the floor in extreme pain gripping my abdomen as if I had been stabbed in the gut. They called an ambulance, and when the paramedics arrived I kept repeating that it was probably only food poisoning, but they all knew if it was food poisoning I would be able to get off the floor. I could not budge.

After a CT scan the emergency room physician came in my room and told me I had appendicitis, and the surgeon on call would be coming in to take over my case.

I was calmed by the immediate thought that this was something that could be fixed. It was not uncommon. But then I recalled, as if my mind was a slow computer finally completing a keyword search of previous conversations, my parents talking about a distant relative who had an appendectomy and later died of cancer.

"He was so young," I remembered them saying.

"Could it be cancer?" I asked, willing the doctor in my mind to deny my fears with a flat, "No."

"Yes," the emergency room doctor said in a nonchalant and disconnected tone. "Dr. Kent will talk to you about that when he gets in."

I was dazed and in tremendous pain, and his words

sounded unreal as if he was speaking to another person. "Game Over, Game Over" flashed in my head like a video game screen of life.

It seemed like a decade before a man entered the room. I was expecting a gorgeous man after the nurse's description, but he seemed quite ordinary like a guy I might see jogging in the park or at the beach with a surfboard in his hands.

"Do I know you?" were the first words out of his mouth.

As a doctor in a small town he probably phrased this question at each meeting in an effort to avoid offending someone he previously met in a social setting or who was his patient.

"No."

"I am Dr. Kent, and it says here you are Lennon Tyler."

"Lennon as in John. My parents were big fans."

He told me he had some patients who were preparing to go into surgery, he was going to monitor my progress and he would decide what the next step would be soon.

It was the longest hour of my life as the pain ripped through my body like a rusty unsharpened machete. He came into the room saying the antibiotics the ER doctor administered did not work as previously hoped, and they would have to operate.

If I could have run out of the room and hopped in my car I would have in mere seconds. I never had the chickenpox or a sprained ankle, so the thought of going under the knife was terrifying. The paralyzing pain numbed my thoughts as I was wheeled into the operating room. I did not even cry, because every inch of my body was screaming in pain for me. I knew that I most definitely was going to die.

However, when I woke up from the surgery the nurse told me they had to remove my appendix, but I was going to be fine.

The moment four days after my emergency surgery when I entered Dr. Kent's office guided by my mother and sister in a blur of pain pills and shock, I was ready for the words that would change my life forever. My parents said after the surgery, while I was in the recovery room, Dr. Kent told them there was a chance that I may have appendiceal cancer. He found what he thought may be a tumor and was sending the tumor tissue to the lab to be tested.

The receptionist said all new patients had to take a photo and she instructed me to smile as she snapped my picture for my medical records, but smiling was the last thing I could do.

It was Friday, May 13, and I knew he was going to say, "Lennon, you have cancer."

But instead when I entered the room, the nurse did not have the results saying they were not sent by the lab. Dr. Kent insisted they find the results, annoyed at the nurse's excuse. Apparently they had been sent over, and she was not looking at the correct screen on the computer. He quickly scrolled down and found the results.

"Good news, Lennon. You don't have cancer."

The obvious reaction would be to jump for joy, but I sat there like a zombie while my mind was filled with images of the past, present and future.

It was at that very moment that I had a life changing experience. I had been given a second chance, and I was going to take advantage of the gift I had been given. What did I want to do most in the world?

I needed a pen and paper. I wanted to write what I was experiencing. I knew I would walk down to the editor's office of the local newspaper as soon as I was well, and I was going to write again. There was no doubt my path had been set.

My mother's face was full of joy and relief as she hugged the doctor and nurse after hearing the good news.

"Thank you, Dr. Kent," I managed to say the words, although my brain was somewhere else entirely.

I peeked down at my physical presence and realized I also needed to start caring about myself again.

"I think I am going to start exercising. When can I start exercising?"

Dr. Kent smirked and let out a half laugh scanning my out of shape form. "What exactly are you going to do?"

And then I knew I was going to exercise and get back into fighting form, and the next time this joker saw me he would be smiling alright.

And he did.

3 IS THAT AN 'S' ON YOUR CHEST?

Ralphie was a cutie pie in his little white outfit sitting on the floor pulling on his Superman Velcro sneakers.

Tara, the queen of multi-tasking, was busily smoothing down her daughter's hair, tying her shoes and talking to the mother beside her. I know she saw me standing there, but she would not acknowledge me. I was surprised she did not put the keys on the floor and kick them behind her so she did not have to turn my way.

The women were all gathered by the tables that overlooked the indoor pool. There was a glass wall separating the pool from the lobby area, but I could still smell the chlorine.

All the women's heads turned when a gorgeous guy with thick black hair and piercing blue eyes exited the strength training class with a gym bag over his shoulder.

Tara dropped the brush in her hand and it skidded on the floor towards him. He reached down and returned it to her with a killer smile. Tara blushed bright red and stood frozen with the brush in her hand. Watching this was better than eating chocolate served by Johnny Depp on a tropical island. The next time she humiliated me in a social setting I would remember this exact foolish look on her face and laugh.

I inched forward unable to keep my eyes off the train wreck with Ralphie by my side tugging at my hand. I approached the group of entranced women, and the man looked in my direction and waved. I immediately flipped my head behind me to see who he was greeting, but there was no one there. Now I was as bright lobster red as Tara. I managed to lift up my hand for the belated wave, but he was already talking to another mom.

High school insecurity washed over me like a tidal wave of braces and awkward moments.

The guy finally made his way through the group of admirers leaving them whispering excitedly amongst themselves. He had the kind of features people sought in plastic surgeons' offices. With strong cheekbones and an awesome physique he was a JFK Jr. look-alike with a faint resemblance to a superhero.

Tara would never break off her conversation now to give me the keys.

"Does your mom have a spare key hidden somewhere?"

"I don't know."

Ralphie shrugged his arms and held up his hands.

Tara actually peered through me, because I am the incredible invisible woman.

"Hi, Tara…," I began.

But she turned back to the group and held up a key ring on her finger which she extended behind her.

"Thank you, Tara. Quinn appreciates it," I said loudly enough so she and the others could hear.

"Well, Ralphie. I think we deserve a big hamburger and french fries."

"With chocolate milk, please."

"Of course, my little man. You would not be my nephew if you didn't like chocolate."

I would save Quinn's veggie lasagna for tomorrow.

After our trip through the drive-thru and a brief stop to feed the ducks at a quaint park, we made our way to my sister's house. Their home was absolutely exquisite. It was a two-story brick structure with a large wrap around porch and various geometrically patterned windows that offered unbelievable views of the river. It took over two years to construct. They moved in a couple of months ago, but it still had that new quality that made you want to take off your shoes at the door and not leave any fingerprints, a dust cloth close beside you to correct any marks you made on the hardwood floors, granite countertops and mahogany furniture.

Ralphie and I set on the porch swing and read a handful of books as the sun set on the glistening river like diamonds had been poured from a hole in the clouds onto its rippling surface. Sally and Sam napped at our feet listening to my voice as I read about pirates and magical ships under a rainbow of cotton candy. We did not go inside until the lightning bugs produced a mini fireworks display in the air of neon green flashes and the bugs starting singing their Bob Marley tunes that only the bugs on our river can belt out during the humid months of summer.

I put Ralphie in bed with his circus nightlight and favorite stuffed animal.

I tiptoed into the kitchen. Everything in the house was either brand new or incredibly old antiques that Jack had inherited from his family. I loved the older furniture. I wished I could interview it, because I knew each loveseat, buffet, wall hanging and side table had an interesting story to tell.

Their home was a space that would easily fit in an interior design magazine. However, when I noticed there were dishes in the sink my head did a double take. There were never dishes in the sink here or at their former home. While I preferred the soak, wait till I get time to scrub it method, as soon as a dish was dirty Quinn rinsed it and placed it in the dishwasher.

I began to search the room for signs of burglars or misfits who would dare enter Quinn's house and leave two wine glasses and a plate in the sink. Maybe she was simply in a hurry. I decided to wash the dishes myself. Before I commenced the ritual I so disliked, I pressed the power button on Quinn's wireless speaker which had her music on deck. As I turned on the music adjusting the volume so I did not wake Ralphie, I began to ponder why the Palmolive lady was always so happy when I used to watch the television commercials as a child.

A musical group I had never heard of came on as I rinsed the glass. It had a nice, soothing sound with a female voice and a jazzy reggae mix. I liked it, but this was not Quinn and Jack. Jack was all Dave Matthews and Quinn's taste was whatever Jack wanted. She would turn on the occasional pop song on the Top 40 station and sing along in the car, but I never heard her listen to anything this out of the ordinary.

4 HITTING THE SEND BUTTON

When Jack and Quinn came home, I was watching Jimmy Fallon sing a song on *The Tonight Show*.

"Hey, Jack."

I thought Jack would stop and say hello, but he walked right past me to their bedroom, slamming the door so loudly I hoped Ralphie did not wake up. I walked over to his door and peeped in, but the kiddo was still snoring those little grunting noises children make which I affectionately compare to small piglets.

I returned to the sofa. This was not good. My imagination started spinning. Maybe the wine glasses in the sink belonged to Jack and his receptionist. I distrusted her demeanor when she interacted with Jack. She seemed too nice and eager to please.

No wonder Quinn wanted me to stay with Ralphie tonight. She was trying to salvage her marriage.

Quinn wearily traipsed in with glassy eyes and the red splotches that always appeared on her cheeks when she cried.

"What did that idiot do?"

"Nothing."

"Yeah, right. I am gonna kill him."

"Lennon, he did not do anything."

"What's wrong? Are you sick? Is he sick? Tell me."

She peered down the hallway at the two closed bedroom doors.

"How is Ralphie?"

"He is fine. We read a million stories, and he is dreaming of candy coated ships sailing on pink lemonade seas in faraway lands."

She slumped over the back of the couch and tears began to fall. I went over to her and hugged her.

"Let's go sit on the pier. I can't talk here."

Her thin body shook as we walked down the pier and set in the two Adirondack chairs. The moon was dancing on the river casting a spell over us, silencing her sobbing.

I was quiet until she began to talk.

"It's me. I am the idiot."

I was puzzled. What was Quinn saying?

"I am the one at fault."

"There are always two sides to a story, possibly three and maybe four, Quinn."

I was careful not to say Jack is not perfect, because with all couples anything you say to a friend or family member who confides in you during a fight is always in the back of their minds when they reconcile.

"He will never forgive me."

"What could you have possibly done? Did you not buy the right tie to match his boring suit, did you forget to pay his golf club dues or was your pasta primavera too garlicky?"

"I had an affair."

I wanted to shout an expletive and jump into the river fully dressed. That was the last thing I would have ever thought would come out of the mouth of my caring, church going sister whose worst sin to this day had been...oh, I could not think of a single sin.

"I am sorry. Did you say something was not fair?"

"No, Lennon. I had an affair with another man."

"Well, we are all human. Did I tell you I am in love with my married doctor?"

"Be serious, Lennon. I need someone I can talk to."

"I am serious. I don't know what came over me. I didn't even find him attractive when I first met him at the hospital. You know I have never really liked blond guys since Bradley Van in the tenth grade. It must be my hormones. He was talking to me today, and I had to muster every muscle in my body to stop from jumping in his lap and ripping off his scrubs."

She began to laugh.

"You know everybody has that same fantasy about Dr. Kent. All the women have adoring googly eyes at him during our board meetings for the homeless shelter. I even heard 85-year-old Vera Milton in Olivia's bridge club talk about the handsome younger doctor she was going to who gave her a hug before he left the room after her checkup. You would think he had ravaged her with kisses by the way she described him."

We both erupted into a fit of silly giggles.

She grabbed my hand.

"Thank you for not telling me I am the worst person in the world."

"I would never tell you that even if you slept with all the men in town between the ages of 25 and 50."

A shocked expression was on Quinn's face in the moonlight.

"I didn't sleep with Drew."

"What? I don't understand. You said you had an affair, and when you say Drew you don't mean your Drew do you?"

"We did not sleep together," she repeated.

"Then what did you do with the man you loved since

21

you were 13 years old and he rescued you from the big wave that knocked you on your bottom at Nags Head?"

"It has only been online."

"What? Quinn, you hardly even use any social media."

"I know this sounds weird, but I got an email from him. He said he got my email address from the list of board contacts on the homeless shelter's website. He is an attorney in Raleigh, and he was doing research for a similar organization and saw my photograph volunteering with last year's holiday donations."

Did Quinn really believe this baloney? I would bet my life that Drew did a computer search of Quinn until he found her email address and made up this story, but I am not in the habit of bursting bubbles so I kept my full lips pressed together.

"We started emailing. He would tell me about his daughter making the basketball team, and I would share how Ralphie lost his first tooth on my organic gluten-free biscuits. It was all innocent."

"When did it start not being innocent?"

"He would tell me about something that was bothering him at work, and I would share how Olivia is driving me crazy."

Hold on. Stop the presses. Quinn does not complain. She never told me anything negative about having to wait on her mother-in-law.

"You began to confide in him."

"Yes. And I began to get used to seeing his name appear on my cell phone. If it didn't appear in a couple of days, I would get upset thinking he had lost interest. Gosh, I even began to get jealous thinking he found someone else to email. I never get jealous. I mean I don't get jealous when Jack's client's wife, the 'been with everybody in town' Mrs. Colin, completely ignores me standing right beside him and asks Jack to meet her for a business dinner every single time we have to attend one of their parties. Drew is married, too, but I was not jealous or envious of his wife. Why was I jealous of a nonexistent person who may or may not be emailing Drew? It is all so confusing."

"You didn't want to be his wife, and he didn't want to be your husband. You guys were just having fun, a pre-midlife crisis," I said, stating the facts.

"Possibly. I thought I was boring him, so I started to flirt."

I had to look at her again. It was like my sister was transforming before my eyes.

"And he flirted back."

"No details, please. Don't tell me he asked you to do any weird stuff. I can see where this is going, and I have to sleep at some point tonight."

"It was not dirty. It was actually quite lovely," she paused, her eyes staring lost in thought. "We talked about our summers growing up in Nags Head, about how it would feel to walk under the stars together and feel the ocean's waves again—how it would feel if we met at some hotel and woke up to a glistening sea."

"Stop. Right. There. You didn't meet him, did you?"

"Of course not," she said, as she twisted her hands and massaged her temples trying to stop an impending migraine. "But I wanted to."

"I found a hotel and everything, but he did not email me back."

"He told me he was old enough to know how to avoid trouble in his life," she said, beginning to cry again with these words.

"Was that all I meant to him, trouble?"

"You are not trouble, Quinn. But you have to see he was right. You could not have a one night stand with Drew like a girl he may pick up in a bar. You let yourself feel too much, and you have too much history with him."

The entire situation was the definition of "trouble," but again I held back my words. I was getting pretty good at this as the night went on.

"I am assuming you told Jack about Drew's emails tonight from the way he came into the house."

"No, he found my emails."

"Are you crazy? Why didn't you delete them? Have you learned nothing from all the political affairs and cable news outlets?"

"I don't know why I did not trash them. I am not ignorant, Lennon. I just wanted proof that whatever was happening with Drew existed, that someone cared about me."

"Come here."

I began to rock her in my arms as the water lapped against the pier until we both fell asleep.

I don't know what time Quinn woke up, but the sunrise on the river was my alarm clock. A steaming mug of hot chocolate and a slightly burnt to perfection bagel with cream cheese was on the table beside me.

Last night had to be a nightmare. My sister could not be embedded in this emotional hurricane that was bound to hurt someone she loved.

I went directly to the driveway, avoiding the house, knowing the family needed their space. I ran a hand through my tangled locks and hoped my lipstick had vanished and not bled down my chin creating a psycho clown effect.

Jogging near the house, a man waved his hand, and I wanted to run for cover like torpedoes were coming at me on the battlefield. I needed a place to hide my scary morning face and wrinkled attire.

Oh no, no. The JFK Jr. look-alike was coming towards me. Of all times to look like warmed over meat loaf. Did I smell like the river? Maybe the hot chocolate had permeated my skin with sweetness. DOUBTFUL. At least it would somewhat camouflage morning breath.

"Hi, my name is Clark. I think we met the other day at the gym."

I nodded like a mute idiot. How could he have possibly remembered me in that crowd of women?

"I am staying at a house up the road for a couple of months," he gestured backward with his thumb. "I'm a photographer, and I would like to take some photographs of your home for a coastal magazine I do some freelance work for on occasion. It is such a unique design."

"No," I spat out the word and smiled as if I had just said something interesting and fantastic.

He frowned, "No?"

He clearly was not accustomed to hearing that word from a woman.

My brain cells were quickly disintegrating.

"I mean, no, this is not my house. It belongs to my sister, Quinn, and her husband, Jack. I am Lennon Tyler."

"Whew, I thought I had lost my touch," he said, wiping fake perspiration from his forehead.

The statement would sound arrogant coming from some men, but when Clark said the words it only gave off a sincere vibe.

"I have to go. Can you give your sister my card?"

He placed it in my palm sending tingles down my spine and was out of sight before I unlocked my car door.

Another good looking man with an email address—I tucked the card in my pocket, fully aware that this was not the best time to give his card to Quinn.

I had to go home and take a quick shower before biking over to the baseball field for an interview with a volunteer baseball coach who spent one year in the minor leagues before becoming an accountant.

* * * * *

"How was your interview today?"

My father was weeding a flower bed by the mailbox as I stopped my bike in the driveway.

"He showed me how to hold a bat, and my hands vibrated as the aluminum hit directly with his guided pitch. It would have gone over the fence, but for some reason it just hovered above my head and landed with a thud in the mud beside my foot."

"My daughter, the jock."

"You are so fun-E, Dad."

"How was everything at Quinn's last night? Your mother told me Quinn said you spent the night."

I had to be very careful with my words. My father was a retired high school history teacher. He had seen his share of B.S., so the least said the better.

"Oh, I just fell asleep watching Jimmy Fallon. They did not have the heart to wake a drooling Lennon," I said.

It was somewhat true.

He chuckled and continued working in his flowers, snapping the orange and yellow balls of sunshine from the marigolds.

I hated lying to my father, but it was not my story to tell. What was I going to say? Your daughter is having an email affair with Drew. You remember him. He was the lifeguard who saved her life when we were teenagers at the beach. She was infatuated with him for two summers in a row. She wants to throw her entire marriage away for a one night stand with a man she has not seen in 25 years.

I walked up my steps, pausing to say hello to the tiny toad I affectionately named Bill who made one of my clay flower pots his home.

The next morning I turned on my laptop and was about to start writing my lead, but the words refused to flow seamlessly. I decided to browse the Internet, and I searched for Drew's latest photograph on his Raleigh law firm's website. It took about two seconds. He still had those dimples I recollected from years ago and a few added wrinkles, but nothing about his eyes said home wrecker.

He had stolen all the girls' hearts in his cool sunglasses and red lifeguard shorts on the beach those many years ago. Quinn turned her back on the waves, something we had always been told never to do, and she was pulled under. Drew rescued her from the rip current, and a small crowd had erupted in applause. From then on, he would wave as we came to the beach. He stopped one late afternoon after he got off duty and asked Quinn what book she was reading. They started talking and every afternoon after he finished his lifeguard duty they would take a long walk and talk. I don't think it ever amounted to anything romantic. I knew she loved him, though.

I copied down his email address, but instead of writing him a scathing message I found myself dodging the bullet and instead doing a search about historical figures from North Carolina.

Ever since Dr. Kent brought up his idea, I had been thinking about ways to incorporate the historical aspect into his children's book series.

I composed a lengthy, witty and somewhat humorous email with possible ideas including the brother and sister time traveling to a different state in each book and learning about its history.

I hesitated at the idea of contacting my physician. He was too busy to answer any frivolous email, and he would undoubtedly reply, "Do I know you?"

He would not remember me or our conversation

about novels in the midst of his numerous patients he saw everyday. Am I going to email the handsome doctor who was simply making small talk to pass the time?

I hit the send button.

I typed his name in the search engine box, and it was all there "plain as day" as my grandfather used to say. There is no privacy in this world anymore. Dr. K was on the local boards of the women's shelter, homeless shelter, food pantry, public library and served as a volunteer assistant coach for the high school's tennis and soccer teams. He went on a mission trip with his church to South America. His social media page was plastered with images of him in warm embraces with his wife, family and multitude of friends.

All his good deeds made me exhausted. His intentions about writing were indeed genuine, and I was going to help him. I owed him everything. He saved my life more than he would ever know. He could delete my silly ideas into the trash and not respond if he so chose. The ball was in his court.

Still, there was something about his smile that made my stomach do flips, and before I knew it I was daydreaming about various scenarios involving his soft lips and expert hands. My silly amorous thoughts were interrupted by the ringtone on my cell.

"Let's go workout."

"I need to. I am dreaming about Dr. Kent again, and I think I caught your email disease. I am going to have to go to Olivia's senior bridge club and ask Vera how she gets a hug from the man."

"She probably brings him her famous walnut brownies."

"That is what all those women had in plates and Tupperware in the waiting room—homemade foods and desserts. I regret that all he is getting from me is a check, a thank you and a smile."

The hip hop dance class had already begun when Quinn arrived. I began to worry, but after a quick inspection I saw no red splotches around her eyes. We teased each other and laughed as the music vibrated through the room and we mimicked the instructor's moves that were out of the latest music videos.

When the 60 minutes were up, the instructor said, "We can't run over, the strength training class is next in this room and they flip tractor tires. I don't want to make those guys mad."

Oh, noooooo. Not again. I shuffled over to the mirrored walls and glanced at my face. My foundation from this morning had run in melted streaks, my clothes were soaking with sweat from the workout and this was not my most flattering pair of yoga pants. My guess is I did not emit a pleasant aroma of hot chocolate either.

Even Quinn in her current state of fog noticed my frenzy.

"What's wrong?"

"Nothing, nothing. Is there another way out of here?"

I glanced at the door where I could see a gathering of men and women in top physical fitness waiting to enter.

"Nope. Did you want to stay for the next class?"

"Absolutely not!"

Maybe if I held my head down and kept walking he would not notice me. I followed closely behind Quinn out the door, as if her petite frame would hide me from his view. My eyes checked the faces quickly, but none of them belonged to the photographer.

Excited about my avoidance of another embarrassing meeting, and knowing Quinn might need to talk I suggested we head over to grab an ice cream and take Ralphie to the park. We had burned off enough calories to consume a fat free vanilla cone.

"He should be finished swimming with my friend and her son."

They were sitting at the round tables in the lobby as we rounded the corner.

"Hey, Mom. Aunt Lennon I held my breath for 10 seconds."

"Wow, buddy!"

Quinn was talking to her friend and some other moms when I felt a tap on my shoulder.

"Hey."

I think I jumped back literally.

"Are you ok?"

"Yes."

Except self-esteem left the building, and she was not coming back soon.

"My class is starting. Nice to see you again, Lennon."

At least he remembered my name.

"Who was that?" asked Ralphie.

"That was Clark."

"Clark like Superman?"

"Superman he is, and Wonder Woman I am certainly not."

The park was full of kids. Quinn was coating Ralphie in a third layer of 50 SPF and wiping off the chocolate ice cream from his hands and chin before he ran off to join some friends he recognized on the swings. Their laughter and voices were a symphony of innocence that was highlighted by a brilliant blue sky with enormous white clouds that seemed to touch the trees in the distance.

The benches were full of mothers, fathers, grandmothers and nannies watching their kids play. I knew Quinn wanted some privacy to talk, so we sat down in the grass far away from the ears of those who may be listening.

I plucked an ant off my knee and began using some of Ralphie's sunscreen to keep my pale porcelain skin from turning Pepto-Bismol pink.

"What's going on?"

I knew she wanted to tell me something, but I was going to have to initiate the conversation. We always had an innate knowledge of what the other was feeling. It must be the sisterly bond or the fact that we were so close. I could not relate to siblings who were not friends. We had our disagreements as children and even as adults, but there is not another person on this planet who knows me better.

"Yesterday morning when I woke up on the pier, I wanted to make everything right. I wanted to fix the broken vase of our marriage, so I got out the glue."

She extended her legs in the sun and stretched forward. She was in excellent physical shape, had my father's olive skin that tanned easily, his straight auburn hair and small facial features that were described as angelic. I was the opposite with my mother's ivory skin, thick full lips and eyebrows that on a good day had been compared to the popular 1980s model Brooke Shields and on a bad day a gypsy fortune teller or Oscar the Grouch. Needless to say, my tweezers were my friend.

"What did you do?"

"I woke up early, and I made his favorite breakfast, a quiche with sausage, bacon, spinach, tomatoes and a special cheese I order from the deli."

"He would not even look at me. He calmly walked over to the counter and let the entire dish slide into the garbage bin."

"Ralphie asked him why he threw it away, and he said he did not think he liked quiche anymore which seemed to be a reasonable answer for Ralphie, because he continued eating his cereal and playing with his toy car."

"I knew he wanted to say something, but Ralphie was in the kitchen. Jack would never yell at me in front of Ralphie. His father had not always been kind to his mother when Jack and his sister were growing up, and he told me he would never fight in front of Ralphie."

Quinn was not exaggerating Jack's calm disposition. It was true that I had never seen Jack raise his voice except when his favorite football team blew a play. I sometimes wondered if he was the type who kept everything pent up inside until it all burst out. I am glad to know he really was a good all around guy when it came to temperament.

Not many guys would have taken Quinn's email affair this quietly. However, that was kind of scary, too. He had to let his frustrations out some way. My hope is that he didn't see a fling with his receptionist or a divorcee with a short skirt as a way to come to terms with Quinn's indiscretions, but again I was keeping my mouth shut.

"I thought all day long about what I could do to fix our situation. I took Ralphie over to Mom and Dad's to spend the night for a grandparents' night. I did not tell them the real reason."

"Don't worry, I won't tell them anything. You could have brought him to stay with me in the apartment."

I knew my parents were not ignorant concerning their daughters' actions. They would have to know something was up with me spending the previous night at Quinn's house, and the next night Quinn suggesting Ralphie have a sleepover with them. They always respected our sisterly bond, but if they thought one of us was going to be hurt they would clearly ask the right questions. An interrogation was inevitable. Hopefully, Quinn and Jack would fix this mess before I had to spill their story. It would not be easy telling my parents about Quinn's email affair, because really I did not understand it myself.

"I did not want to bother you."

"Did you guys get a chance to talk?"

"Well, no, not really."

"What did you do then?"

She blushed.

"I was ready to have a long conversation with him, but when he came in from work he ignored me and went to the bathroom to take a shower. I had to do something."

She stopped and looked around her to see if anyone could hear, but no one was close.

"Luckily, I had thought ahead of time to wear the lingerie I had purchased for our anniversary trip to Costa Rica last year but never used because we both got food poisoning."

"I undressed except for my red lacey panties and bra and followed him into the shower."

"Well, that is a way to get his attention. I am guessing he did not ignore you."

"No. He was so passionate, he took me in his arms and kissed me and we did things, lots of things. The water was so intoxicating falling over us. It was the sexiest moment we have ever had in our marriage."

"So, everything is alright now?"

"I think Jack has forgiven me, but it is all still so new."

"How about you? Have you closed your email account for good?"

Her head was focused on the children playing, watching Ralphie as he took his turn on the slide. A tear slid from under her wide sunglasses down her cheek.

"I thought about him."

"What do you mean?"

I was perplexed.

"When I was making love with Jack, I was thinking about Drew."

This was not going to end well, I thought. Numerous movies flashed in my mind of star crossed lovers. I hoped Quinn would wake up before it was too late.

As Quinn drove me back to the gym to fetch my vehicle, my phone buzzed. It was an email from my editor with a story idea. I had come to the realization that Dr. Kent was never going to return my email. I felt like a fool thinking he was serious about writing a book. I did want to thank him for saving my life, and really in the long run it had inspired me to change my life.

It was often easier for me to write my emotions than to communicate them with actual conversation, so I would write him an email that he could not ignore.

From: Lennon Tyler
To: Dr. Dean Kent

Dr. K,

I had fun brainstorming ideas for your children's book series. You really saved my life when you performed the surgery for my appendicitis. That painful and terrifying moment made me realize how brief life can be, so I decided to pick up the pen again. It had been several years since I had written any articles or anything...I had given up on my dream and sunk into the daily routine.

I just wanted to say thanks for giving me back my dream.

Lennon Tyler

5 YOU MADE ME DREAM AGAIN

I was lounging on my purple couch with a massive bowl of popcorn, watching some dramas on television when my phone buzzed. It had only been an hour since I sent the email to Dr. Kent, and I knew it could not be him. I had some regrets sending the gushy email moments after I hit send, and I thought if all was right in the world it would go to his spam folder and never be seen again.

I picked up the phone and the screen email notification read, Dean Kent. I dropped the phone onto the purple cushion like I had pulled it out of the oven. I stared at it like it might bite me with venom. I did not want to read his reply. It had been nice when it was all a fantasy, but this was real. There was another person at the end of this message. How did Quinn do it?

I did a load of laundry, painted my fingernails and gave myself a pedicure with the same color of flattering red.

I glared at the phone, but I could not pick it up. I soaked in a bubble bath and turned up the Black Keys as loud as I could without waking my parents or any neighbors.

I slipped on a well-worn UNC T-shirt and dove under the covers of my antique oak bed with a giant headboard that I cleaned up after locating it in a thrift store for fifty dollars. I tossed and turned, and finally I turned on the lights and retrieved my phone from the sofa.

"You won," I said to the gadget in my hand.

"You wrecked my sister's life, and now you are going to ruin mine."

I clicked on the email.

From: Dr. Dean Kent
To: Lennon Tyler

Thank you for making me dream about all these things once again.

We should get together and we can brainstorm ideas.

Dean

Talk about cryptic. Either it was really simple, or there was another meaning behind the words.

I completed another search of "Dr. Dean Kent" and stared at his distinguished hospital photograph. I concluded it was really simple. The email was a courteous reply. He was telling me he appreciated my email. I knew we would never "get together" to share story ideas. I had a follow-up appointment in a couple of days, and I decided I would not mention our correspondence. It was awkward enough to be wearing a potato sack hospital gown while the man you found attractive examined your body.

I woke up to the buzz of my phone. Numerous news reports said it was unhealthy to sleep near your cell phone, but I had gone to sleep with the phone in my hand staring at the message from Dr. K. The irony is I still found it weird to call him Dean out of respect.

It was a voicemail from Quinn.

"Lennon, who is Clark? Ralphie keeps mentioning Superman, and I am beginning to worry if his imagination has run wild. I hope he has not picked up on my conflict with Jack. Hopefully, it is just a phase. Give me a call."

I still had the man of steel's business card on my kitchen counter. I neglected to share it with Quinn, but I knew she would say yes to Superman taking photographs of her home. He is not the kind of man that is rejected by anyone for anything.

"Hey, Quinn. There is a Superman and he wants to take photographs of your house."

"What? Is everybody trying to drive me crazy this morning?"

"Relax. His name is Clark Vincent. Ralphie met him at the gym after hip hop class with me. He said he is staying at a house on your street, and he wants to take photographs of your home for some freelance gig he has at a magazine."

"Lennon, that sounds pretty shady. He could be a serial killer or something. I can't just allow anyone into my home who claims to be a photographer."

"He sent Tara and the mommy gang of gossips fluttering the other day. She seemed to know who he is—maybe you should ask her for a reference."

"I will ask Jack and see what he says."

Having never been married it is difficult for me to swallow comments like this without a bit of sarcasm leaking from my mouth. I wanted to shout, "You are a grown woman, get a spine and don't ask permission for anything."

But marriage is a partnership where communication is vital to its sustainability, and she would probably want

Jack to ask her before having a photographer come over if the roles were reversed. Besides the last thing she needs right now is to ignite a quarrel over some insignificant event while the Drew escapade looms in the background.

"I really doubt he is a serial killer. Not many serial killers live in your upscale neighborhood. I would guarantee it would be a first. Although, Olivia does have many gardeners and repairmen, but I never see them return. You might want to check her basement for bodies."

"I am not going to ask Jack to take off work on a weekday or miss his golf game on Saturday, so I am counting on you to be my bodyguard when Mr. Vincent arrives with his lens."

"Ok."

"What's up? I didn't have to bribe you with lasagna or guilt-trip you to come over. What would Sherlock say about this conundrum?"

"Are you going to give him a call, or do you want me to call him since you are so clearly afraid of stranger neighbors with camera equipment?"

"Hmmm. You avoided the question, and you volunteered to call the man. Suddenly, my image of a sinister old scaly bearded fellow has been shattered. Make sure when he comes over you wear that sleeveless red dress with the V neckline and those strappy sandals with heels that highlight those amazing legs you have developed riding your bike everywhere."

"He isn't cute."

I did not lie. Cute is the last word anyone would use to describe Clark Vincent.

"Wear the dress."

I did not continue with a reply, but the thought of getting dressed up for a man who could have anyone in town, state, country or universe made me want to find comfort in a pair of jeans, flip flops and T-shirt. It was something about the idea of being rejected at the audition when I did not want the part.

"Tell him I can do Wednesday or Thursday afternoon. I need to know at least the day before in order to clean up the house."

"Your house is beautiful, Quinn. Please don't drive yourself crazy rearranging furniture and scrubbing floors that are already shining. Besides if there was even a tiny microscopic fleck of dust he could airbrush it away like they do the movie stars' wrinkles and cellulite."

"Just let me know so I can be prepared."

Maybe this project was the distraction she needed right now. If she wanted to clean, scrub and dust until her fingers bled I would not stop her. At least it was keeping her mind on something else beside an attorney who was playing dangerously with her heart.

An alarm on my phone reminded me of an interview I had with a local veterinarian who was trying to start a free rabies shot clinic for people who could not afford the vaccination for their animals. Directly after that I had to drive over to an adjacent town to interview a pharmacist who was retiring after 50 years of service. I could not imagine going to work at the same job and doing the same task everyday for five decades. I definitely wanted to discover her secret to happiness, because no one continues at a job for that long without finding contentment in waking up every morning and driving to work. Perhaps it was because she found a way to combine both her passions into one by serving her fresh baked goods and sweets in the pharmacy. I could not wait to sample some of her famous ice cream, fudge and cheese straws. Maybe that is what kept her going all these years, a spoonful of butter pecan, chocolate, lemon and peach.

6 OVERTHINKING THE APPLE

The sun was setting on the end of a long day as I drove home, reviewing the conversations I had conducted with people about their lives. My notebook was full and my stomach was empty except for the cup of chocolate ice cream I devoured at the pharmacy.

On the ride home, I debated whether I should email, text or call Clark. If I emailed him or sent a text I would have to wait for him to reply, and I was tired of waiting for people to reply to my messages. I would give him a call, and Superman could answer me in his phone booth. My thoughts sidetracked to the last time I even saw one of those claustrophobic contraptions. They were probably all in a landfill somewhere, and 50 years from now a person will think it is neat to set up an antique phone booth in their hallway.

I wondered if the mommy gang had invited Clark on a date yet with one of the recent divorcees in the group. He was a catch in a small town where the pond of single men of a certain age was limited to a few bottom feeding catfish.

I immediately increased the volume on my radio

when I heard the first few notes of my favorite U2 song. My windows were rolled down letting in the afternoon breeze as I sang along with Bono.

A large black SUV was coming towards me on the opposite side of the road, and I recognized Dr. K behind the wheel in his turquoise scrub top that I knew made his brown eyes and wavy golden hair stand out even in the distance.

In a split second I had to decide whether to do a Miss America wave, beep, nod or try that finger point guys in pickup trucks do to gesture hello.

Before I committed on the correct greeting he had already passed me, and I can only guess I was looking straight ahead gripping the wheel. He would think I was a snob, space cadet lost in thought or the most painful realization that he would not even recognize me.

He did not gesture to me, so maybe he was lost in thought as well after a long day performing surgeries, paperwork and the business aspect of physician's duties which the public often neglects to associate with a physician, thinking his main responsibilities are only with medical procedures. I learned after working in public relations with the non-profit how much data and paperwork is involved in running any successful business.

As usual, I was overthinking everything. It was my gift.

My cell phone was buzzing in my handbag, but I had carelessly thrown it on the backseat. Whatever message was being sent would have to wait.

When I arrived home, my parents were sitting on their porch playing a game of rummy and sipping on a putrid concoction of green that was similar to what you cough up with a bad case of the flu.

"What are you drinking? It looks like swamp water."

"It's a kale smoothie."

"Swamp water is about right."

Dad was clearly unhappy with his beverage and grunted with displeasure.

"Your father received his blood work today from his physical, and he needs to lower his cholesterol and blood pressure."

"She threw away my potato chips. Can you believe that? A few chips are not going to send me to the cardiologist, Rachael."

"No, they are not, because you are not going to eat them, Patrick."

She said his name in a long six-syllable Southern drawl when she meant business.

"Are you ok, Dad?"

"I am fine, honey."

He patted my shoulder and abruptly went inside the house.

"He's worried. His friend, Pete, had a heart attack last week. He was in the greatest shape, running marathons and always so fit."

"That is terrible."

"We went by the health food store, and the young clerk recommended this recipe, but it tastes awful and I am not so sure it even helps lower cholesterol."

"There are a lot of websites online, and I interviewed a dietitian who Dad should go see. He could help devise a nutrition plan that is individualized towards Dad's health needs. He could help himself by reducing the portion sizes he consumes. I will give you the dietitian's name and contact information. If you want, I can give him a call."

"Thank you, Lennon. I will give him a call, but I don't know if your father is ready for all this right now. It is so hard getting old, watching your friends fall apart and your own body age and decline. Sometimes I look in the mirror before I take a shower, and I wonder who is that old lady? And then I realize it is me."

"Maybe you guys need a trip. Why don't you get out of here, and take a tropical island cruise? Isn't that the best aspect of being retired, having no restrictions of the daily grind?"

"I get terribly seasick on boats, and your father does not like to travel. He says if he wants to experience another country, he can do it on the World Travel Channel on his big screen television."

"Well, what about the beach? We used to spend a few weeks there every summer for vacation."

"I don't know, Lennon. It has changed with the traffic, all the tourists and who wants to see your dad and me in our bathing suits?"

"You have to live, Mom. We never know if there will be a tomorrow. I experienced that firsthand."

"And we thank God everyday for that."

She came over and kissed the top of my head.

"You want some baked chicken? I attempted preparing a healthy meal tonight, but it may be a bit bland. You can add some spices to it, and it may be edible."

"Thanks, I have some leftover veggie lasagna that Quinn made. It is only a couple of days old, so it should not kill me."

Mom paused as if she remembered something on her mental checklist.

"How is Quinn doing? She brought Ralph over the other night."

"Did you guys watch a movie? He loves playing with all our old toys and books. I can't believe you saved them all these years. You know kids these days constantly have a screen in front of them that you would think any other toy would not keep them entertained. I see so many toddlers with their parents' cell phones in their hands."

I rambled on until I was out of breath to avoid her underlying question.

Mom could sense I was about to break from my intense rambling, but she did not push the issue forward. Her plate was full tonight with a husband coming to terms with his mortality.

"I love you, Mom."

"Goodnight, sweetheart."

Before she closed the door she added, "We are always right here if you need us."

I walked up the stairs and felt cramps in my stomach, lower back and thighs reaching all the way to my knees. It always surprised me when I would hear a woman say she never has cramps. I had them my entire life each month since I was 11 years old. I guess I was not one of the lucky ones.

After I ate a small portion of the scrumptious lasagna, I took three ibuprofen and collapsed down on the sofa with a mug of hot tea. I was about to check my message on the phone that I was not able to see earlier when I was driving as it began to ring.

"Hello."

"You sound tired," said Quinn. "I won't keep you long on the phone."

"I will be alright."

"Try to rest, and use that microwaveable heating pad I found at the drug store. I have one, and it always helps me when I feel bad."

"I made some hot tea."

"Good. I wanted to let you know that you can set up a time with the photographer. I mentioned his name to Jack. He said he knew him, and he is a good guy. Evidently he lived here with his grandparents for a year when they were in the same fifth grade class. He is renting his grandparents' home from his uncle who inherited it when they passed away. Anyway that is what

Tara told Steve who told Jack."

"I will give him a call tomorrow."

"Get some sleep. Love ya, bye."

I put the phone down, and grabbed the remote to see if there was something on television to get my mind off my pain. How did Tara know about Clark? She probably already set him up with her bestie, Genevieve, who recently moved back to town after her husband caught her having an affair with a partner in his real estate firm. Genevieve could have started life anew with no one in town knowing the details of the dissolution of her marriage in Seattle where she lived with her husband, but social media makes gossip universal.

I could not picture Clark with Genevieve and her two Pug dogs following close behind as they went shopping for his and her monogrammed pillows. He seemed too smart to be trapped in that superficial flypaper.

Perhaps Tara had visited him with a basket of muffins herself. I could not blame her if she did. No human being should have to live with Tara's husband, Steve.

I nestled under my blanket and sipped my hot tea. Did other people have imaginations like mine that spur wildly out of control? I wondered what it would feel like to just view the apple as red and not question where it came from and why it existed.

I was about to doze off to voices on a shopping channel which has a rather calming effect and is the ultimate sleeping pill. I decided to finally view the message that appeared on my phone while I was driving earlier in the evening. When the screen lit up I saw the email notification was from Dean Kent.

My mug of hot tea sloshed over my pajamas, and I let out a shriek. The liquid had cooled to warm, but I stripped out of my soaking clothes and changed into a gown after wiping off my legs with a fluffy towel.

Luckily, I was the only victim of the hot tea clumsy fiasco with my phone and sofa miraculously avoiding the spill.

I climbed into bed with my cell phone in my hand. Going to bed with my cell phone was a habit that needed to end. I swiped the screen and tapped on Dr. K's email.

From: Dr. Dean Kent
To: Lennon Tyler

You didn't wave

I kicked the covers off me and went to the bathroom to splash some water on my face. I tapped the screen again and reread the message to make sure my eyes were not deceiving me.

And so this is how it begins.

7 TOO NICE TO SEE THE TRUTH

Every half hour I would glance at the vicious neon eyes of my alarm clock and flip my pillow over to find the cool spot, but my mind would not rest.

Three words had sent my head spinning on a carousel ride of scenarios.

Clearly Dr. K felt something for me, but I was clueless as to what it was that he felt exactly. Maybe his feelings were equivalent to the same swelling up in my chest I felt for a lovable dog with downcast eyes that I met while at the animal shelter yesterday interviewing the vet who volunteered his medical services for animals without homes.

When Dr. K saw me he saw that same sad heart wrenching puppy, the shattered in pain individual he had rescued at the hospital.

At least that was what I had concocted the entire night staring at a darkened ceiling in my bedroom. As soon as the sunlight entered through the curtains in my bedroom, I grabbed a notepad and pen from my night table. They were always there where I could easily access them. Often I would awaken from a dream with an image that I needed to put into words, and it would be forgotten if I did not jot it down in somewhat legible scribble before I drifted off to sleep again.

People did not act on whims. It was their subconscious, direct intent or perhaps fate.

The question proposed was why did he email me?

My neon green notepad was full of possible scenarios in hot pink ink:

1. he wanted me to help him with his book series
2. he wanted me to write a flattering article about him—(scratch that, he ignored my calls for an interview)
3. I was just one of 500 women he emails (no man is an angel, especially a dashing doctor who melts hearts like chocolate candy on a hot summer day)
4. he was bored and email and social media were habitual technology mind play to pass the time

I read the list and ripped it to shreds, embarrassed at my thoughts. He sent me an email. Get over yourself, Lennon. I was as bad as Vera embellishing her hug to the bridge club.

I got dressed and rode my bike downtown to the farmer's market letting the breeze awaken my senses. Maybe the fresh orangeade they served would help stimulate my brain cells that needed to be shaken like an Etch-A-Sketch until all nonsense about Dr. K disappeared.

I was sipping on the sweet citrus beverage when I noticed a sign in one of the tented booths that read, "All Natural Health Remedies."

"That one is good for the heart and irritable bowel syndrome."

I held the small herb growing in a plastic green container as the man with a long ponytail and tie-dyed shirt proceeded to tell me about its digestive health benefits in unfiltered detail.

I felt a presence beside me.

Out of the corner of my eye I spied him attempting to stifle a laugh, but it came out like a big bellow bursting from seams of ridiculousness which he could retain no longer.

I put down the plant in a huff and walked away frustrated that I was not able to control the situation whenever Clark was near.

"Wait. I was not laughing at you. Come on, Lennon," he said, catching up with me in two long strides.

Suddenly, I remembered the photo shoot, and tried not to let my embarrassment override a way to help my sister forget her troubles with the opportunity Clark offered. He had no idea about the powerful effect of his lens in maintaining a peaceful balance in her household.

I realized I was acting a bit bratty and gave him a weak smile.

"You always seem to run into me at the most awkward moments. My father recently became aware that his cholesterol is high, and I was looking for some way to ease his transition into a healthy lifestyle. My mother cleaned out his junk food stash, and I am afraid their 40 year marriage will not survive. I think he may run off with the donut shop girl if I don't soon find him some tasty low cholesterol alternatives."

He laughed at my obvious attempt at humor.

"I had really high cholesterol, too, so I know how he feels."

I gave the toned man in remarkably great shape a once over from top to bottom before I knew what I was doing and shook my head slightly hoping to wake up my inner self from my apparent goggle fest.

"How could you have trouble with cholesterol?"

"I did before I made a life change, started eating

healthy and exercising regularly. I was never really unhealthy in my habits, but my doc said sometimes it is just genetic."

"You will have to talk to my dad," I said.

"Sure."

Again I was reminded of his sincerity. Usually I was a pessimist when sizing up crass, arrogant characters, but Clark seemed genuine in his words.

"By the way, my sister and Jack agreed to have you come over to photograph their house if you are still interested."

"Absolutely. I have one favor to ask," he said.

"Ok."

"I have seen your column in the newspaper. You are so descriptive that I can visualize everything you write. You are truly talented."

I blushed brighter than Tara and all of the mommy mob put together.

"Thank you."

"I would like you to write a piece to accompany my photographs of your sister's home. I need about 400 words. It's short, but the magazine will pay you well."

"Thank you so much. This is a wonderful opportunity."

The next few minutes I attempted to remain calm so as not to alert him of my extreme giddiness at landing my first magazine byline. We set a time and date for the photo shoot at Quinn's house. My lips were moving, but I could not hear the words as I was in that tunnel of light where everything seemed so far away and in muffled voices.

As soon as he left I scanned the park for a private place, so bystanders would not send for a straight jacket. I spotted a discrete corner of the park under a tree by the river where I did my little dance swinging my hips and jumping up and down.

I immediately texted Quinn with my fantastic news.

My parents had so much faith in me and never once told me I should not quit my stable job with benefits and a retirement plan to pursue my dream. I wanted to bring them some flowers from the farmer's market and surprise them with my new opportunity in person.

The path to my destiny was set. I lingered on by the sailboat dock and contemplated my new opportunity while viewing the tranquil river scene before me. The river was dark blue with flecks of black in its ripples transforming it into an impressionist's vision that should be placed on canvas. A fisherman with a straw hat waited patiently in his small boat for the tug of the line.

I envisioned people reading my article as they opened their mailboxes on a country road, grocery store aisle, office waiting rooms and on their tablets as they rode the train home from work on their lengthy commutes in the afternoons. My words would take a journey in a nationwide publication, and it was amazing.

I never doubted my ability, but my practicality tried to extinguish my joy with doubt that Clark's offer was viable.

A ring from my phone jostled me from my contradicting thoughts.

"I got your text. That is awesome, Lennon!" said Quinn.

"I know, but it does not seem like I am in the present. It is not real for me yet."

A bunch of Queen Anne's lace and white daisies were bound by a bright blue ribbon in my basket as I pedaled home letting the sunshine warm my skin. I smiled at every car that passed and every person I saw. Even a small baby rabbit in a yard was a recipient of a smile from me, and he seemed to stop munching on his lunch of grass and weeds and twinkled his nose back in return. Just call me Snow White Writer.

A couple was jogging on the opposite side of the road. The woman was talking as the man stared in my direction. I was about to wave, but my hand stopped mid-air.

I recognized the woman as the owner of a jewelry store. A lot of talk in town especially by the mommy mob and even some of my mother's age group surrounded the middle aged woman. She had stolen an older man away from his wife when she was younger and years later, he repeated the pattern trading her in for a newer model. It was told she gained a formidable sum of money to open the shop in the divorce. It was also the gossip that she kept several sugar daddies, as Mom's friends called them, to maintain the upkeep of the business.

Sometimes I would see her walking about town, but I could not determine anything about her that would attract men to give her money. She did not exude that floozy vibe as Mom's group called her or the younger mommy gang's skank label that they related to certain women of questionable morals. She was indistinct from others her age with that familiar purplish burgundy dyed hair and her figure was somewhat frumpy even though she obviously jogged. Her curves were not defined with a drooping top and bottom as described by the ladies. She waited on Quinn and me when we chose an anniversary gift for our mom and dad last year, but there was not any kind of outgoing or sensational personality that would warrant the gossip that plagued her. She was not particularly nice or funny, somewhat cold in her professional style, but perhaps she had heard the mommy gang's comments and associated us with them.

I remember saying that I did not think she looked like the type to be able to obtain gifts from men to a group of Mom's friends at lunch one day when she walked past the restaurant's window downtown.

They told me I was too nice to see the truth, and they were probably right.

"It does not matter what you look like when the lights are off, honey," said Sophia.

Sophia should know, having been married three times herself, and currently seeing a man who was two years younger than her daughter.

"I heard she makes her money in an unconventional way," said another member of the group, who I had never heard mention a negative word about anyone.

"Dot, stop, you know that is not true," said Mom, who did not like to participate in gossip even if it was true.

"Look at her, girls. It is more likely she is cooking them up fattening cupcakes, corn fritters and fried chicken," said another woman, and they all laughed in unison.

"She is probably into role-playing or something, as a lady, I will fail to mention at our dignified table," said Sophia, knowingly, and all of their voices hushed.

"Do you think so, Sophia?" asked several of the women, as Sophia had undoubtedly grabbed the attention of the senior ladies group.

"Let's just say some men have different tastes," said Sophia, in a tone of a professor to her students.

As these memories passed through my mind, I glanced at the man beside her. He continued staring in my direction as they jogged towards me.

It was difficult to see with the sunlight in my eyes across the street, but he was a tall, lean blond man with a penetrating look. I had to admit the women were correct. She really must have a secret to be jogging with such a handsome man.

My bicycle almost hit the curb as my mouth flung open.

He did not wave this time either, and I was too

stunned to do anything but attempt to keep my balance on my bike.

I stopped with my feet skidding the ground, Fred Flintstone-like, instead of using my pedals to break. I turned around to catch another glimpse, but the couple had turned the corner.

That could not be him.

I must be going insane. It was a mirage. Certainly, if I saw the two people again, I would clearly see it was not the athletic, handsome, smart, man of my dreams and possible writing partner, Dr. Dean Kent.

Why would a married man who is known to everyone in the community be jogging with a woman with a peculiar reputation out in public if they were actually having an affair?

The positive angel in me validated the mirage with various possibilities. Maybe they were just friends, he had a second career as a personal trainer or they happened to meet while jogging and started up a conversation.

The pessimistic side of my journalistic background went straight to the meat of the matter. They were having an affair. He was possibly one of her sugar daddies, or he was hooked on whatever bait she dealt out to the men of the city. I popped that idea balloon of utter depravity with one fierce reminder that this was indeed the man who saved my life.

No, it definitely could not be him.

Why did I care if it was him? He was only my physician, and as far as helping him write his book that was going nowhere. He had been unresponsive to my emails with suggestions for characters or plot.

Was Dr. Kent a phony good-deeder? Did he really have a secret life?

And then I remembered I had a doctor's appointment the following afternoon. If anyone could discover the truth behind the man, it was me.

8 THE MYTH OF THE HONEST MAN

How would this play out? My life had to be a plot for a sitcom episode somewhere in the land of reruns that I had bypassed with the remote one late night unable to sleep in search of a television sedative.

At least with the distraction of Dr. Kent's possible dual identity I was not consumed with the potentiality of tumors, ulcer and cancer ravaging my body while I waited in the blue room among several people with various ailments. All I could think of was what would I say to get the information I wanted. Did I even want to know that Santa did not exist?

It was easier to believe in the myth of the honest man.

I drew circles on my notepad. But wasn't the fact that he was emailing me enough to knock him off his untarnished pedestal?

I contradicted myself. No, our emails were completely innocent. I almost started to ask the women around me if Dr. Kent ever emailed them. But as I was about to speak, a woman burst into the room and said emphatically to the receptionist at the glass window,

"Dr. Kent just texted me and said he could see me now."

So, there you have it. He engaged in technology with his patients to provide the best feasible health care. I was not special. I was number 505 and counting.

A toddler began to scream while a few kids started throwing foam blocks at each other in the corner, and I wrote on my pad, "Remember to tell Quinn how lucky she is to have Ralphie."

Idly searching my phone about my symptoms, I had previously come across a blog about patients' health which recommended writing down your questions for your physician, so you would not forget to voice your concerns in the brief time they spent with you before a door was shut in your face and you were left guessing.

I wrote down all my questions about my symptoms in my notebook, so I would not forget anything. At the bottom I included a question that had plagued me.

I would never dare ask the good doc directly, but I desperately wanted to know, "Was that you jogging yesterday?"

My name was finally called, and the nurse led me to the last room at the end of the hallway.

"What are we seeing you for today, Lennon?" asked the nurse.

"I am following up on my appendectomy, and I also have been suffering from pain which he thinks might be an ulcer."

I felt like I was reading lines that had been written for me on a cue card, and she was going to say in a director's megaphone, "Let's try that again with more feeling this time."

"Well, we can take care of you for the follow-up. You should see your primary physician for the possible ulcer."

She turned and looked at my puzzled face. "But then again, he likes you."

I laughed, expecting her to do the same, but she did not. How did she know he liked me? This had to be a standard comment she made to everyone.

"Well, I am sure he likes everyone," I said.

She did not reply. "Undress and put on the gown on the table. He will see you in a few minutes."

I glared at the horrid gown. With all the fashion designers in the world, couldn't someone stitch together something less depressing?

Every time I heard a door close and a man's voice in the hallway outside my room, I thought he would knock and come in, but he never did.

I searched for a clock on the wall that did not exist and dug my phone out of my handbag and found I had been sitting on the exam table for an hour and 45 minutes.

The office was quiet, and I thought they had left for the day, forgetting about me sitting somewhat patiently on an exam table for hours like an imbecile. How embarrassing would it be for me to walk out of a closed locked building sounding the alarm because I was so forgettable?

My fantasies were diminished as I heard a knock on the door. I had to be the last patient of the day. Had he done this on purpose so that we would have time to talk about the book? My overthinker mind was at work once again with various possibilities for being moved back until I was his last patient of the day.

He thudded into the room with a heaviness associated at the end of a tiresome workday. The nurse followed behind him, closing the door. He smiled and mumbled a greeting and began the examination.

After he was finished, I breathed an audible sigh and the nurse left the room to begin her end of the day duties. He sat on a stool and typed on his computer.

"Everything pretty much looks the same. From the

examination your pain seems to be lessening, so the medication must be working. Do you have any questions or concerns today, ah…ah?"

Did he forget my name? I know it was on the screen in front of him.

It was so weird. This was a man I had been emailing, who had been consuming my thoughts, and he did not act like he even knew me. I definitely was number 505.

"Lennon," I said, quietly.

He laughed loudly. "I know."

My teeth chattered and my lips quivered either from the fact that I was half-naked in an air conditioned freezer, or because for the first time in my life I could not sum up a situation. I was the person who always knew who committed the crime in a mystery novel and when a couple in my social circle of friends was doomed to fail or excel. I knew how to read people and situations, but this guy was a force that was new to me.

"You're cold," he said softly, stating the obvious.

He opened a cabinet door, pulled out a sheet and came towards me. He wrapped it around my shoulders enveloping me in warmth. I wanted to wrap my arms around him and pull him under the sheet feeling his breath linger on my skin.

What was wrong with me? Did he know the effect he had on me with his actions? Of course he did.

He stepped slowly away and returned to his stool.

Unable to look at his face again for fear that he would see my emotions plastered like a billboard in my eyes, I lowered my head and began to read the questions I had written in my notebook about the exercises, diet and medication that could help alleviate the pain from my surgery and possible ulcers.

I must have been reading too slow, because in mid-sentence he snatched my notebook away and read them aloud clicking off the answers in seconds.

I gazed at his abruptness with mild shock.

When he came to the final question, he looked ambivalent.

"What does this mean about jogging? Was this question for me?"

It was like a dawn had awakened inside of me. It could not have been him jogging with the disreputable woman or he would have come up with a quick excuse or maybe a joke. Guilty people often resorted to humor to dispel a serious situation.

"Exercise is always good," he said.

"Do you jog?" I pressed the question.

"Well, I was on the track team in high school a long time ago. I play basketball with my kids and volunteer with the high school soccer team. It is nice to be around some young people full of energy and spirit," he said.

He continued talking for several minutes about sports and something in the news about a famous basketball player who was signing with another team. I wondered if I was the only person who managed to have an educated knowledge and passion for basketball that he was able to talk to today. I garnered from his elevated interest in the topic at hand that most of his patients or staff he would engage with in a similar conversation would reply with a blank stare of utter disinterest.

I kept waiting through our conversation that lasted longer than my examination to hear him speak of characters, time travel, history or writing in general, but he did not mention the book or our emails. It was driving me crazy. Had he forgotten our emails and our discussion during my last appointment?

Did he receive so many emails from women that they were like Ralphie's finger painting that transformed all singular bright colors eventually into one brown blur?

As he was about to leave, I had to know. I nervously shouted out the words before I could contemplate their tone.

"Do you want me to keep emailing you? I don't want to be a nuisance about your book."

He paused and thought for a while before answering. "Yes, but I am so busy. I want to write it, but..."

My heart sunk at all the "buts." I was determined to laugh it off. I could not believe it. I could feel hot wetness beginning at the corner of my eyes. If I had to blow every birthday wish from now until I was dead, I silently pleaded do not let them fall down my cheeks like rivers of melancholy. Thankfully, they did not fall.

"Well, if my emails become bothersome, just block me. It is real easy to do," I said, my lips twitching at my feeble attempt to present a nonchalant response.

We both laughed uneasily, and he walked towards the door.

He turned back towards me, staring at the wall behind me without looking me in the eyes.

"Good night, Lennon."

The door shut, and it was over.

It was obvious I would never receive another email from him again.

9 THE PERFECT SHOT

I turned off my headlights in Quinn's driveway. I could stay up all night and write, but if you asked me to get up this early in the morning and complete a single sentence it may not be coherent. I gathered my notebook and pens and lumbered up the steps.

Quinn would not be pleased with my attire. The last thing I wanted to do when my evil alarm started beeping this morning was slip into a sexy, silk red dress. I did collect myself enough to put on some lipstick, and my hair was thankfully frizz free this morning with that wavy just got out of bed look. My jeans were snug and form flattering with a cute black scoop neck sleeveless top, some attractive leather sandals with crossed straps on the ankles and a silver medallion filigree necklace hung at just the right length on my chest.

As I approached the door I had an odd memory flash. The last time I wore the necklace I was at Dr. Kent's office, and as he performed my exam he looked down and said, "What's that?"

"Excuse me," I said.

"Your necklace. Does it have some meaning?"

"No, it's just the style, Dr. Kent."

Actually, I had no idea if the necklace had any meaning. It was in my grandmother's jewelry box when I was teenager, and she told me it belonged to me after she saw it on my neck.

"It looks beautiful on you, Lennon," she said, as we both looked in the floor length standing mirror in her bedroom.

We were so alike in our appearances that it was like a fast forward and rewind button had been set when each of us looked at the other's reflection.

I wished I had asked her those years ago where she had obtained the piece of jewelry and if it had any special significance, but when we are young we only look to the future disregarding the past.

I touched the necklace, and caught myself doing that which I promised I would not do again.

Why in the world was I obsessed with Dr. Kent? After he basically told me in a roundabout way that he was not interested in writing a book, I still found myself daydreaming about what might happen in the historical book series. It had so much potential.

I sent him one final email again thanking him for everything he had done for my health. I attached a document of all my notes on the book series if he ever wished to use them.

I did not receive a reply. Not even a thank you or an abbreviated "ty."

He was not interested.

I knocked on the door before opening it and walked in like I always did when I entered Quinn's home. However, it felt strange to be so comfortable in a setting where I would have to gain a fresh perspective as I wrote the article.

Jack was drinking a cup of coffee and reading the paper.

"Hey, do you know I have a famous sister-in-law? She is going to be published in a national magazine."

I smiled at Jack. It was nice to see things were getting back to normal.

"I still can't believe it. Thanks so much you guys. If it wasn't for your spectacular house, I would not be able to accomplish my lifetime goal of national publication."

"I want a nice write up in the dedication of your novel…to the best, most intelligent, handsome brother-in-law in the world. And I think Brad Pitt should play me in the movie."

I punched him in the arm and he laughed. "O…k, best brother-in-law in the world."

Quinn placed a mug of hot chocolate and bagel with cream cheese on the granite counter island in front of me. Everything was in place. As soon as we finished our breakfast, Quinn would erase any trace of crumbs or water rings from glasses left behind.

"And you are definitely my most favorite sister in the whole wide world," I said, sipping my hot chocolate which she had perfected by adding a couple of marshmallows floating around in the top.

I felt a weight leaning on my knee. Ralphie was half awake dressed in a pair of khakis and a checkered button up shirt that was too adorable.

"Aunt Lennon, let's watch toons."

Before he could lead me to the television, Clark walked into the room from the French doors at the back of the house where a peek of sunlight began to sneak through the azure sky and whisper on the river.

He had not shaved with light stubble, but his blue eyes were alert and his body moved in quick motions. He seemed not to be aware that it was too early in the morning to be alive.

"Listen up everyone, the sun has created a beautiful shot for us this morning, so let's move to the pier," said

Clark, who evidently had been setting up his gear outside.

"Yum. A bagel with cream cheese. May I?"

"Help yourself."

He grabbed half and devoured it in a couple of swallows. Jeez, now I know why he was always jogging and working out at the gym.

I was careful not to be in anyone's way as he managed to capture a shot from the angle of Olivia's yard next door. He kneeled on the ground to present a view of the house and river as the sun poured out of the sky onto the family. I recognized a grin on his face not when they posed stiffly, but when they thought he had stopped shooting and relaxed. That was when he snuck in his winning shots.

I did not talk to him the entire time, afraid that I would break his creative drive.

When I would write, I would occasionally leave the television or music on in the background, but a conversation would break the flow like a crystal vase falling from a podium with a microphone vibrating its shattering pieces through an empty auditorium.

Occasionally, he would direct me to position this equipment here or move a screen in a certain direction. His tone was not bossy or demeaning, but simply calm and directed.

He moved his body in different positions that even my friends who prided themselves on their yoga flexibility would find difficult.

Jack, Quinn and Ralphie were perfection. It was so hard to look at them and not have the demon of nausea taint my stomach with that "knowing" I was plagued with of the reality that remained.

My grandmother always had this sense of knowing things. It could be seen as perceptiveness, an abundance of both intelligence and common sense or maybe a little of the gypsy crystal ball knowledge that I laugh about and people often disregard as irrelevant in modern society.

I don't really know what it was that made me recognize and identify so clearly the character of people and often the paths that they would take in general. There was a possibility I was simply a good listener.

When I looked at my family moving about from place to place on the dewy grass posing for the camera, I became ill with the knowledge of their fate.

I hoped I was wrong this time. I loved them. I wanted this picture to stay the same forever. But that is not reality. Life moves on.

"Beautiful. Absolutely beautiful," said Clark taking a brief break to linger in the new sun.

"I know."

"Isn't it a shame it can't last forever?" he asked me too directly.

"What?"

I was stunned. How did he know? Had Jack shared Quinn's indiscretions with his friends, or had Quinn been so naïve to think she could trust one of the mommy gang with her secret?

"The light from the sun in the morning—I wish it could last forever."

I nodded, and the speechless overthinker that I am was relieved.

Sally and Sam's tails were wagging as Quinn opened a jar of dog biscuits. Ralphie slurped a big purple bowl of his cereal and Jack sipped his second cup of coffee by the large window over the sink with views of the flower garden. Clark remained silent while snapping photographs of the family.

I began scribbling notes on the style of the furniture, the layout and design of the rooms and the overall atmosphere as the family moved throughout the space.

I closed my eyes and opened them seeing the people in front of me not as my family, but as strangers who allowed me into their home viewing it for the first time.

I did not see a delicate pottery bowl as the dish our grandmother had served Watergate Salad in every Christmas, but as a fine piece of art that was now sitting on a side table. I picked it up, and discovered it was a signed piece dated decades ago. I took out my phone and snapped a pic that I would use to search later on the web for clues to its origins.

As I began to question where our grandparents had found this piece of pottery, I heard a loud bell echo throughout the room. I looked at Quinn, and from her horrific expression of pure terror, I knew who it must be. Jack opened the front door, and I imagined we could feel the chill of doom down the hallway.

"I heard all this loud ruckus next door, and I had to come see what was going on," said Olivia.

"Mother, I told you we were having a photographer coming over to take pictures of the house. Quinn asked you to come, but you said you did not want to disturb us."

Olivia ignored her son. "Ralphie, come here, my darling boy."

"Hey, Grandma Olivia."

He rushed over to give his grandmother a hug. The boy was an angel.

Olivia had insisted on being called Olivia from the night Ralphie was born in the hospital when a nurse asked if the grandmother wanted to see the newborn.

"My name is Olivia, and that is what he shall call me. Do I look like I could be anyone's grandmother?" she said to the nurse, her son and my sister who had just finished a long painful labor.

It was the only time I have ever heard Quinn defend herself against the wrath of Olivia.

"Ralph will call you Grandmother Olivia," said Quinn, still in a daze from the labor.

My parents, Jack and I were all in the room, and we looked to see what Olivia would say. We expected her words to rattle the hallways with her contempt, but it was if she was struck by a spell of kindness.

"As you wish," she said, as she gazed at the baby cradled in Jack's arms.

Ralph never screamed even when he was born. His eyes seemed to look about the room, and he made these small cooing noises. He had always been an angel.

"I have to send my handyman over here," Olivia said, frowning in the kitchen and hugging her grandson.

"Why, mother?"

"Well, obviously your clothes washer is broken. Ralph's monogrammed shirt must be dirty that I bought him for his birthday," she said, innocently.

"No, it's not broken," said Jack.

"Oh, Quinn is so dedicated to going to the gym and all those meetings at the homeless shelter. THEY should certainly benefit from her efforts. You could have brought your laundry to my house, son."

"So she could get her maid to do it, and make you feel guilty, as well," I whispered to Quinn beside me.

She did not respond, but looked down solemnly as if she had been reprimanded for a chore undone. I hated the way Olivia treated Quinn. Quinn took care of Olivia better than Jack's sister. She only came home for Christmas, and sent an occasional card or email that Quinn would read aloud to Olivia.

Quinn would mention to me that when she helped out at one of Olivia's luncheons, book club or bridge club, Olivia would talk endlessly to her friends about her daughter, who was a law professor at a university in Maine, was married to a judge and had two children.

"Olivia, have you met Clark?" I said, attempting to

guide the monster away from ruining Quinn's smile.

Quinn had been as happy as I had seen her since the whole Drew email affair debacle earlier when Clark was taking the photographs outside, but Olivia had eliminated the entire good mood of the house.

Olivia turned to Clark seeing him for the first time, and her facial expression softened to something I had not seen before. It was if she had been overtaken by an alien Botox presence and a youthful glow appeared. Her posture straightened as she lifted her chest and chin, batting her eyelashes.

Really, Olivia, I thought as I looked at the woman in her 70s stare at the much, much younger man. I knew my mouth was so open it was catching flies, which was another one of my grandfather's favorite sayings I loved.

"Clark…?"

She paused, waiting for someone to say his last name.

"Vincent."

Olivia's eyes grew wide, and she started to cough.

"Here, Olivia, have a drink of water."

Quinn's face was worried as she immediately became the faithful daughter-in-law, handing her a glass of filtered water.

I did not know how she could have such compassion for a woman who treated her so badly with disregard every day of her life.

"I just need to sit down a minute."

"You guys can take a break while I shoot some of the interior rooms and the master bedroom," said Clark.

Olivia was as entranced by Clark as the mommy mob. He definitely had an effect on women.

After a few minutes on the sofa with a cup of tea and saltines, Olivia had her compact out and was fixing her lipstick and combing her camera ready bob of peach colored hair. She had managed to place herself in the final photo with the family on the porch.

Clark motioned the family outside with the wave of his arm. As they began to find a place to sit and pose, he had already taken his best shot of the day. The river was behind them as the leaves of the trees sparkled in the sunlight with a mixture of colors as the family shown their true selves. Jack was playing with Ralphie and the two dogs, as Quinn looked over at them with a warm smile leaning on the railing of the porch while Olivia was already seated in a rocking chair throne regally directing where everyone should be while no one listened.

I could not help but smile at Clark. He had found them through his lens.

By midnight, I had finished the story. When my fingertips began to glide over the keyboard they did not halt. As I reread the words over and over, I was proud with the outcome. I did not trust the spell check, checking every word and comma before I would email it to the editor of the magazine.

Clark had given me the woman's contact information after the shoot, and he said she would need the article a month from today. I did not need the time. It was done. I thought about waiting at least a week before I sent it, so I would not seem too overeager. But I had an awful thought that I would lose my article in a freak accident where my entire backup drive was extinguished, my email accounts cleared and clouds vanished. I was going to send it that night.

I thought about reading it to Quinn first or even my parents, but I knew it was good. I did not want to doubt myself. Any hesitation from them would send me into unnecessary rewrites and edits. I had to muster the confidence in my ability to be published in a national magazine.

So, with the click of the mouse, it was sent. My first article would be published in a magazine.

I stared at the screen as if I would receive a reply in the middle of the night from the magazine editor. This would not happen for days or weeks, but I still waited in my chair for a reply that would not come that night. I finally gave up on my staring contest with my computer screen, and shut down the device that just sent my destiny across states to an office somewhere in New York City. Actually, it would be in her inbox wherever she was, maybe in the Hamptons with her laptop or even across the world traveling to a coast I had never heard of on her mobile device of choice—that was the simple beauty of email.

I brushed my teeth, washed my face and moisturized everything in sight, but my body still seemed on edge with excitement. I completed a few yoga poses, and climbed into bed pulling the sheets over me.

I twisted this way and that, but I was so ecstatic I could not even think about closing my eyes and going to sleep. I put on a pair of comfy pants and faded cotton shirt that was once a neon pink, and opened the door to step out and gaze at the full moon in the sky.

Everybody I knew would ask me if I was crazy if they learned of what I did next. I grabbed my bike, and pedaled towards the river. I was a shadow in the darkness, riding between the street lights of the abandoned downtown. It was not the safest place for a woman to be by herself at 3 a.m., but I did not care.

I felt like the purity of the sky and river would protect me from any sinister outcome. It was highly illogical and perhaps incredibly stupid. However, it was what my heart and mind needed to celebrate such a feat that I had dreamed of my entire life.

I sat on a bench, listening to the sounds that surrounded me until the sun broke through the clouds and rose over the river.

10 COOL INSECURITIES

Cool.
My phone jingled a beat, waking me up from a dream. I swiped the new email open and found this dreadful four letter word.

He was not a writer. What did I expect? Obviously, I was hoping for something more than an overused four letter word describing my life changing article.

After staying up the entire night by the river, I had returned home. The excitement had finished coursing through my body, and I fell into a deep sleep sitting straight up on my couch reviewing notes for my next article.

I remembered seeing my grandfather fall asleep sitting straight up in his recliner every Sunday afternoon after church watching a football game. I always wondered how someone could fall asleep sitting straight up. Now I knew. He worked hard all his life. When you give yourself over to your job, sleep is a luxury taken at any brief chance during the day.

I gazed at my phone screen at the word for a few more minutes, and I concluded Clark did not like the article. Would the editor feel the same way? I panicked at the thought that my dream would suddenly vanish with a mere click of my email into the trash by the editor. She would subsequently send another freelancer to step into Quinn's home to get a real story by a real writer.

I began to feel nauseous. I had to find out what was going on. Before I knew what I was doing, I hopped in the shower, dried off, slipped on some clothes and drove over to Clark's house. I did not know what I would say if he happened to be at home, but I had to know what "cool" meant.

Quinn told me in an earlier conversation where Clark lived in her neighborhood, and I immediately recognized the home. It was a large brick and stone house on the river that looked like a small castle to me as a young girl when we passed by in my mom's station wagon on the occasion that we would drive down this road.

I recollect imagining this was where a fairytale may have taken place. Fairytales had always been my favorite books growing up, and even now I fondly recall a specific version of Cinderella with magnificent illustrations that I asked my mother to read to me each night before I went to bed. She was diligent in reminding me that it was a make believe story, and a princess often has to save herself by obtaining an education so she could buy her own shoes and get her own home to move out of her stepmother's house. Then, a prince may or may not come. However, it never stopped me from dreaming of a pumpkin turning into a chariot and whisking me away to a ball where a prince would fall madly in love with me in my sparkling new gown. All of this occurring after I earned my college degree, of course.

There was a truck in the driveway with California license plates, so I assumed he was home. I told myself to maintain my fortitude. I would not concede and reverse out the driveway like a mute fool.

There was a huge knocker on the door that I lifted and let fall to a resounding noise that conveyed a sense of endlessness. I almost backed down at that very second, but Clark opened the door and looked bewildered at my presence at his home.

"Lennon. Hi, what's up? Are you alright?"

I frowned.

"Yes. I mean no. I mean why? Do you think something is wrong?"

"Well," he said, reaching out towards my neck his fingertips just touching my skin, sending a shiver through my body.

I stepped back.

"Your tag is…I think your shirt is on backwards and inside out."

I touched my shirt with my hand around my neck, and I expected my face was as red as the shirt that I had thrown on haphazardly before I rushed over to confront him.

"You must think I am a complete wreck, but I need to talk to you."

"Sure. Come in."

The inside of Clark's home reminded me of the time when I visited the Duke University campus and saw the Gothic style architecture of the buildings. Arches formed at each entryway and exposed wooden beams emitted a dark haunting quality. I expected to see gargoyles and organ music playing in the background, but to my disappointment both were missing from the perfectly staged horror movie setting.

"I was making some tea, and editing the photographs I took yesterday. Would you like to see them?"

He poured me some tea in a divine, delicate china cup and saucer.

Evidently, he was aware of my thoughts that were painted on my face.

"I am sorry. This is all the serving ware I have. A bit fanciful for me, but it might as well be used instead of just collecting cobwebs."

I laughed.

"What?"

"You look so ludicrous. I mean I can envision you playing football with your friends or climbing a mountain with a thermos, but holding a dainty teacup with your pinkie out is very surprising," I said.

"I have done all of those things with a camera in my hand. But I also enjoy my tea as well, Miss Lennon. In the end we can't all be so fashion forward," he teased, reminding me of my obvious snafu with my shirt.

"It's all the style in Paris," I said.

"The next time I am there I will have to check," he said.

"Have you really been to Paris?" I asked like an enthusiastic teenager.

"Yes."

"I have always wanted to travel."

"What's stopping you?"

I was about to reply, but I did not have an answer.

"I don't know."

"All writers should travel."

And then I was reminded of why I came to see him with a sea rushing over my confidence, sending it drowning in a tsunami of inescapable doom.

"Is that why you think my story is bad? I am too inexperienced."

He stared at me.

"I know it is terrible," I rambled on.

"Lennon, it was wonderful. What are you talking about?"

"You described it as cool."

"Yes, it was very cool. Sometimes when I read words like yours I don't even think my photographs are necessary."

I wanted to hug him and cry tears of joy. I stopped myself before he perceived I was even more of a needy freak than he possibly already guessed.

"Thank you."

"Let me show you those photos."

I followed him into a large dark room where every surface was a type of wood. A chaise lounge in an off-white textured fabric was the only light hued feature in the entire room. It was primarily a massive library with built in shelves and one of those ladders on wheels I had seen in movies.

"You know I always wanted to be a librarian growing up. Those books are calling out to me. Do you mind if I borrow a few?"

"They have not been read in years. I would donate them to a museum or library, but my uncle refuses to move anything from the home. He has a hard time letting go of things. I hope not to inherit the same trait."

For the first time I recognized Clark as being uncomfortable and even saddened. I did not like seeing him this way, so I did what I do best. I attempted a humorous comment to lift the tension.

"I have to admit this ladder is like an aphrodisiac. If I found you in any way attractive, I would have to take you on a spinning ride around this room," I said with a wicked smile, letting my arm drape over the ladder flirtatiously.

"Well, it is a good thing you don't find me attractive. I would hate to ruin the reputation of a would be librarian."

"In your dreams, sir. In your dreams."

He laughed, and it was great to see the smile return to his face.

Clark leaned over a large desk which held an enormous flat screen computer monitor.

"Come here. You have to see these. They are better than I could have imagined."

He swiped the screen with his fingers, loading the pictures.

The images were fantastic. I knew when he was taking them they would be good, but this was on an entirely different plane. This was art.

"You are an artist. They are phenomenal."

I pulled up a wooden chair behind the desk, and he began to narrate each photo, telling me why he chose a certain perspective. He loved his work.

When he came to the photo of the family on the porch, I was overcome with emotion. Any tears I did not use the other day in Dr. Kent's office now flowed out of my eyes without barrier.

I was not embarrassed. It was pure unabashed emotion for my family.

Clark handed me a tissue from what I could only guess was a secret wooden compartment in the room as tears blinded my eyes.

"I don't have to use that one, but it is my favorite," he said.

"Oh, you must use it. My emotion has more to do with my family and what they have been going through lately."

Clark remained silent.

My words continued leaking from my mouth like the dripping faucet in my tub after I ran too much hot water. It was not my story to share, but for some unknown reason I felt like I could tell Clark anything and everything regardless of the fact that he was almost a complete stranger. Conceivably, it was because he was not close to the situation that I was able to confide in him.

"Quinn and Jack are going through a rough period, and I am afraid they will not be able to pull out of it."

He leaned back in a chair that he pulled close to the desk, and his hands were clasped in front of him as if he were contemplating my every word.

"She is having an affair with a man we knew as teenagers a long time ago," I said, observing his face that did not flinch.

I could not believe I just said those words, but something in me wanted to continue on the topic to explain my sister's actions.

"It is not actually an affair. They just communicate online, but I think she wants more, and I am terrified she can't see the big picture," I continued on without hesitation.

"She has a beautiful family, and she may give it up for what? Hot romance for a month fizzles when reality strikes with stinky socks on the floor and shaving cream in the sink."

Clark's pensive stare spread into a wide grin.

"You are something you know. Stinky socks and shaving cream? Is that all it takes to make you run for the border?"

My lips pursed into a pout, and my eyes narrowed.

"Is that seriously all you have to say? You are the only person I have spilled my guts to about my family's conflict, and you are making a joke."

"Whoah. Hold on, you are not going to knock me out are you?" he said, laughing even harder.

I got up and paced the shelves searching for a book, unable to directly focus at his intense eyes for fear that I would say something that I would regret forever.

"Come on, Lennon. Everybody has problems."

I ignored him, gently running my fingertips over the spines, trying to locate a title I would take home with me that would hopefully help me forget that I just betrayed my sister to a man who did not even show the slightest bit of empathy for the situation.

I pulled out my favorite book on the planet. I had several print copies and an electronic version on my eReader, but there was something about this leather bound copy of Jane Austen's most famous novel that inspired me to read it once again.

"You don't mind if I borrow this?" I asked, tugging the book under my arm and waving good-bye with a swift flick of my hand.

"No, but wait, Lennon. Stop. Thank you for sharing about your sister. Marriage is difficult."

"And I guess you are the authority?"

I was instantly taken aback by my own cold reply. I was not accustomed to being this forthright and rude. I was overreacting, and I suddenly needed to apologize to cleanse my being from this uncharacteristic combative behavior.

Before I could lament, he replied, "Yeah, I know all about bad marriages."

He rubbed his chin with his fingers and tilted his head up to the ceiling as if something were about to appear to him from beyond the large wooden beams.

"Clark, I am sorry. Please forgive me. I am not usually this rash. I guess I am so protective of my family, and I should not have shared their private conflict with you."

I perched on the chaise lounge, still gripping the book in my hand.

He swiped the screen and turned off the computer.

"I know it is none of my business, but what happened?"

I could not help but ask the question. The story was out there, and my journalistic side leapt on it like a tiger presented with raw meat.

"Do people always tell you everything about

themselves?"

"Kind of," I said, and we were both finally smiling again.

"I don't want to bore you with the details. I was married. It did not last."

"Bore me. I have all day. Besides whatever you tell me will only end up in the local paper," I said, jokingly.

He twisted the pen on the desk until it spun around in a circle.

"We were both very young. I met her while I was an assistant on a photo shoot for a swimsuit catalog. It was my first time working with models, and she was absolutely gorgeous."

"She was a swimsuit model?"

I glanced down at my inside out shirt and ran my tongue over my teeth hoping my lipstick had not ended up there during our conversation. This man was used to being in the presence of models. I must look like a before photo in a daytime makeover show to him.

"Yes. We married soon after. Our jobs had us traveling in different directions, so it was inevitable that we would split apart."

"What about now? No offense, but she must have aged out of her career by now. Have you ever thought of getting back together?"

"No. She still does some modeling, but truthfully it was more than the job that broke us apart."

"Was it infidelity?"

"No. I am not saying there was not cheating, however. I knew she had her affairs. People would talk, and I would hear things. I was not an angel either to be honest. There is so much temptation for a young man in this business. But I did not leave her because of adultery. It was because she did not love me, and I did not want to spend the rest of my life with someone who just tolerated my existence."

"How did you know she did not love you?"

I threw the question out there as if I was asking how was your day instead of why did your wife not love you.

He seemed transfixed on a spot in the wall, attempting to supply an answer to my question that would validate his actions.

"I was sick in the hospital. I was not suffering from a life threatening condition, but I was in pain with a severe back injury from an accident on my mountain bike. She was in town, but she chose to go out with her friends and did not even stop by to check up on me."

He looked directly at me. "It was simple. I knew she did not love me. And I did not love her. If I were in her position, I would not have left an important shoot to visit her if she was in the hospital. I mean it was not life threatening."

He paused and nodded his head as if agreeing with his own thoughts.

"We were both too selfish to love each other more than ourselves."

"At least you ended it before you had children."

"I will probably look back and one day wish I had children. I mean that Ralph is something special."

"My nephew is one-of-a-kind."

"Don't be so gloomy, Clark. You are a man. You can still be baby making until you are in your 80s, and I am sure you will be able to find some young woman who finds your false teeth a turn on."

He picked up a small burgundy wine colored pillow that had been on the back of his wooden chair and threw it in my direction, but I dodged it and threw a counter pillow from the chaise lounge in his direction.

I had not laughed so much in a long time. It was weird how we could be talking about such serious topics and still discover humor in each other's words.

As I was driving back home, I turned up the radio

and began to sing. The doubt about my writing had disappeared and had been replaced with something I could not describe.

And then I hit the brakes, not on my car, but my actual flow of thought.

"Do not crush on him, Lennon," I repeated to myself. "You love to fall for an unattainable man. I repeat, do not start mooning over this guy."

I looked at my eyes in the rearview mirror, hoping they would see what my heart would not.

And then I heard a ring coming from my cell phone once again lost in the bottom of my giant handbag irretrievable on the backseat.

It was odd, but for some unknown reason I felt like it was a message I needed to read. I pulled over on a side street and recovered my phone.

The notification read "Dean Kent."

11 KITCHEN FLOOR
CONVERSATIONS

Every time I received a message from Dr. K it surprised me like a snake under my feet.

I jumped back and stared at the reptile not knowing which way it would go and if it would harm me.

It was safe when I was filling up his inbox with messages that he did not reply to about his book. Whether he was too busy, too disinterested or they just were spam to him, I had continued on my tenacious drive to persuade him to write. After my appointment he had extinguished my hope, and I sent a final email as a way to end the game that evidently only I had wanted to play.

And then he sends me an email, puncturing the bubble that I had created to protect myself from disappointment. What could it possibly say? Please let it be an advertisement sent out to all his patients about some kind of awareness month or health tips. If it was anything else it would restore hope in a venture I had already buried.

Why did I care so much? If this was my optometrist,

who like Dr. Kent is a kind and attractive man, I may have been interested in helping him write a book if he asked me. But I would have probably made up some excuse not to help him if he did not respond to even one of my emails.

What was it about Dr. Kent that made me want to help him? I think I knew, but I was not ready to acknowledge the answer.

I did not open the message on my phone, but took a detour to Quinn's house to tell her about my meeting with Clark and the exquisite photographs he took of her home and family.

Quinn opened the door, and her smile turned into a look of concern.

"What's wrong?"

"Nothing. Why do you say that?"

"Yes, there is something wrong. I can see it on your face."

I shrugged and did not reply.

"I am making some brownies. Ralphie is on a play date. Come in and have one or a few."

I followed the pungent aroma of cocoa to the kitchen which was a topsy-turvy of broken egg shells, mixing bowls and whisks with chocolate waiting to be licked by some lucky person whom I hoped would be me.

"They smell heavenly," I said, holding a warm moist brownie in my palm in Quinn's kitchen.

I did not even want a plate, feeling the gooey warmth between my fingertips as I pinched off a small piece at a time to savor the chocolate bliss.

As I was about to take another bite of the sinful treat I asked, "So does this have some hidden zucchini or vegetable puree?"

"No. Actually, it is just a full fat good mix from a box."

"What? Am I missing something? Maybe I should be

the one asking if everything is alright with you."

She stood by the counter and was about to begin straightening up the mess but stopped to stare out the window.

"I am fine. Sometimes you just have to enjoy life and not be so worried about the consequences."

This carefree version of Quinn was pleasant, but it worried me because I knew there was something triggering this new identity, and I hoped it was not Drew.

"Well, I would love a glass of milk and if you pull out a gallon from the fridge that is not fat free I am calling the FBI, because my sister has been kidnapped and there is an alien imposter in her kitchen."

"You won't have to do that," she said, pouring a glass of fat free milk for me.

"This is fabulous, Quinn. I am going to have to walk five more miles today to burn it off, but I will be dreaming of chocolate tonight."

She sat on the floor, and I did the same, feeling the cool hardwood beneath me. We always liked to lounge on the kitchen floor and talk while our mother was cooking as youngsters. As we became teenagers, we would grab a snack at night and talk for hours about boy or school trouble and really any conflict in our lives. The last time we sat on her kitchen floor I told her I was quitting my job to become a writer.

"Ok, so now that you are on your sugar high, can you please tell me what is bothering you?"

"I drove over to Clark's house this morning."

"Very interesting."

"Oh, no. It was not like that. I sent him my story, and he sent back the word 'cool.'"

"That's good."

"No, I thought it was bad. I overreacted with a fit of low self-confidence, and I went to his house like a lunatic on a mission."

"Please tell me you were not wearing that, or at least tell me it was inside out when you left his house not when you got there."

She pointed to my backwards shirt that now had chocolate crumbs lodged in its wrinkly surface.

"Yes, I wore this. I hate to shatter your bodice ripping romance novel fantasy, but we are just working together."

"Lennon. He's a nice guy, and besides you don't have to marry him. Just go out to dinner and have some fun."

"I am not interested," I said the words so even I halfway believed them. "I found out he liked my story, and that is all that matters."

"Is that all that happened? I was sensing more from the look on your face when you walked in."

"Pretty much. By the way, I saw your pictures. They were phenomenal! You will be really pleased."

"Great! I was so worried my eyes would do that crazy blinking thing in all the pictures. Do you think he will send me some copies?"

"I will ask him. I am sure it is no problem."

"Hold on. I am thrilled about the photos, but you sidetracked the question."

I could not tell her the real reason I was upset was my email from Dr. K, so I came up with something even more believable.

"Clark was married."

"Really, how did that come up?"

"I don't know."

I did not like varying from the truth, but I was not going to admit I shared her personal life with a stranger. I still could not conceive how I betrayed her secret so freely with Clark.

"I think you should ask him out."

"Clark?"

"Who else? You are acting like I put some special ingredient in those brownies, Sister."

"That is not going to happen. There is no way he would even go out with me or anyone around here. He was married to a swimsuit model."

"Seriously, you are joking, right?"

"Nope. It is the truth."

"Let's look her up. Maybe it was a special catalog with those granny swimsuits with the skirts. I am sure you are prettier than her."

"Doubtful."

We both rushed over to her tablet to search for Clark's ex.

It was not long before we found his wedding announcement with her name. Quinn showed me the wedding picture from the newspaper announcement archive. It was a nice photo, but all brides have that special glow.

"See if you can find one of her swimsuit modeling photographs."

Quinn swiped and read for a few moments and swiped her finger again. Her eyes widened, and she powered down the tablet.

"She's ok. Nothing special."

"Let me see," I said, turning on the tablet and reviewing the history on her browser.

"Probably not a good idea."

The photos were a decade old from the catalog dates, but if Clark had been with a woman with a body like this he would never be able to date any women around here.

"I am never eating again, and I am making an appointment with Dr. Clyde for a total makeover tomorrow," Quinn said, sarcastically.

"Quinn, you are perfect. Besides everyone knows all these pictures are airbrushed. I think we both look beautiful," I said, looking at my rumpled attire and the chocolate smudges on her neck, chin and mouth. "As a matter of fact, we are gorgeous. Give me another brownie."

And we both erupted in a fit of giggles, not unlike the kitchen chat sessions we had when we were children.

"Speaking of doctors. You never told me how everything was at your appointment."

"I meant to tell you, but I forgot. Everything seems to be fine. I have to keep monitoring my symptoms. He told me to contact his office if I noticed any changes."

"That is the best news I have heard today," she said, hugging me.

I wanted so badly to confess my feelings about Dr. K to my sister who was my best friend and the person I trusted most in this world.

"I think I am obsessed with a man who does not even know my name. I think there is an Alicia Keys song about it," I would say to Quinn, and we would laugh.

I knew after the laughter she would advise me to end it, and make an appointment with another doctor.

But I would never tell her or anyone I emailed Dr. K. It sounded absurd, me working with him to write a novel. No one would believe that was all we were doing. They would think we were clearly up to no good.

12 THE PATIENT PATIENT

It was midnight before I decided to open Dr. Kent's email.

From: Dr. Dean Kent
To: Lennon Tyler

I think we should write the book. Let's get together for a set schedule. Please be patient with me. I know it will only work if we meet regularly. Agreed?

I had to laugh. I wanted to respond that I was the woman who waited idiotically for a doctor on an exam table for almost two hours. Patience is a virtue I not only practiced but supremely achieved with this man.

We emailed back and forth for the next couple of days, determining a date and time to meet. I suggested meeting in a coffee shop, the hospital, his office or even a bar to scribble some notes and get a plan down on paper.

Each time I was rebuffed with a "no" or totally

ignored.

I did not understand what he wanted. Was he afraid to meet with me in public for some reason? That definitely could not have been him jogging with the woman of a certain reputation if he was this set on appearances.

Finally, we decided to meet at his office on a Sunday morning.

As I was getting ready for the meeting, I glanced at my phone. I emailed him the night before to confirm the time, but I had yet to receive a reply.

I stared at the red dress Quinn had asked me to wear for Clark's photo shoot, but I decided that was not the impression I wanted to give off. It looked fantastic, but I wanted to look professional. I grabbed the standard V neck black dress that fit like a glove. I had worn it on many interviews, and I always received nice compliments and quite a few approving looks whenever I wore it.

I thought about wearing flats, but I instead reached for black high heel sandals that made my calves look great and added a few inches to my height.

I added my grandmother's silver necklace and some large silver hoop earrings to finish off the look. I caught a glimpse of myself in my bathroom mirror as I was getting ready, and I realized a lot had changed since my operation. Those polyester pants and turtleneck I was wearing the night of my emergency surgery no longer fit, and I had mercifully given them a new home at the thrift store.

I had a new life and a zeal for writing that spurred me to live. The radiance in my skin and overall persona had taken a twirl on the merry-go-round of possibilities that led to a healthier and happier me.

I owed much of my renewal to Dr. Kent, and I once again promised myself I would finally tell him face-to-face how he had saved my life in more ways than he knew. It was easy to write things in an email, but I found it much more difficult to share my feelings in person.

I sprayed on a light dusting of Chanel Mademoiselle, checked my teeth for red lipstick marks and was on my way to his office.

I parked in the parking lot and waited, but I did not see another vehicle near his office. I knocked on the locked door, but there was no answer.

This was not good. It was apparent that I was being stood up.

Perhaps he was called to the hospital on an emergency. I sent him an email telling him I must have missed him, and we could schedule another date and time.

I received a reply to my email on my phone.

From: Dr. Dean Kent
To: Lennon Tyler

Are you available now? Why don't you come out to my home?

If I had received this message from someone else for an interview, I would have definitely thought it was a bad sign. Why did he not want to meet in his office?

The circumstances were quite odd. Usually Quinn was the one with the pessimistic scared of her shadow thoughts that often led to possible kidnappings and serial killers in the midst.

I cast away all the dire daydreams of mischief and deceit. Dr. Kent was not a man to be afraid of, and I wanted to finally sit down with him to talk about his book. I decided to take a leap of faith.

From: Lennon Tyler
To: Dr. Dean Kent

I can meet you in about 15 minutes. Text me your address. No vicious Dobermans I hope.

Dr. Kent responded with his address and the words, "They don't bite."

I laughed at his quick response.

Since I started writing again for the paper, I always set up interviews in public places where I knew my surroundings. I did not like relinquishing my control in any situation, and Dr. K seemed to always have me at his advantage.

I drove away from the city to the rural part of the area passing rows of crops. I followed the directions on my phone, and turned down a dirt road.

I looked in the rearview mirror, but the dusty dirt kicked up by my tires made the vision unclear. I could not look back, only forward.

A massive forest of pine trees engulfed the area creating a dimly lit narrow passageway to an unknown destination. Every now and then the sun and blue clouds above would wink to me through the forest.

My mind began to rattle away with the things I would say to him when we would finally meet. Was this all a ploy to seduce me in his hideaway cabin?

I had lived in this area all of my life, but I knew nothing about this part of the land. Anything could be waiting for me at the end of the road.

I finally neared a circular driveway and an ordinary two-story yellow aluminum siding home that could be found in any neighborhood around town. A woman was standing by a minivan talking to whoever was in the vehicle while two adolescent children were near with a rambunctious little white scruffy dog running in circles around them.

I looked down at my clothing, and came to the conclusion I had once again chosen the wrong outfit to wear.

The woman with short orange-blonde hair the color of a creamsicle and freckles covering her arms wore a faded yellow t-shirt, white shorts and flip flops. I could only devise from her attire that this must be a cleaning lady or a babysitter, but as I opened my car door I heard a child yell to her from the steps of the house, "Mom."

I was not a snob in the least. It had been my experience that wives of men with a certain economic distinction all maintained the same general look of tan skin Botoxed and peeled to their youthful desire, Pilates to almost starvation bodies and plain but simply expensive attire. Many of the mommy gang fit this paper doll aesthetic. I would never fit that gel mold, and Dr. K's wife was far from the average as well. I immediately had respect for the couple who did not conform.

I wondered what he had said to her and his family about me. Did she even know I was coming?

I approached her tentatively, hoping not to interrupt her conversation. I waited for a minute or two, but she never looked my way. I was disappointed, guessing the invisible woman that Tara often ignored was also present today. I finally decided to speak up.

"I'm here to see Dr. Kent. I am Lennon Tyler."

She glanced at me for a second and said, "He's in the house."

She continued her conversation with whoever was in the minivan. She did not greet me with her name or even show me the way. It was quite odd.

I walked up the brick steps and rang the doorbell, but no one answered. Similar to my last appointment where I waited in a cold room on an exam table for two hours, Dr. K had me in a position where I felt like a total imbecile. Except this time I was like an unwanted salesperson selling some door to door trinket that no one apparently wished to buy.

Finally, a young boy about the age of 12 came spiraling up the stairs and opened the door. I decided to follow him in and asked, "Is Dr. Kent at home?"

"He's upstairs."

He knew I was coming. I thought it was extremely awkward that he did not meet me at the door.

"Can you tell him Lennon Tyler is here? Please ask him if he wants me to meet him upstairs."

Maybe he just expected me to come up to meet him. Perhaps that is where he had his office. I had surmised it was a laid back atmosphere where obviously no rules of strict etiquette were being assessed.

While I waited standing in my heels on the wooden floor, I took a moment to observe the surroundings. I was waiting in the kitchen where a small island held liter sodas with their caps left unscrewed, bags of pretzels and chips and a plastic bag of bread that was left untied with the slices in danger of slipping off the counter onto the floor. None of the appliances were new, and the dining table for the large family had a vinyl checkered table cloth that looked like something from a chain pizza restaurant. If Quinn were here she would have cleaned up the kitchen while she waited for the doctor. It was a house with many children a nice person would say describing the décor.

It was very surprising, because one could only assume that the doctor had accumulated a sizable income. The river was at his backdoor, but I knew from real estate that it could not have cost as much as the more upscale homes I had visited of other professionals in the area. Maybe the good hearted man had given most of his money to charity.

A tumbling noise came from the stairs as the young

boy ran past me, and his father followed behind him.

He looked at me as if he saw a ghost.

"Hello, Lennon."

"Hi, Dr. Kent. I am so glad we are finally going to write."

"Come on out here."

We walked through the kitchen towards the back of the home where there was an open empty room. There were only a couple of weights on the floor and an abandoned fishing pole. He pushed open the screen door to the deck where there was an adjacent screened in porch area facing the river. I almost tripped over a pair of extremely large sneakers that could only have belonged to Dr. K. He gestured for me to sit in the wicker cushioned chair, and he plopped down onto a matching couch.

The late August air was hot and humid with a few breezes sending minute relief in spurts.

"You must have just come from church," he said, taking in my formal outfit.

"No."

I was about to place my notebook on the coffee table, but it was covered in a layer of dust. I wondered why he brought me to a place in his house that was only used for storage or to air out funky shoes.

"I am sorry I missed you this morning at the office. Did you not get my email last night?"

"I did not see it, but I am glad you came here because I wanted you to see this."

He gestured behind me.

I turned around and was mesmerized. I sat back slowly in the chair and did not speak for several minutes. I had never seen the river more beautiful. The sun reflected off the ripples in a radiant dusting of pure heaven touched by nature in a way that could not be replicated by words, film or artist's hand.

I could not speak for a while as the words caught in my throat at the sheer magnificence of the water. My thoughts rewound to the night I celebrated my magazine article, riding my bike downtown and sitting by the river. I wondered if at the very same time he was across the way lounging on his wicker couch from his screened in porch, writing his words and eventually staring at the sunrise on the water. When I awoke from my midday dream, Dr. Kent was looking at me.

The sounds of his children playing and his dog barking in the background as we sat in the screened porch jostled me from where I was about to go in my mind. It was unbelievably perplexing to be sitting with a man who just showed me the most inspiring landscape. My heart tightened at his words while I was submerged in an ice bath of reality.

"I guess you like it," he smiled.

Still unable to speak I simply gazed at him, and then began to flip through my notes on the book series. I handed them to him, and he read fast scanning each page swiftly without any emotion on his face.

"Wow," he said.

"I know it is a bit um…I really think it is a great idea, and kids will love it."

He was reaching under the sofa and pulled out several yellow legal pads in a stack bound by the largest rubber band I had ever seen.

"I have not shown this to anyone except my family, and they have not really read all of it. It has been something I have worked on for quite a while."

He handed me the large stack.

"I would sit out here and write nights by this lamp or in the early mornings when the sun rose on the river and I could not sleep."

"Are these notes on your book series?"

"No. That was just for fun. This is real."

"I don't understand. Do you want me to read this?"

"Lennon, I am not a writer. You are the writer. I need someone to put it all together."

"You want me to edit your book."

"It's about a young boy growing up in the Midwest who finds his calling in the medical field."

"Is it your life story?"

"Yes and no. Some aspects come directly from life, but most are fiction."

I looked at the handwritten chapters before me, and I felt myself about to make some joke about doctor's handwriting. But I held back all attempts at humor, afraid that he would take the yellow pads back that I yearned to read. It was if he had given me gold, a story untold to anyone's eyes but mine.

No one had ever shared a piece of themselves with me like this before. I thought I was number 505 on Dr. K's most emailed list. I found it jarring to accept that I was the only one he would share his writing with in such a personal way.

"I am honored. Did you want me to read it right now, or can I take it with me?"

The kids were making a lot of noise in the yard, and then they proceeded to bounce a basketball back and forth to each other on the deck.

"Maybe you should take it with you."

"Are you sure?"

Suddenly, the idea of holding this man's only copy of his life story made me frantic with worry. A swift breeze through my open car window sending the papers blowing out onto a field as I drove home, or a spilled cup of hot tea as I read the final page erasing every word in a melted ink mess were just some of the images that popped like giant warning signs in my head.

"I trust you."

"The first thing I am going to do is scan them on my

computer, save them on my drive, cloud, USB and send them to you in an email."

"That is fine."

What was wrong with this man? How could he hand his work over to me like this without a backup? He must really trust me.

He stood up, and I followed him back through his house. As we entered the kitchen the little furry dog ran alongside my legs and licked my ankle, surprising me as I almost tripped.

I laughed. "I guess I have a new boyfriend. What is your name?"

"Jupiter," said Dr. Kent's wife.

I turned towards the windows where the river could be seen.

"You have a spectacular view."

"It was the reason we bought it. The realtor showed it to me, and we made an offer on the spot."

Dr. K was munching on a small plastic bag of pretzels and drinking a soda while his wife talked to me.

It was odd that neither of them thought to introduce her to me or me to her. It was beyond a laid back atmosphere.

"Lennon is going to help me write my book about growing up back home."

"Oh."

She seemed bored and continued to move around things without actually cleaning up.

She eventually lost interest and went to another room, and he showed me out the door. I had a sudden pang of guilt that I let myself think this was anything but a writing partnership.

I was walking towards my car when I heard him say from behind me, "Thank you, Lennon."

I turned back towards him and mumbled a "you're welcome."

I was transfixed by his dark brown-eyed stare and confused entirely by the last hour of my life.

13 IT MUST BE LOVE IF YOU
IGNORE YOUR PIZZA

I completed a final fact check on my article and hit send.

Dr. Kent's stack of yellow legal pads containing the book of his life was safe on my shelf. As soon as I had returned home from my strange visit I wanted to read them, but I knew if I did not write my article first I would not meet my deadline.

I always met my deadline. Even when we had wind gusts that knocked out the power and I wrote by candlelight or when I was sick with the flu I managed to type out a story after interviewing a portrait photographer sounding like a hoarse frog. I put on some red lipstick and tried not to cough all over her photographs that she showed me on her tablet as we talked over a cappuccino in a coffee shop in a blur of cold medicine. The story meant everything to me, and nothing could stop me from meeting a deadline.

I was about to sit down and read Dean's story, curious if there would be any sensational tidbits about his life or if it would be a horribly lackluster journal entry that I would invariably lie and say was fantastic. The thought of a disappointing read led me to call my sister instead.

"Hey, let's go get a pizza."

"Fine. I need to talk. Jack is with Ralph at the soccer field."

The pizza burned the roof of my mouth with gooey mozzarella on top of a thin crust layered with spinach, marinara, onions, green peppers, mushrooms and tomatoes.

Quinn did not touch her slice.

There was 1950s crooner music playing in the background, and no one could hear our conversation above their own at the booths at the pizzeria.

Dark purplish circles were under Quinn's eyes, a sign that she was not feeling well or she was worried and without sleep. The only other time I had seen her like this is when she was not accepted into a graduate arts program at a school in New York which had devastated her plans for the future. She returned home and started dating Jack who had been a friend for years, and then he became so much more to her. I remembered receiving emails from her while I was at Chapel Hill commenting on their dates, but I could not believe it when they were married a year later. I thought she was too young to settle down. I always thought she had given up, but when I saw them together I felt like they were a compatible couple. They seemed to ease into their roles like a comfortable pair of slippers.

"Quinn, eat your pizza. It will make you feel better."

I knew I sounded like our mom, but her endless zombie-like staring was scaring me, and for some reason I thought food would help.

She pulled off her onions from her slice and pinched a miniscule piece of cheese and put it in her mouth.

"What's wrong? You are terrifying me. Please tell me

how I can help, Quinn."

"I can't stop thinking about Drew."

"Are you still emailing him? Is he still emailing you?"

"Yes and yes."

She tied knots in her empty straw wrapper while she continued to talk.

"I tried to stop. He tried to stop. But we can't. I am not sure, but I think I love him."

I chose to ignore the love comment.

"What do you mean you can't stop emailing him? Of course you can. All you have to do is set up a new email account. Don't turn on your phone. Block his messages."

I could not help but take a demonstrative tone. My sister could not destroy her life with this infatuation that would last a month, maybe two. How could they not see that they were just living out some fantasy?

It was easy for me to see how wrong Quinn was about her relationship with Drew. I wonder what she would say about my working with Dr. K on his book, and how it had disturbed my soul.

"What are you going to do, Quinn?"

"I don't know, but if I don't do something I think I may seriously lose my mind."

The waitress came to the table just as Quinn finished her sentence.

"Can I get you anything? How is the pizza?" she said, looking at Quinn's hardly touched slice.

"It's wonderful. Thank you," I said, and she left the table.

"Quinn, you can't be serious. You have a handsome, nice husband and a magazine worthy home."

I straightened my back and pushed my plate away from me. I realized those factors seemed less than plausible when faced with the love component, but I knew something that was worth more than the entire sum of the fractured parts of her life.

"Ralphie, you can't do this to Ralphie. I won't let you do it to him."

"I don't think it is your decision to make. You have no idea what it is like to be married or to be in love. When was the last time you actually even cared about a man you were dating? When was the last time you had a date?"

They were words that were supposed to cut, but they did not even leave a scratch.

I could not and would not tell her how I felt so confused about Dean. I could not argue with her words. I did not let anyone get close to me. This was why it was so easy for me to fall for an unattainable man. It is simple to give your soul over to someone when in the long run you know it is fiction. We were writing a story together, and I was living a dream.

I would not even let myself think about Clark. In my mind he was beyond unattainable if such a category existed.

"You are right. I don't know how you feel."

She sat quietly for a few minutes. I don't think she was expecting me to agree with her.

"If you leave Jack are you going to move to Raleigh? I don't see Drew moving here. It is not like they could open competing law firms."

"No."

"I could see that as a reality show. Let's spin it for the networks."

Quinn laughed finally at my words, and I was relieved.

"Quinn, I hate to ask this, but is he leaving his wife? In these situations it is often always one person who ends up living in the sad divorce apartment with joint custody while the other person ends the affair and goes back to his or her spouse."

"I don't know. He has never mentioned leaving her."

"Then he probably won't."

"But it is not just Drew. I feel like I am getting older, and I have not accomplished anything. I don't paint anymore. You are a writer. You are living your passion."

I could not object to anything she said. It would be devastating to live an entire life for everyone else but yourself. Sometimes it is too late when you finally get a chance to be free to follow your destined path professionally or personally. Sometimes I wish society would reconsider letting you take one of your retirement years while in your 30s and 40s and then return to work until the mandatory retirement age in most professions.

I would have never quit my job if I had not had my life affirming emergency surgery.

I did not understand, however, if it was just her art that Quinn was missing in her life. Quinn had time to paint. Ralphie would soon be in school, and she would be able to work studio hours.

It had to be more than her art that she was missing. Perhaps she never really loved Jack. I sped through their marriage in the photo book of my memories where there was always a smiling couple.

14 YOUR EX IS A WHAT?

The eight-year-old's bone protruded out of his ripped skin on his arm. The two young brothers had been climbing a tree overlooking a corn field where they had just finished racing through the rows. The limb had snapped, and as George reached out to grab something on his way down the bone in his arm fractured.

It was the early 1980s before screens replaced the need for any outdoor play, and the fields had been a world of imaginative adventure for the boys.

Several miles away from their home, Dean instinctively knew what to do. He took off his T-shirt and placed it lightly over his brother's arm.

He could see his brother panicking, and he started to talk to him about a basketball game they had watched the previous night to calm him down.

As I read Dean's words I could imagine his young self finding his calling as he guided his brother to safety.

I had no idea he was so talented. I stopped reading and closed my eyes envisioning Dean writing his story on his comfy dusty couch on his screened in porch while watching the river before him.

My cell phone ringtone which I had changed to a flick of crystal sound disturbed my thoughts.

"Hey, it's Clark."

I almost dropped my phone. It was 7:30 on a Friday night. I would think he would be busy somewhere with someone.

"Hi."

"I have a proposition for you, but you will have to come over to see it."

"Ok. That statement could result in a variety of replies depending on the proposition itself."

"You only need one reply. Yes."

I pretended to ponder a possible Friday night outing.

"I guess I can clear my schedule tonight."

"Well, I would appreciate it and you will, too."

"I am way too easy."

"That is not a bad thing."

This flirty banter made me smile. There were no misconceptions in this conversation like Dean's house of mirrors.

Clark wanted me to come over which was really difficult to believe after viewing the photographs of his wife. Maybe he was using me for my mind. Now that is a statement that is very rare. It was most definitely another working opportunity, but I still decided to forgo the jeans and inside out workout attire for a more flattering ensemble.

I slipped on a flower patterned shift, flat sandals, a long gold chain necklace, small gold hoop earrings and my hair was pulled back in a loose French twist. It was very becoming, but with a high neckline my outfit was saying I like to look nice, but that is all. I was not trying to compete with a swimsuit model. I was here for a professional purpose, I thought.

Unlike the time I had previously been to Clark's house, it was nighttime accentuating the architecture of the house and instilling a haunting quality that spurred my imagination with visions of dark fairytales and looming witches.

"Come on in. I prepared a few appetizers to munch on while we talk as a means of bribery."

"They smell fantastic. Bribe me anytime."

"Where did you learn to cook like this?"

"I dated a sous chef while I lived in Paris."

"Are you serious? A swimsuit model, a sous chef, did you ever date any normal women?"

"Well, when I was in high school, I dated a girl named Jillian."

"I bet she was the homecoming queen."

"No, but she was runner-up for Miss Teen Massachusetts."

"You make me sick."

He laughed and placed a platter of scrumptious looking tiny bites of undetermined origin in front of me.

"I suddenly feel much better."

I plopped one of them in my mouth. It was a mixture of unfamiliar tastes that melted in my mouth, and I craved another immediately.

"I love that you did not even ask me what it was before you dove in."

"Life is too short to be cautious of anything that smells and looks so delicious. You aren't going to tell me they are some kind of reptile or fungus you have doctored up with spices hopefully. Even so they were terrific."

"No crocodile. They are pissaladieres."

I attempted a nod like I was familiar with the dish.

"They have olives and anchovies like a French caramelized onion tart."

"I don't like olives or anchovies, but these are extraordinary."

"Try these grilled peaches wrapped in bacon with a

balsamic glaze, and this is sweet potato and roasted chili ravioli."

He sat two small trays on the ceramic tiled kitchen counter top.

I tasted the spicy sweet ravioli and reached for the glass of sparkling water he had poured to counteract the heat.

"That is amazing."

"Now that I see you are in a good mood, I can tell you why I asked you over."

"Let's go to the library."

"My favorite place."

"I remember."

His grin sent a flutter through my stomach, but then again it could be the appetizers.

He turned on a lamp that created a soft warm glow in the room. He swiped the screen, and breathtaking images of the ocean appeared.

"Did you take these photographs of Nags Head?"

"Yes."

"How did you know they were of the Outer Banks and not some other East Coast destination?"

"I have lived close to the beach my entire life. The sea becomes a part of you. I know it as I know myself, probably better unfortunately."

"That is amazing."

I looked at all of the images, each one presenting a unique perspective on the landscape.

"I am publishing a book of my photographs of the Outer Banks. That is one of the main reasons I came back here for a few months to work on the project."

"The publisher was going to send a writer from New York to write the accompanying foreword. I can't allow that. I needed to find someone who knows the Outer Banks, not a weekend visitor. I want someone whose spirit is with the salt of the air and the rhythm of the waves."

I stopped looking at the photographs and noticed that he was observing my every move.

"I want you to write the foreword to my book of photographs."

I was speechless, and then I started to jump up and down happy that I was in my flat sandals and not in my ridiculous high heels.

"I am guessing you agree?"

"Most definitely."

I did another mini jump in the air not caring how I looked. "Most definitely," I repeated.

"I am going to the beach to photograph a wedding for a senator's daughter next weekend in Corolla, and I would like you to come along."

"They are giving me a large suite. You can have the bedroom. I have slept on many couches before."

My sassy personality wanted to reply with, "I bet."

However, I took another route and asked the most logical question.

"What does a wedding have to do with your book?"

"Well, it will not take up my entire weekend, and I thought I could get some shots in for the book. It would also be a nice opportunity for you to actually experience some of the exact locations where I took the photographs I showed you tonight."

"I will have to check my schedule. If I can get my articles done in time for the paper I am sure I can take the weekend off."

I paused, and the opportunity immediately became so clear. This was one of those moments you would regret for a lifetime if you turned it down. I would probably never get another chance to stay at such a luxurious resort in Corolla.

"What am I saying? Yes. Absolutely. Yes, I will go."

"Is it alright that I am staying in your suite? I mean

will the wedding party be ok with that?"

He nodded and grinned. "I assume they will be fine with it. It was in my contract that I have a room and a guest."

When you have a certain professional reputation, a man like Clark can pretty much do as he pleases.

Clark already knew months ahead that he would have a guest with him.

"Are you sure you wouldn't want to bring a model or a former Miss America instead of a boring writer?"

"You are hardly boring, Lennon. Anyway my stay here in North Carolina did not include time for interludes with women."

Oh, now I see the full picture. I was not a person who could tempt him away from completing his book.

"I am going to email you some of the photos and the address and milepost of each location so you can take my car and go to any of these places while I am shooting photographs for the wedding."

"I won't be driving my own car?"

"I thought we could ride down together. It's more than an hour away, and we can discuss some of the photographs on the drive."

"I will bring my tablet so I can pull them up in the car."

The thought of writing about the beach stirred all kinds of emotions. Living so close to the ocean my entire life I had found that it had become a part of my soul. But this was Clark's story, and I wanted to portray his view. The photographs I had seen were indeed beautiful. However, there was also an equally melancholy aspect to some that I hoped to unveil the meaning behind as we spent the weekend together.

I decided to take my first approach at uncovering this certain tone in the photographs with a light question about his year spent here as a child with his grandparents. I assumed they had a cottage at the beach. Most wealthy families in the area owned one of the cottages on the Nags Head oceanfront. Signs with their family names hung on each of the weathered shingled homes that had survived many hurricanes and nor'easters.

The newer homes, which were primarily rentals, were pastels and bright Easter egg colors with several floors to entertain many families vacationing together.

As he was about to answer my question the phone rang.

"Excuse me. I was expecting an important call. Do you mind?"

"No, please go ahead. I will see myself out."

"I'll email you the details and photos for our trip."

I was back on my sofa at midnight finishing up some stories to get a head start on next week, so I could free up my weekend for the beach.

My phone's email notification popped up with a ring. I decided to keep working on my stories thinking it was just ads or spam this late at night. No one I knew would email me at midnight. If it was an emergency they would just call.

I started writing again on my laptop when a memory from my conversation with Quinn made me pause, my hands hovering over the keys. I kept putting her conflict aside in my head hoping it would fix itself like a knot on a chain necklace eventually working itself with the right pull or maneuver to hang elegantly on a neck. My fear was that the knot Quinn was creating was more of a noose.

I couldn't help myself. I opened another tab and visited Drew's social media page for some investigative work. Multiple photographs of a happy family were on the page along with postings about his daughter's scholarship and early acceptance to her favorite university. I then located his wife's page, and there were posts about an anniversary trip to Hawaii where they snorkeled and enjoyed the honeymoon suite. Did Quinn really think this man was going to leave his family and move with her to some unicorn dreamland where everyone would be happy?

A cricket sang somewhere in the room, but I could not see him. I tried to remember if it was bad luck to kill a cricket. Just to be safe I would leave him alone to sing until his heart was content.

I hoped Quinn would not do anything rash, but it was not in Quinn's nature to hurt the people she loved, so I knew she would never leave them.

I decided to send her a text. If she was not awake she would have turned her phone to silent or off.

When I turned my phone on the email notification said an email was sent by Dean Kent. It was odd that he was emailing me so late at night. Maybe he was on call at the hospital, he had a free moment between surgeries and he wanted to remind me to return his manuscript.

From: Dr. Dean Kent
To: Lennon Tyler

Listening to music, looking at the moon on the river

What was this man doing to me?

He sends me an email in the middle of the night. He was obviously thinking about me, or maybe this was his reminder to me to send him some feedback as I read the words on the yellow legal pads.

No, if he wanted my feedback he would have asked directly.

I searched online about relationships looking for a reason for my crush, but it only resulted in a list of mainly lewd topics that were definitely not helpful with my situation. I could not believe I was the only person on earth who could not understand the actions of a man. I thought about starting an anonymous blog for those with helpless heartaches. I am sure the ice cream companies would be one of my best sponsors with advertising banners flickering above the blog reminding people the cure was in the carton.

As a matter of fact when I went to open my freezer there was none, and I went into an immediate need for an ice cream fix. I looked down and thought twice about going to the grocery store in my pajamas, so I found my parents' spare key in a drawer in my kitchen and walked quietly over to their home.

I opened the door and it squeaked open, but I knew they would be sound asleep on the other side of the house.

The freezer was void of any ice cream. I completely forgot. Mom had thrown away all the good stuff for Dad's lower cholesterol diet. I sat at the bar and rubbed my head which was throbbing from staring at a computer screen, lack of ice cream and a man who was messing with my mind. I used to be so proud of myself for having never let any person discombobulate my thinking. I had always been in control which had led to me building a brick wall to protect myself from caring too much about another human being who was not a family member.

Why did I let this man get past this brick barrier? I had never thought it was possible. I had always been the smart pig, but this brown-eyed wolf was going to blow my brick house down.

"Hey, honey. Are you okay?"

My father was yawning as he came into the room wearing his favorite Yankees T-shirt and pajama pants Quinn and I had given him for a birthday when we were teenagers. They still fit him. He was not any larger in weight now than he was then. He was not going to run a marathon anytime soon, but he was not out of shape. I guess age and genetics were playing a role in his high cholesterol.

"I was trying to find some ice cream," I said.

"You are not going to find anything with any taste in that ice box. If you promise not to tell your mother I will let you have some of my stash."

He went over to the cabinet and shuffled around some things before pulling out a handful of candy bars.

"Take your pick," he said, with a variety of chocolate treats in his hands.

I chose the Dove bar, immediately ripping into the package and snapping off a piece of the smooth chocolate.

"They used to have these awesome sayings inside the wrapper. I thought it would be neat to be the person who wrote them."

He yawned and listened in a half way sleep daze and was about to go to bed when he turned back around as if he remembered something.

"Your head. Is it alright? I saw you rubbing it when I came in."

This was an out of the ordinary comment from my dad. He always cared for his children, but never had a medical sense that parents often do when they know their children are unwell. It was shocking for him to comment on my health.

"I am ok, Dad. Thank you for asking."

"Your mom keeps some headache pills for me in the cabinet above the sink in the bathroom if you need any."

"No, I am fine. I will be alright. Don't worry about me."

I gave him a hug. "Thank you for caring so much. I am lucky to have a dad like you."

He smiled, but a look of concern remained on his face as he left the kitchen. I saw the television flickering in the darkness from the living room. Dad would always get up and watch TV when he could not sleep or something was worrying him.

15 CINDERELLA DID NOT WEAR A BACKLESS DRESS

"If you are going to spend a weekend with Clark you will definitely need to pack something special."

"And what exactly is wrong with my favorite pair of jeans, a couple of tops, some sunscreen and my bathing suit? I am going to the beach."

Quinn was in her walk-in closet searching through racks of clothing organized by season and function. Her shoes were an entire treasure trove of eclectic and stylish from cheap knockoff styles to red bottom big money brands that she had maintained since we were in college. It was a shame she wore a 9 and I wore an 8, or I would constantly borrow from her collection.

"His photographs are amazing. Look at these."

I was holding a tablet, studying the pictures of the Outer Banks he emailed to me.

She ignored my attempt at a diversion continuing to slide hanger after hanger over like she was in a mad 75 percent off sale in search of a deal.

"This one of the sunset on the Wright Memorial Bridge overlooking the sound is mesmerizing. I have so many words and feelings that I associate with all of these photographs, but I don't know if it is too personal to include in his book of photos."

"He knows your style of writing. Evidently that is what he wanted when he asked you to write his foreword. I can't think of anyone who could do a better job."

"Thanks. You are kind of biased on the subject, however."

"I would love your writing even if we did not know each other. People constantly tell me how they enjoy reading your articles. I am rather envious of your success at your craft."

"Why don't you start painting again? I know some of the people at the art gallery downtown, and they would definitely show your work."

She was silent as I continued to hear the hangers move and the swish of clothing moving down a succession of discarded styles.

"I think this is what you need."

"That is beautiful, but there is no way it will fit. Where am I going to wear it?"

"Just do me a favor, and try it on. You should always be prepared for anything."

The dress was a nude color similar to my skin tone with millions of sparkles. The high neckline was offset by an open back that was beyond daring.

"I am glad I never got that tattoo on my back. I knew there was a reason," I said, jokingly.

"I think the real reason is that you faint at the sight of blood and needles."

"Where did you wear this dress?"

"I don't remember any particular occasion."

She seemed rattled at the question.

"I bought it for an event that never happened."

I held the dress in my hands, wondering if she could

be talking about her rendezvous with Drew that never occurred after he called her "trouble" which she would have been in this dress. I did not know how she could have continued to email and obsess over this man after he used such a derogatory word in correlation with her character.

I went into her bathroom and closed the door, still not crazy about showing off my body even though I had worked diligently to get back into shape since my surgery. There was no way this dress was even going to fit over my shoulders much less my hips.

I peeled off my clothing in her bathroom with the claw foot tub, massive shower and double sinks that will be the envy of all in town after the photographs of her home are published in the magazine.

I pulled the dress over my head and let it slide over my body. I looked in the mirror and was stunned. It was absolutely gorgeous. How did Quinn know this would look so great on me?

"You need to be a personal shopper. I would have never guessed this would have fit, but I think it does."

"Wow! It does not just fit, Lennon. It looks like it was made for you. It never goes back in my closet again. It is yours forever."

"Are you sure?"

"Positive."

"Now that I have my Cinderella dress, I need some place to go."

"If you wear this dress, Clark will find a place to take you."

I looked at myself in the mirror, and I think it was the first time I ever allowed myself to think I was beautiful. Your parents say it, your friends say it, your boyfriends say it, sometimes even strangers on the street say it, but I never truly felt beautiful until this moment. I don't know if it was because after my surgery I started seeing everything clearer and I lost some of my inhibitions and insecurities.

As I was putting my ordinary clothes back on in her bathroom, I looked out the grand window by her tub and a single sailboat was in the middle of the river with a white sail picking up the wind.

Quinn was combing through her jewelry box in a manic search for something.

"Did you lose something?"

"No, I thought of the perfect accessory."

She pulled out a long gold chain with a single small star hanging down.

"This will be perfect hanging down your back with the dress."

She wrapped it around my neck fastening it so the star hung just above the waistband of my pants.

"Do you think it is a bit daring?"

"Well, if you mean sexy, yes it is very sexy. That is the entire point."

"Clark is handsome and funny, but Quinn we are so incompatible. What exactly is my point in playing dress-up for this man?"

"It is not for him. It is for you. You need something to make you feel special."

She began straightening up her closet where she had pushed aside several choices in an effort to be the fairy godmother of my storybook weekend at the beach.

"We all need something to make us feel special. How are you doing?"

She plopped on the floor, hanging her head over her legs which she had pulled up to her stomach.

"I tried to end it very cordially, telling him thank you for being such a good friend. I gave him some lame excuse about how the homeless shelter was keeping me busy this fall so I probably would not have time to email."

"What did he say?"

I already knew the answer from the way she was curled in desperation on her walk-in closet floor.

"He replied quicker than any other email I have sent with something about not giving up. It was very ambiguous, and I responded and he replied. We continued several back and forth emails about everything going on in our lives like I had never tried to end it."

"What would you have done if he had listened to your email, and never replied back or replied back with an ok and the conversation ended forever between you both?"

"I am glad he did not stop emailing. I guess I was testing him or me. I don't know. But I guess we both failed, or maybe we passed. I don't know."

I thought about telling her about Dean. His actions and emails were so obtuse I could not understand their meaning. Her phone rang as I was about to share the complete story with her to get her mind off her own troubles before she broke down into a million pieces.

She picked herself up from the floor with the gracefulness of a ballerina and answered the phone in a completely normal voice.

"That is fine. If we are already asleep when you get home there is she crab bisque I made in the refrigerator that you can warm up. Remember to use the bowl that doesn't splatter. The other one you like to use splatters everywhere."

She nodded even though he could not see her.

"Love you, too."

She went back to cleaning up her closet.

"Is everything ok?"

"Yes. He is busy with a real estate deal. He has not been home for the last couple of nights."

I wondered if Drew made the same excuse when he ventured off from his family to email Quinn. Then I had a more repelling thought. Could he be emailing her from his phone in front of his family while they watched television, played rummy or were eating supper? But when I pictured Drew's family with him holding his phone, it was not Drew but Dean and his family.

Was it wrong for me to be communicating with a married man with children? His wife seemed to be aware of who I was when I visited. An even more nauseous thought popped into my mind. Did his wife read my emails and even take the phone and respond? Was I a joke to them?

"Lennon. Lennon."

Quinn was standing beside me.

"I have been talking to you for the last 10 minutes, and you are completely zoned out. I know that look. Are you already worrying about what you will do with Clark this weekend?"

"You know me well," I said, my stomach curling at my deceptiveness.

"Come on. Let's go get Ralphie from his art camp. It should be wrapping up around now. I made bisque, but I think I want something else. Let's grab some tacos from the Taco Shack and go to the park."

"That sounds great!"

The woman standing in front of me was talking about eating fast food. I was seriously worried about my sister.

16 TARA'S HALL PASS

"**I** made it just the way you like it with plenty of whipped cream."

"It's heavenly, Will," I said to the short stout man wearing an apron behind the counter at the Pemberley Deli & Bistro.

"I read your article about Tom. I have known him my entire life, but I still didn't know some of the things you wrote about him, and the article the other day about the animal shelter benefit was great, too."

"Thanks."

It always made me feel content when I realized people were reading and enjoying my words.

I sat down at my usual small table by the window that overlooked the brick street, which was a historical landmark and difficult to drive upon.

Will's wife, Martha, came in through the font door with a burst of energy. They were high school sweethearts and had been married for two decades. I wondered if being together for so long since a young age had been the reason for them adapting to each other's shape and personality like a matching pair of figurines you place on a shelf. They worked together, had two mini-me children and finished each other's sentences around the kitchen. They always looked happy.

This couple was entirely different from the last couple I saw in the deli about to spill coffee on my article. They were in the first stages of a passion filled relationship. It made me ponder what made one stage progress into another and what kept the chain from breaking mid-cycle. What was Will and Martha's secret?

Looking at them, however, I don't know if I would ever desire that kind of relationship where you are so close your identity becomes one unit. Maybe I was too selfish or in a dreamland of yearning for a passion that never exists.

My bagel was slightly burnt on its edges. The crunchy taste with the smooth cream cheese was scrumptious. I closed my eyes and savored each bite with a sip of hot chocolate letting the flavor linger on my tongue. It could be concluded that their marriage was like my hot chocolate, plain to others but so fulfilling.

"I read your silly little column the other day."

I refused to open my eyes hoping the monster would go away. Her persistent chatter lingered, and my face scrunched up as if I were at a garbage dump.

Tara was repellant with her words and actions. I did not want to acknowledge her presence. However, if I continued to ignore her she might attack like a vicious animal with gossip slewing on all social media of her experience with Lennon Tyler at the Pemberley Deli & Bistro. The posts would not be pretty.

"Good morning, Tara. How are you today?"

"I will be much better when school starts," she said, standing with a hand on the hip of her shorts.

Her arms began to move excitedly sending the short sleeves of her peach shirt hiking into her armpits. I imagined her wedge heels about to kick up dirt like a bull in a fighting ring.

"Teachers have it so easy with their long summer vacations and holidays all year. The children should be at school now learning something."

I decided not to ask where her three lovely children were at the moment, because they obviously were not with her. I did contemplate mentioning that they were not of school age yet at 1, 3 and 4 years old.

I took another long gulp of hot chocolate. She pulled out the chair across from me wiping a nonexistent crumb from the seat before sitting down, crossing her legs and clutching her purse in her lap as if someone might snatch it at any moment.

"Oh, that's right. You were a teacher before you decided to quit and become Charlotte Bronte."

She actually knew an author's name. Congratulations Tara! Evidently you did learn something in school from those teachers you are complaining about.

"Actually, I was in public relations for a non-profit."

"Hmph. Same difference. Although, you certainly do look better now that you have lost the black glasses, are wearing contacts and actually have a nice figure."

I would have fallen on the floor with the sheer surprise of an actual compliment coming from Tara's mouth if Will had not arrived with her tea and bran muffin.

She ignored him, but I nodded appreciatively at him and he winked.

Tara definitely wanted something, and it must be substantial.

Her straight blonde hair was pulled back into a tight ponytail that bobbed up and down when she talked. It looked as if her eyes were being pulled tight by the hairdo, but Quinn had told me Tara was already venturing to the plastic surgeon for prevention cosmetics. She had a large dark mole on her collarbone visible from the scoop neck shirt she was wearing that undoubtedly could pay for my entire grocery bill for a week. I thought it was odd her plastic surgeon had not recommended removing the mole.

She continued to rattle on, but I lost focus on her words concentrating on the mole who I had named Beatrice out of boredom and survival of this conversation.

"Lennon. Hello? I was asking you about Quinn's magazine article."

"Yes."

I was not going to offer any details.

"Jack told Steve about it, and he said Clark Vincent was the photographer."

"Yes."

So this was the reason for our conversation.

"Is he single?"

Wow. She was not very subtle.

"I don't know."

It really was not a lie. Clark had never clearly said if he had a current girlfriend, fiancée or a regular date for the ball.

Her attention was caught by something on the other side of the window.

"She has some nerve walking down the street like she owns it."

I thought again of the bull and imagined this woman on the sidewalk was definitely fueling Tara like a red cape. She did look better today than the day I saw her in the shop or jogging, almost like she might be happy.

"That old skank stole Yvette's daddy from her momma when we were in college. Thank goodness he caught her cheating and got rid of her before Yvette's baby boy had to call her grandma."

I did not contradict the story which I had been told so many times. I did not argue that Yvette's father is now engaged to his 24-year-old receptionist.

"Not only did she ruin their family, now she is doing it again."

I swallowed hard.

"I heard that she is having some affair with a doctor who is married and has children. I mean I can see it happening with someone who is hot, but she is definitely not."

Don't say it. Don't say it. Don't say it. I silently repeated to myself.

She mentioned how they were spotted at a local bar and their cars were at a cheap motel for everyone to see like they did not even care.

I could not stand it any longer. I would rip it off like a Band-Aid.

"Who is the doctor?"

She finally stopped talking, pausing before she recovered with, "I promised I would not tell."

This meant either she did not want to share her secret with me, or more likely she did not know.

If anybody could get someone to spill information it was me. It came so easily as I asked people to tell me their most personal details of their lives everyday as a reporter.

"I was at the doctor's office the other day. They are so busy I don't know how any of them would have time for an affair."

"They can make time, Lennon," she said, looking at me as if that was the stupidest thing she had ever heard.

"I had a good appointment. My doctor is the best in the region."

Her eyes lit with fire, and I could see the bull's nostrils inflame. She took the bait so easily.

"That is not possible. My doctor is the best."

"Oh, really. What's his name?"

"Dr. Kent."

She said his name without hesitation. I knew if he was the doctor who was having an affair she would let her cards show now, but she did not flinch. If she did know the name of the doctor who was having an affair it was not Dean. On the other hand, if she was bluffing and did not know, it could be Dean.

"Dr. Kent is my doctor, too. So we both have the best doc," I said, smiling.

"He is a hottie, don't you think?"

I knew my face was blushing red as I felt the heat rise on my neck, so I coughed to mask my embarrassing feelings.

"He's ok. He reminds me of a lot of the guys I knew in college."

"You have got to be kidding, Lennon. He is gorgeous."

"He is nice looking for around here, but place him in a large population of fish and he is just a minnow."

"I told Steve, Dr. Kent is my hall pass if he ever becomes available," said Tara.

TMI. I thought I would gag on my last bit of bagel.

I wondered why Tara would have the need to see a surgeon, but I remembered Quinn telling me she went to several different doctors for a variety of unusual reasons. It takes many medical professionals to keep Tara Frankenstein together.

A promising thought also came into my mind that if all the women in town lusted after Dean why would he choose to commit adultery with the woman who just walked by the window.

"So anyway, back to Quinn's magazine shoot and Clark."

She finished off her bran muffin, and took a sip of her tea.

"I have a friend who is interested in him."

I bet.

"Quinn said you were working with him. Can you please give him Genevieve's number? She just had a dreadful divorce, and I think they would be perfect together."

"I can try, but I don't know if he will be interested."

"I am texting you her contact information, including her social media accounts so he can see her. He will be interested. It's not like there is anyone else around here that is dateable," she said, and looked at me and laughed.

The bull was in fighting form, but I did not take the bait.

"Have a good day, Tara," I said, leaving a tip and setting off for a new day of interviews.

17 SHE TOLD ME IT WAS ONLY EMAILS

Jack's ancient 1985 Volvo was in my parents' driveway. He always bragged about its long life even though it spent more time getting its own kind of automotive Botox than Tara. You could hear its breaks squealing several blocks away, it had a tape player that sometimes functioned playing Jack's mix tapes from a century ago and the air conditioner never worked to my knowledge with Jack commenting that he preferred the fresh air.

Jack and his mechanic were on a first name basis.

It was odd that Quinn and Ralphie would be riding with Jack in his car, because when they usually came over it was in Quinn's silver minivan, the standard for all the mommy gang.

I also noticed that my mom's car was not in the driveway, which was out of the ordinary if Quinn and her family had stopped by for a visit.

As I neared the corner of the house, I saw Jack sitting in a chair on the porch scanning his phone with an intense look.

"Hey, Jack. What's up?"

"Lennon, do you have a few minutes to talk?"

He was already out of his chair and walking down the steps towards me.

"Is Quinn here?"

"No. Nobody is here. I guess your parents went out to dinner, so I just waited on the porch."

"Come on up. Do you want something to drink or eat? I should have something in the fridge."

"No, thank you."

I had a sick feeling in my stomach. Until he said the words that I knew he came here to say, I was going to keep on rambling, boring him into a trance so that he would forget his purpose for coming over.

I didn't know what I was saying, but it was a mixture of sports and news of the day.

He responded with a few replies as we made our way upstairs to my apartment.

"Have a seat."

I gestured toward the purple couch and rolled over my desk chair to be close enough to hear him, but far enough away from the interrogations of an attorney with a mission.

"Are you sure you don't want something to eat?"

"No. I'm fine. Kyle ordered me Japanese takeout before I left the office."

"That was nice of her."

I bet that was not the only thing his receptionist would like to do for him.

He put his ankle on his knee and began to tap the edge of his shoe with his finger. Was this a lawyer mesmerizing trick to hypnotize me into spilling my guts?

"That was some amazing photo shoot with Clark. Quinn told me you guys were in elementary school together."

"Yes. He was here living with his grandparents for a

year. I think something happened with his parents. I remember hearing my parents mention something about it, but divorce and financial troubles are not of interest to a 10-year-old boy so I really did not listen. He stayed for the whole school year, but then he moved back with his father I think. I am not really sure. When you are young you don't question those things."

He paused for a moment to adjust the pillow that was sinking behind him.

"Well, not those kinds of things anyway. More like Mom why can't I go skateboarding with Freddie, can I stay up to watch a movie on TV or why do I have to make up my bed?"

"It would be nice if life was always that simple," I said.

"Life is never simple, or it has not been for me."

The conversation was getting heavier than the tractor tires the strength training class participants flipped. I wanted to make a joke to lighten the atmosphere, but I knew it would fall flat for Jack.

"I am fixing us a snack. You can eat it or not."

I began to pour two tall glasses of ginger ale that sizzled over the ice. My mother would always fix Quinn and I ginger ale when we were sick, and it always made us feel better. Hopefully, this would ease Jack's pain, as well. I popped a bag of popcorn in the microwave and divided it into two bowls.

Jack took a sip of his ginger ale and grabbed a handful of popcorn.

"Is this how you trick all these men into falling for you, popcorn and ginger ale?"

"What can I say? I have my tricks."

His intense eyes scanned the room as he ran a hand through his brown hair which curled at the back of his neck just like Ralphie's. It had been a long time since I had seen Jack's hair that long. He usually kept it closely trimmed.

"I know you know."

I almost choked on my popcorn at his abrupt segue. Quinn is my sister and best friend. I refused to share anything with her husband that she told me in confidence. He had to know coming to me was a dead end, so why was he here?

"What do you mean?"

He rolled his eyes. "I know you know about him."

I plastered a vague look on my face. It might get me a good review for a role in a community theater production if the lights were low, and the reviewer sat a great distance from the stage.

"Really, Lennon. Come on we are adults. You were there the other night, and you guys fell asleep on the pier talking about what happened."

"Jack, I am not the person who you should be having this conversation with tonight."

"I was hoping to find some answers. I can't talk to her about it, because I am afraid of hearing words I don't want to hear and saying things to her I will regret saying in anger."

He paused, taking another sip of the ginger ale.

"Once certain words are said they are never forgotten. People can go to therapy or revive a dead marriage, but it always lingers waiting to strike at any future disagreement."

"Jack, I love you as a brother-in-law, but I love my sister more. She is my blood, and I would do anything for her. What exactly do you want me to say?"

"I know you love her, and that is the reason I am coming to you. She is letting him rip our lives apart. It is killing her."

His voice heightened with distress. "Don't you see the way she looks?"

"What do you mean?"

"I don't mean that she looks bad. She looks the same physically, but it is the way she stares like a vacant person who is never in the present always wanting to be somewhere else."

I felt for him, but I would not budge on the subject. I could not let my barriers down.

"If not me, think of Ralphie. It is an entire family she is letting him destroy."

"That is a low blow, Mr. Attorney. You know he means the world to me."

"I am desperate to know the truth. She told me it was just emails, but she is not the same person. It is like I am living with a shell of a woman. It is evident from her actions that she no longer wants to be with me. She only wants him."

I wanted to tell him that Drew was part of her past not her future, but really I did not know her true feelings. I don't even know if Quinn knew what she was doing. From looking at his social media posts, I knew Drew was nowhere near leaving his family. I did not understand his motive in his communication with Quinn.

I could not tell Jack any of these things out of loyalty to my sister.

"I don't want her to leave. It would break me. I love her. I have loved her since we were in high school, and I was a senior walking by her freshman art class. She was painting a picture of the beach, and I felt like someone had punched me in the stomach. It was crazy how much I adored her."

He began to smile at his recollection of memories.

"We did not see each other for years. Soon after she graduated from college and moved back to town I was in the courthouse lobby and she walked in through the doors to make a tax payment for your parents, and I knew that I would ask her to marry me. She was so beautiful."

Jack was a straight shooter direct person, but I was stunned by his candor about how he felt about my sister. I still could not give him the answers he wanted to hear.

"You know I have to tell her we talked."

"I knew you would, but please convince her to do what is best for our family."

"I love her. She needs to know that if nothing else."

I wanted to scream at the ridiculousness of the statement. He lived with her, slept with her and spent most of his life with her. Why did I need to tell her something he could so easily say through words or even actions?

"Lennon, I am terrified. I can't sleep, eat or concentrate on work. My constant thoughts are on how to make her love me again if she ever did. I am not used to losing anything in my life. I can't lose Quinn."

"Ok. I will tell her how you feel, but try telling her yourself tonight."

He shrugged and thumbed his keys in his hands.

"Promise me you will try, Jack."

I patted him on the shoulder as he walked out the door. Mom and Dad were driving up as Jack was descending the stairs.

I did not think this evening could get anymore uncomfortable, but I was wrong.

"I am glad both of you are here," said Mom with a smile as if she saw her son-in-law coming out of her daughter's apartment everyday. "We just went to the market and they had a special on Rocky Hock watermelons. Grab one and take it home with you, Jack."

"Thank you, Rachael. Can I help you bring in the others?"

"No thanks, Jack. It is part of my cardio workout for today," said my dad, lugging two in his arms.

"I better get going then, if you are sure you don't

want any help, Patrick?"

"I'm good."

"Bye, Jack. Tell Ralphie and Quinn we love them," Mom said, waving goodbye with one hand and holding a bag of apples in the other.

I almost laughed out loud. If there is so much love going around why is Quinn so miserable? I wished she would find fulfillment soon.

"Lennon, take a watermelon, too. Have you eaten supper?"

I thought it was sweet how my parents were concerned about my appetite, but sometimes it could be rather annoying. I was a grown woman capable of cooking very well if I was in the mood. Tonight I was famished, however, so I accepted the invitation knowing very well that there would be questions I could no longer dodge.

I followed them into the house. I would text Quinn tomorrow morning, giving Jack ample time to find courage to be honest with his wife about his feelings.

The large colorful Dansk bowl that we had purchased on a shopping trip to a Williamsburg outlet several summers ago held a stir-fry mixture of chicken, pineapple, broccoli, snow peas and carrots over homemade squash pasta.

"This is to die for, Mom. You could open up a restaurant."

She took out her cell phone and snapped a photo of the dish.

"I posted it on social media."

I frowned. "You are not becoming one of those people who document everything they do on social media."

"No, honey. The girls are having a contest to see who can come up with the most screen savory dish. The best looking photo wins."

"What do you win?"

"Nothing. But the winner does get to cook the dish for our next book club."

"Is that really a prize?" I asked, thinking of all the preparations that would send Mom into a frenzy to achieve perfection.

Quinn inherited Mom's need for perfection and making everything Goldilocks "just right" at all social occasions, whereas, I inherited my father's sense of if they don't like it they don't have to eat it.

"They aren't coming here are they?" Dad grumbled.

"Thank you, Patrick, for your obvious confidence in my winning dish," she said, kissing him on the head. "And yes, they are coming here."

"You know you like having all those women coming over, Dad. They are always telling you how handsome you are and how Mom is so lucky to have you."

He twisted his pasta with a fork collecting it with a spoon into a delicious bite.

"What can I say? I am a stud."

We all laughed. He had taken the news of his health hard. It was so nice to see him smiling again. Mom looked relieved.

He looked at Mom. "But don't worry. My eyes are only for you."

"Where else would they be?"

My parents never lacked self-confidence. I did not know where I fell so short in that department.

After I finished washing the dishes, I came into the den to watch some TV with Dad while Mom worked on her Sudoku.

I cuddled up on the sofa and grabbed a blanket from the chill of the air conditioner which they always kept on high.

"It helps me breathe easier," Dad always said when I complained that it was freezing in the room.

The last time I had been as frozen cold I was in Dean's office. I felt the heat surface on my face at the very thought of him wrapping his arms around me. I wished I could stop this infatuation with an unattainable man.

"What's up buttercup?" said Mom.

I immediately brought my hand to my cheek thinking she had noticed me blush.

"Tell us what is going on in our daughters' lives."

They had not noticed the blush fortunately.

I hesitated. I could lie, but they would see through me like a transparent glass about to crack from the fall of betrayal. I did not think they needed to hear the entire story. They did not need that kind of worry right now. I decided on avoidance. It had worked on Jack, but only for a few minutes.

"I am writing the foreword for Clark Vincent's book."

"Congratulations!"

Mom came over and gave me a giant hug.

"What is the book about?" my father asked, turning down the volume on the TV signifying his immediate interest.

"It is a book of photographs of the Outer Banks."

"Does he have a publisher?"

"Yes. I can't believe he chose me. He could have any professional well-known writer his publisher recommended."

"You would know the subject better than any of those people. Your diaper was your first bathing suit. You were born with salt in your veins. I remember holding you in my arms, and your little hand reached out to the ocean wanting to grab it in the distance," Mom said.

"You are a wonderful writer. There is not another better choice out there anywhere period," said Dad.

"I am so excited. I was talking with some people who

have been writing for years in my online writers' group, and some of them have never been published in a magazine and very few have written books or contributed to books."

"It is your gift."

"Thanks. We are going to the beach this weekend. Clark is shooting the wedding for a politician's daughter in Corolla, and he wants me to visit some of the locations of his photos."

"That sounds lovely. Where are you staying?"

"They are giving him this luxury suite."

"Excuse me. What does his suite have to do with where you are staying?"

"It's not like that with us, Dad. It is purely professional."

"Patrick, she is an adult. My goodness, Lennon, it sounds like a very nice weekend you have planned."

Dad turned up the volume on the TV.

"Come on in the kitchen. I will fix us an apple for dessert."

"I rather have my Rocky Road ice cream, thank you very much," he said, audibly above the sound of a mystery drama.

Mom began peeling the apple leaving a skin of perfect circles on the countertop.

"How do you do that?"

"Practice. Do you know how many potatoes I peeled growing up on the farm with your grandparents?"

I picked up the spiral, and it formed an apple shape.

"The girls tell me Mr. Vincent is gorgeous."

"He is very nice looking, but I really don't see him that way."

Mom glared at me with a look of incredulity while continuing to peel. It was like a piano player not having to look at the keys, but it still freaked me out to see her holding a knife guided by her thumb blindly cutting away.

"Dot kept rattling on and on the other day at lunch about how he is renting his grandparents' home from his uncle, and he saw her across the street and helped her take in her groceries. We did not hear the end of it. She kept repeating how he was such a mannerly and handsome man."

"I think he is both. He lived with his grandparents for a year when he was a child. Did you know his parents?"

"No. I believe they were older than your father and me. They were probably more the age of Jack's parents. I do remember your dad saying his grandparents always donated a large sum of money to the high school library each year."

"That was commendable. He got this funny look on his face the other day when he mentioned his similar inability to let things go when he was referring to his uncle."

"I have no idea why people do the things they do or say the things they say. Most of the time their actions are not ruled by logic but by pure spontaneous emotional response."

She did not know how true her words were in relation to her own daughters.

"Why don't you ask him out to dinner? I think it would be good for you to have some fun. You are still young. Don't wait until you are older to have regrets."

"Do you have any regrets?"

"Yes. We all do. But none of them involve a man. Your dad was the second best thing that ever happened to me. You girls are the best thing, but I could not have you if it was not for him."

It was not the first or last time I would hear these words. She said them in front of Dad all the time, and he would always agree that Quinn and I were their best achievements in life.

It made me wonder if I would ever have that same feeling of maternal love. I loved Ralphie, and that would have to be enough for now and maybe forever. After my surgery, Dr. Kent emphasized that it would in no way have an effect my fertility, but he was always very encouraging. I unfortunately knew better.

I never told him or anyone else, but when I went for my first OB/GYN appointment in high school the physician assistant, an older grandmotherly type who was about to retire, informed me that I had a severe case of endometriosis and would never be able to have a baby. I remember sitting on the exam table thinking how my preconceptions of my first exam had been absurd and trivial in comparison. I thought I would enter the appointment with the worst thing being an uncomfortable exam. I left the appointment devastated and unable to share the news that I would never be a mother to anyone. If I acknowledged it openly it would be true.

"Lennon. Lennon are you awake?"

"I am sorry, Mom. I drifted off. I think I am tired."

"This probably isn't the best time to ask you why your sister's husband was leaving your apartment tonight, but I am going to anyway."

"Do we really have to talk about this tonight?"

"Your father and I have been worried for some time. If Jack is coming to see you by himself we can't ignore it any longer."

"I told her you would be asking, and she told me not to worry you with the details."

"Are they getting a divorce?"

"No," I said, rather louder than I imagined.

"Good."

"I really don't know why he came over tonight except that he is desperate. He wants me to help him plead his case, but I have the faintest idea how that might be accomplished. I know there is love between them, but sometimes that is not enough."

"Love is all you should ever strive for in this life."

"Is everything all right in here? I heard Lennon yelling. Your Mom did not try to get you to eat that nasty tofu frozen yogurt did she?"

"No, Dad. Everything's ok."

"I asked Lennon if Quinn and Jack were getting a divorce and that was her reply."

I felt a deep knot form between my eyes.

"Lennon, I don't keep secrets from your father, and we both have been worried. We have known something was going on with them for a while."

"You will understand someday when you are a parent," said Dad. "You can tell when your child is hurting."

18 HE DID NOT SING TO ME

White puffs of cotton were the pillows of my sky as I lay on the surface of the river's smile and closed my eyes. I could hear the fluid motions of my arms and legs through the water, but evidently I could not hear Quinn.

A small neon green ball landed right beside my head, sprinkling the brown river on my face.

I jerked my body upright instinctively feeling the mushy bottom of the river sinking between my toes.

"Good morning, Sis. Do you want some breakfast?"

"Sure. That sounds great."

By the time I climbed the ladder by the pier and dried off with my fluffy beach towel, a little rocket of energy burst out of the back door balancing a plate in each small hand.

"Aunt Lennon, Mom said we could eat on the pier."

"What do you have there?"

"Waffles. They are so good!"

Quinn followed behind him with a tray holding a pitcher of orange juice and a bowl of fruit.

I placed a spoonful of fresh strawberries and

blueberries on top of my waffle letting the juices soak into the small squares.

"Between the meals you and mom are cooking I will definitely not be able to wear that dress this weekend. Although, I don't think I would have a chance to wear it anyway."

"The waffles are oatmeal, so they are healthy. Besides you look terrific. I wish I had your body."

"Yeah, right."

"No. I have always admired your frame, and you are in shape now."

"Thank you."

It was both a compliment and a dagger to my self-esteem when someone would say those words. It was if before I lost my weight I was a monstrosity not fit for public viewing.

"Tell me what is wrong. Are you nervous about this weekend?"

"Why would you think I was nervous?"

"Because when I looked out the window this morning and saw you swimming, I knew there was a conflict weighing on your mind. The only time you wake up this early to swim is when something is bothering you."

I looked over at Ralphie who had already eaten his three bites and was steadfast in moving his toy truck in the wooden grooves in the pier.

"It is not something I can talk about with little listening ears present."

"Ok. Now you have me worried. This must be more than man troubles worrying you."

I thought to myself that Jack evidently did not have the courage to face his wife with the truth about his feelings last night. Maybe he did not deserve my sister if he did not have the guts to ask the questions he wanted answered.

My grandmother always told me that it was wise to

never look for trouble. I think this would be the right approach for Jack if he had not already confronted Quinn that night several weeks ago. But now both of them knew what was at stake, and he was too afraid to engage the truth.

"Get out your phone, and text the words you can't say."

"Are we really going to become these people. Mom was posting photographs of the stir-fry she made on her social media page last night."

"I'll be sure to like it on my page I just created as soon as we finish this conversation. Now get out your phone."

I took a deep breath and imagined myself floating on my back in the river once again.

"He came by to see me last night."

"Who?"

I picked up my phone and typed, "Jack."

"He came to your apartment? That is so unlike him. What did he want?"

I texted, "He is worried."

She looked at the text on her phone with a baffled expression and placed it in her lap taking a few minutes to absorb the full meaning of the words.

"I don't understand. What is he worried about?"

I typed, "YOU, Duh."

"He is, he is," she stammered and clenched her fist.

She did not even bother to type, but said the word "unbelievable."

"I spent weeks trying to communicate with him ever since he found the emails, and he chooses not to respond while my insides are being eaten away with acid at the thought of him finally blowing up with anger," she clicks away on her phone noticing her son close by.

"Sorry, texting is not made for these kinds of talks," she said, after having broken down the message into parts before she sent it in a series of messages.

"He wanted me to tell you he loved you."

"Like that is going to solve anything."

"It doesn't? I am confused as usual."

"Why doesn't he tell me he loves me?" she sends.

"He is scared of losing you and his family." I write back adding, "What would you want him to say?"

"I don't know what he could say that would change things at this point. I know you don't want to hear this, but I look forward to any emails or texts I receive from Drew. All of my conversations with Jack seem like a chore."

I put down the phone. "Do you ever email or text Jack your feelings? Maybe it would be easier for you all to communicate this way to ease back into normality."

"I could try."

I saw that she was contemplating this suggestion, and the mood was lifted somewhat until I would have to fess up to my next obliteration of the sister pact.

"You are not going to like this, and remember your reaction around Ralphie."

"You certainly are full of great news this morning, Lennon."

"Mom and Dad saw Jack leaving my apartment last night. They gave him a watermelon."

"Oh, that's where that came from. He did not say anything about it. I just assumed it came from one of his clients. They are always bringing him things they have grown in their gardens."

This was not the reaction I was expecting, but I will take it. It was a relief that she was not angry with me.

"They would have to know at some point. It was actually easier this way."

I held my tongue deciding not to reply with how difficult it had been for me to share her story with them.

She took a blueberry between her fingers and mashed

it until the purple juice slid in droplets down her fingers.

I handed her a napkin, but it would take more than a delicate white flowered cloth to clean up this mess of a situation.

I could not sleep at all that night. I got up and fixed a bowl of cereal, but I was not hungry and it remained in a soggy clump in the bowl. I turned on the TV, but even the voices on the shopping channel could not lull me into a slumber land. My head was pounding, and my pillow felt like iron spikes were sticking into my skull.

It was a mixture of the stress of watching my sister's marriage fall apart, the possibility of whatever was happening with Clark and my ludicrous crush slash writing partnership with my physician who was plainly ignoring my emails. They were the ingredients for a migraine of a certain magnitude. Mrs. Migraine laughed at the presumption that medication and yoga could in any way ease the pain or grip she held on my skull. I had found it was easier to name situations or health problems therefore making them accessible to being overcome.

I noticed Dean's legal pads sitting on my desk. Since I read those first few chapters describing when he helped his brother after a bad fall from a tree, I had sent more than a few emails for suggestions as to where we could meet to discuss his story. Finally, content with the idea that he did not want to be alone with me in a public setting I decided to propose emailing our ideas back and forth, but that email was also floating without a reply. I checked the email address, and it was correct. Maybe there was something wrong with my email account, but my editor had responded to my emails every day. It was not a technical problem. It was a human problem. I could not figure out which human was at fault—him for ignoring my emails or me for consistently attempting to gain a reply from a man who could care less about writing a book.

I decided to write him a message. I would drop off his book in the form of a stack of yellow legal pads with his receptionist at his office. I had to move on before this became an obsession. I was spending more time thinking about his book than about my own writing.

From: Lennon Tyler
To: Dr. Dean Kent

Thank you for saving my life and inspiring me to write. If you ever want to write you know where I am located.

Lennon

I stared at the message on the phone until my hand was numb from holding it. I debated whether to send it to Dean. It was more personal than a patient should be with her doctor I realized as I reread the words. However, when he asked me to his home and shared his book with me he opened a door that I could have never unlocked as a mere number among the throngs of his patients.

I searched his name online once again which was becoming an unhealthy habit. All of his reviews on the physician ratings sites by patients described how he spent time talking with them, and almost all of them mentioned him singing to them at every appointment.

This must not have been the same physician. There had to be another Dean Kent. I had racked up many office visits since my surgery, but he never sang once to me. What did that mean? Did he not like me as much as the others, or did he like me more than the average patient refusing to use his parlor tricks with me? I laughed at myself. He did not sing to me, because he talked with me about sports to fill the gaps in the conversation. Nothing more, nothing less. I kept forgetting that I was patient number 505.

My thoughts about Dean were an endless contradiction.

I had to cease this crush on the man and his book. He did not want to write with me or he would have replied.

With the tap of my screen, the message was sent.

I went to bed and snuggled up under the cool sheets, and sleep washed over me with the relief that my obsession was finally over. I had said goodbye and that was the end.

A panic arose all over my body two hours later after a dream of pure black darkness sent me gasping for air. I was absolutely out of my mind. How could I have given up on a story that could be grand and a man who had saved my life?

I prayed that this message would go answered just like the rest sitting in his inbox. It would be like a weed that would eventually be picked with many others and tossed in the bin without notice that it contained gripping thorns.

I shuffled over to the stack of legal pads and began to read them again. I wondered if Dean could also not sleep. He might be writing on his porch and staring at the stars in the darkened sky as the water lapped against the pier.

My phone rang an email notification. It was 3:06 a.m.

From: Dr. Dean Kent
To: Lennon Tyler

When are we going to meet? Sausage and cheese biscuits this Sunday at my house?

Self-control was my friend. Don't do something you will regret later, I told myself.

I wanted to call up Dean, regardless of the hour, and ask him what exactly was his plan. His number was in my contacts. All I had to do was hit the phone icon and I would be talking with Dean. If I called him I might wake up his wife and children, and I was not that kind of person. Although, they were probably used to late night calls with his profession of saving lives. If I knew he was at the hospital, I might actually give him a call. I was about to call the hospital's main line to see if Dr. Kent was at the hospital when it hit me in the face.

I had been asking this man for weeks to meet with me, and my emails were ignored. Stop chasing the ball, and let it come to you.

Why was it so hard for him to sit down with me to talk about his book? Evidently he had time. He was constantly updating his social media accounts I shamelessly checked frequently. It made me frustrated that he had the time to "like" an irrelevant site or tweet a ridiculous comment, while obviously ignoring my emails about a book that had so much potential.

Was he hesitant to talk about his books because he did not want a critique from me? I had already told him his words were incredibly vivid in my emails. He had to know I loved his book. As a matter of fact I think I even wrote those words.

He chooses now to ask me over to his home on the weekend I had planned with Clark that would go towards attaining one of my professional goals of being published in a book.

From: Lennon Tyler
To: Dr. Dean Kent

I am sorry I can't make it this weekend. I will be out of town. Can we reschedule for next weekend?

I waited for a response, but none came.

I slipped back under my covers. This man was definitely messing with my mind. I thought Drew was taking advantage of Quinn. Now, as I reflected in a semi-dozing state, I recognized at least there was some sort of relationship at the foundation of their communication. I was nothing but Dean's patient. I was waiting for his emails just like I had waited for him on the exam table in his office. I had never been the girl who waited by the phone for a man to call.

I don't know what time I finally fell back asleep, but it was around 8 a.m. on my alarm clock beside my bed as the sun came through the blinds in my bedroom waking me from my hard sleep that left my sheets in tangled disorder.

I checked my phone and there was one text. Dean always emailed, so I did not expect it was him, but there was still a lingering amount of hope that he would have replied in some form to my message.

I clicked on the text icon, and it was from Clark.

"Leaving now. Bride had wedding photo emergency. Your room key will be at the front desk of the resort."

The text time was 6:30 a.m., almost two hours earlier.

I was thoroughly disappointed. I had been looking forward to the drive to the beach with Clark. I would have been able to ask him the questions I needed to know about why he was making a book of photographs about the Outer Banks.

I felt like there was a deeper meaning he was not sharing, and riding in a car would have been the perfect setting for me to ask broad questions that would narrow as we passed each field on the highway with crops in their perfect rows situated between fast food restaurants, gas stations and businesses that had popped up as if planted with a seed.

I was tempted to once again snuggle back under the

covers of my bed until it was closer to the time Clark said he would be available this afternoon to show me the locations of his photographs. However, the beach was calling out to me.

19 TALKING TO THE SEA

The first thing I always did when I crossed the Wright Memorial Bridge onto the Outer Banks was roll down the windows, breathe in the salt air and say hello to the water.

Yes, I actually spoke to the water, and if you are true to her she will reply.

One of my first tumbles with the sea occurred when I was about eight years old. I was standing at the water's edge watching my feet sink into the sand with each extension of the wave's arm foaming over the shore. I was mesmerized by the back and forth motion, the sound of the waves as they sizzled and the tiny shells turning over as if being washed in an enormous machine. I stepped closer and closer until my knees were emerged in her grasp feeling the sun warm my skin as the seagulls chattered above me. Quinn ran up beside me and kicked the foam with her toes. The waves were higher than average, with many surfers dotting the landscape. I inched a little further in to feel the waves splash over my legs as the sun had made me hot and the cool ocean was a relief. I must not have noticed how far I had traveled in because the water was only just above my ankles. I was looking down and I heard her before I saw her crashing right on top of me. As the wall of dark blue broke over my body I was pulled under, my feet sliding out beneath me. I began to panic with my instinct to push toward the surface for air, but I could not. The weight of the water above me was like a brick wall, so I stopped struggling against the wave and let it rock my body back and forth like the shells I had been watching. I looked over and Quinn had also been pulled under and was still in a fight to emerge from the wave. It was suddenly peaceful with the sunlight's rays cascading through the water, and the struggle was almost over, but then she pushed us back out to the shore. It was not our time.

I remember Quinn running back to our parents who had been lost in books and had not seen the episode. It happened in an instant even though it seemed like eternity beneath the sea. There were no tears in her eyes, but she was in shock and would remain by our parents the rest of the day. It was not until our next summer at the beach when her memory faded that she would venture near the water. I was the complete opposite embracing the waves as soon as I emerged splashing in the water, unafraid, because I had never been so at peace in my life even to this day.

I reflected about how Quinn's later mishap with the ocean that sent Drew from his white horse lifeguard stand to save her might be a similar issue she is in conflict with now. I analyzed in my notebook brain that she is searching for someone to save her from her current life. I and everyone around her fail to understand what she needs saving from, and that is the problem.

The lobby of the resort in Corolla was full of people in a bustling chatter of activity. A cloud of a mixture of heavy and expensive perfumes sent my stomach spinning as I opened my purse and found a peppermint to suck on to settle its rumbles. It was like someone had opened a hundred fashion magazines and ripped the free perfume samples from them all. I would have stepped outside for a moment, but I was finally near the front of the line and an end point was in sight.

Two young women in their 20s stood in front of me in stiletto heels, outrageously short tennis skirts and tank tops. Their skin was a shade of orangeade fake tan, but their long extensions were relatively realistic if not for the fact that no one has hair that thick that has been processed and dyed.

"My sister is highly allergic to chlorine," the one with the bleach blonde locks said to the desk clerk.

The desk clerk smiled and said, "All of the rooms in the resort have been reserved by the wedding party. I am sorry there is not another one available."

Her sister with dark black hair was texting on her phone.

"Who got the ocean views? We are her best friends. There has got to be like a million rooms by the ocean."

The desk clerk bit her tongue deciding not to argue with the million room logic.

"If a room becomes available, we will certainly honor your request."

She had evidently lost the women's attention as they were both looking at their phones smirking at something on the screen and erupting into cackles. If Cinderella had modern stepsisters, these would fit the mold.

They turned around and looked at me their noses scrunching up as if they smelled something rotten. The blonde one's eyes took in my entire form from my shoes to my head like a cyborg listing all of my faults in a screen behind her eyes.

"I guess Cassandra invited everyone she ever met."

These girls made Tara look like a teddy bear.

The clerk exhaled as I approached the desk. I smiled

to let her know I was not another vicious guest on attack mode.

"Hi, I am Lennon Tyler. Clark Vincent said he was leaving a key for me at the front desk."

When she heard Clark's name she giggled a bit, and a gigantic toothy grin spread across her reddened face.

"Mr. Vincent left you a package. She handed me the card key with the room number and then she retrieved something from behind the desk. A black gift bag with an immaculately tied pink bow was placed on the desk before me.

"He is a very nice man. You are a very lucky lady," she said, giggling again.

"Oh, no he is not my," I said.

As I was about to finish the sentence she had moved on to the next person in line. There was no need to ruin her fantasy bubble with the truth. I found myself pulling my small rolling luggage to the elevator after denying help from the bellhop seeing that he was needed by other guests waiting in the lobby.

The room was unlike anything I had ever stayed in at a hotel. Its layout was spacious with a clean white interior design. The wooden floors created a nice contrast that made it feel as if the old beach had embraced the new. There were three doors that exited the sitting area. I opened the one nearest to me and it was the bathroom with a large Jacuzzi tub and an adjacent shower with new fixtures and sparkling tile that made you forget others had ever been there before you. I ran my fingertips along the soft towels that hung on a rack by the door before moving on to the next door.

It was a bedroom with a full bed and a suitcase was already propped by the dresser. Clark had made his pick, and I would be left with the seconds which was only fair because I was his guest, professional acquaintance and nothing more. I should be happy he even invited me. I turned the knob on my bedroom door and was astonished by the massive California King. I was about to run and jump on the massive bed when my eyes were transfixed by the enormous glass doors that led to a balcony with an ocean view.

I felt bad about my initial reaction that Clark had taken the better room. After consideration perhaps Clark did not look in this room or the bellhop brought his luggage to the first bedroom. Whatever the reasoning, I was not about to roll my luggage into what was obviously the room meant for Clark, so I placed it in the other bedroom.

I knew I was once again overthinking everything.

I decided it would not hurt to take advantage of the view while he was not here, so I opened the doors sending the curtains flowing through the air behind me. The ocean breeze covered my body in a salt cocoon of contentment. The beach was littered with figures in various forms of activity in between colorful umbrellas and tents. Among the waves was a man attempting to paddleboard. His family watched holding their arms at a distance in front of them no doubt snapping shots with their cell phones of their vacation on the Outer Banks. The poor guy would never live down his bellyflops and slips off the paddleboard.

I contemplated what was in the package Clark left for me while I watched as several people walked to and from the beach on the long wooden walkway from the resort. I gave the bow a tug, and felt around the crinkling tissue discovering something hard and smooth. I laughed out loud as I pulled out an oblong orange plastic container with the words Waterproof SPF 75.

I texted him, "Ty for the gift. They didn't have 100 SPF?"

Minutes later I received a reply with a smiley face wink and the word, "enjoy."

He followed up with the text, "See you around 5."

I had plenty of time, so I stripped out of my clothes and pulled on my black strapless one piece bathing suit. When I saw it hanging on the rack, I thought it was boring but I tried it on and the high cut sides made my legs look long and the curve around the chest enhanced my figure. I caught a glimpse of myself in the floor length mirror in the bathroom. I looked pretty wow. Don't do it, I told myself. You are in a good mood, don't go looking for the imperfections. Don't turn around. You won't like what you see. No woman is ever very happy with the rear view. Either it is too big, too small, too flat, too wide or cellulite prone. I decided not to spin around and smoothed out my bathing suit on the back with my hands making sure everything was in the right place, and I wasn't too cheeky.

I grabbed a large hat and sunglasses, refreshed my red lipstick and made my way downstairs in my flip flops, cover up and my bag of goodies which contained my music, beach towel, sunscreen, bottle of water and my notebook to jot down my thoughts.

The pathway to the beach sent you through the pool area where almost every lounge chair was occupied and several people were swimming in the pool. Even though the pool itself was enticing, I still did not understand the concept of vacationing at a beach and spending all your time by a pool which could be done anywhere.

The staff outfitted in Bermudas and golf shirts were standing beside a long buffet table filled with fruit, drinks, shrimp, small bite sized sandwiches and an assortment of chocolate muffins and other scrumptious baked goods. Pictures of the happy couple eating at various places were staggered in between the food dishes that appeared in the photos. There was one of them sharing a pretzel at a baseball park which was kind of neat. I would have snagged a soft pretzel on my way to the beach, but I decided since I was not a part of the wedding I should not help myself to the buffet.

I passed many people who gave me the stare down. A few women started whispering, and I knew by the way they glanced at me I was the focus of their conversation. I heard something about "Clark" and "new girlfriend."

I wondered how these people would know about Clark and why they would think I was his new girlfriend. Assumptions are the worst when it comes to uncomfortable and unfamiliar social situations.

"Hello," I heard a voice calling toward me from the few women who had moved their lounge chairs into a semicircle.

I waved and the woman urged me over with one hand while balancing a drink in the other.

I recognized among the women were the two who had been in line in front of me in the lobby.

I did not mean to stare but they all had some kind of glistening oil on their orange looking skin. I wondered if you could naturally tan over a fake tan. I would have to search that interesting quandary later on my tablet.

The woman who called me over had her dark brown hair pulled back in a tight ponytail with enormous diamond stud earrings. She said, "My friends overheard you in the lobby. You are Clark Vincent's…?"

The question was left hanging in the air while they all froze and scowled at me waiting for an answer they would not receive.

I did not want to say I was just a professional acquaintance writing the foreword to his book. He was hired to photograph this wedding so it would be inappropriate if they thought he was dedicating more time to his own work. Knowing his professionalism he had already told the politician and his daughter about me coming with him, but I did not feel comfortable sharing his business with complete strangers.

I simply answered, "Yes."

If they thought they could get any juicy gossip out of me, they were talking to the wrong woman. Everything they asked I answered vaguely with brief replies and a sunny smile.

"Well, I am on my way to the beach," I said, waving goodbye to my new friends.

"Ooh, too much sand," said one of the women, and they all nodded in agreement.

My eyes rolled behind my oversized black sunglasses.

"Please tell Clark, Angel is flying in to make it to the rehearsal dinner," she said with a malicious grin.

"Sure."

If this name was supposed to spur some reaction from me, the ladies were certainly disappointed. Evidently Angel was a current or previous girlfriend. She was probably another supermodel or rocket scientist who also modeled on the Paris runways if Clark's track record held current.

As I walked away I heard them say, "She is certainly white. Maybe he found her at one of those burlesque shows."

"She does have great legs. Angel will be so jealous."

"I think Clark found himself a vampire vixen. I bet she knows how to…"

Thank goodness a resort staffer asked me at that same moment if I would like a beach umbrella that he would place on the beach for me, so I would not have to hear her finish that horrible comment.

"Thank you. That would be nice."

It was unbelievable how crass and vicious the women had been. It was like how the women in town had gossiped about the jewelry shop owner downtown. She had probably overheard their snide remarks, as well. The chatter about her having an affair with a married physician had piqued my interest for obvious reasons similarly to how these women dove into the Q&A session with me. I thought I should warn Clark about the Angel character so he would not be surprised at the rehearsal dinner.

The resort staffer led me to a vacant red and blue umbrella on the beach as my flip flops kicked hot sand onto the back of my legs. I loved the gritty hot feeling of the sand. I placed my bag on the ground, abandoned my flip flops and ran into the ocean as if I was a child letting the cool sea splash against my body. After I greeted the ocean with a dive through the center of her wave cutting through and emerging on the other side, I surfaced reenergized and now able to laugh at the women's comments. They thought I was a burlesque performer. I would definitely have to text that one to Quinn. She deserved a smile.

I rolled out my soft beach towel, and layered myself in Clark's gift which had the faint scent of cocoa butter. The umbrella provided a cool shade from the sun while still allowing views of the tranquil blue sky with white cotton ball clouds. It did not take long before the sea sang me to sleep with the rhythm of her waves.

When I opened my eyes the shadow of a man was in view. I turned around and Clark was standing behind me smiling in cargo pants, a white button up shirt that was rolled up to his elbows and a camera hanging around his neck. I could not see his eyes behind his sunglasses but I knew from his grin that there was a bit of mischief in them. I immediately touched my top to make sure my bathing suit was still in the right place which it was, and I ran a finger by my lips to wipe off any drool but there was none. Why was he smiling? Most of the time I was an embarrassing wreck in Clark's presence, so I could only conclude that I was snoring up a storm.

"Was I snoring?"

"No," he laughed. "You are so unlike any woman I have ever met."

"What does that mean? Do I have a third eye?"

"You are completely honest, and that is totally unique at least in my experience."

He sat down in the sand beside me.

"Well, honestly this is absolutely the best afternoon I had in a while. The suite is magnificent, and being able to walk to the ocean is a dream."

"It is heaven isn't it?"

"I do have to ask. Some women approached me from the wedding party, and wanted to know who I am. I avoided their questions. Are your clients aware of who I am?"

"Don't worry. I am doing them the favor, so they were fine with me bringing an author to the resort who is working on my book."

The word author sounded good coming from his lips.

"I think the women were afraid I was your new girlfriend."

"They are just jealous. Look at you."

"Thank you for the compliment."

He began to shuffle his feet under the sand where the layers were cooler. A few seagulls flew above our heads singing their songs in our silence.

"They did want me to tell you an Angel would be at the rehearsal dinner."

He did not answer, but looked out into the sea for a while.

I jumped up and straightened my large black straw hat that made me think of Audrey Hepburn in *Breakfast at Tiffany's*. I would not let those plastic dreadful women place Clark in a bad mood.

"How much time do you have before you have to start snapping away?"

"They begin the dinner activities in about an hour,"

he said, looking at his watch. "What do you have in mind?"

"That is perfect. Let's go for a walk. This is my favorite part of the day at the beach."

He stood up and brushed the sand off his bottom. I bet those girls would love to help him with that particular chore. He clicked a few photos of the ocean as we started on our stroll through the sand.

I took the position nearest to the ocean letting the water rush over my feet and legs while he walked beside me not getting as wet with his camera. We passed a few people walking their dogs and a woman jogging in her sneakers in the sand. A man was sitting in his chair with a huggie around his beer and a fishing line.

"Now, he is definitely snoring," said Clark, and we laughed passing the man whose line was tugging.

"Shall we tell him that he has hooked one?" I asked.

"No. If it is meant to be it will happen. Besides I think he is enjoying his nap a little more than a possible fish."

"Wouldn't it be wonderful to live here, get off work and go to the beach?"

"Yes. That could be a problem. You might never want to leave the beach, and people would miss reading all of those fantastic stories."

"Are you for real, Clark Vincent?"

He held out his arms and peered at his hands. "I don't think I am an apparition."

"Is that how you steal all those hearts?"

"I have my ways."

"Oh, I bet you do."

"And you don't? Have you not noticed how every man we have passed stares at you? I am surprised the snoring fisherman did not awaken as you passed by."

"You are crazy."

A little boy and girl ran past us with a yellow and

orange sun kite on a string blowing in the breeze. Clark snapped a shot of the kite as a pelican flew by in a race against the sky.

I noticed a purple and white fragment of a shell that caught my eye and stopped to bend down and pick it up.

"Did you find a treasure?"

"Every time I visit the beach I pick up a shell to remember the day."

"What will you remember about this day?"

I paused. "I will remember walking on the beach with a man who made my first magazine publication possible and who is now giving me the opportunity to be a published author in a book."

He looked at me absorbing the words.

"I owe him more than I could ever repay."

"Someone would have given you the opportunity. I am just glad it was me."

"Me, too."

This was getting way too real for me. I needed to change the topic fast before I did something embarrassingly crazy like run into his tan muscular arms and kiss his soft lips. I shook my head forcing myself to think about something else. We were only professional acquaintances.

"Did you get any great shots of the bride and groom today?"

"I spent the morning alternating between a tea with the ladies and a golf luncheon with the men. Tomorrow will be more eventful according to the agenda they emailed me a few hours ago."

"I never wanted a wedding. I rather get married by Elvis in Las Vegas. He will sing "Fools Rush In" while Johnny Depp and I walk down the aisle wearing my favorite red dress and heels. We will eat at one of the city's fantastic restaurants and go back to the room waking up together stress free and deliriously happy.

Then we will fly to the Caribbean, dance on the beach in the moonlight and wake up swimming in the crystal clear blue waters."

"Sounds pretty great to me."

"I am pretty sure it is going to happen," I said, dryly.

My calves felt warm from all the exercise of walking in wet sand. My bare feet sunk into the ground with each step while Clark walked swiftly beside me on the harder patches without as much resistance. I looked up and saw a faint line of black tiny licorice sticks in the distance that I knew was the pier.

"Wow. We have walked a long time. I can almost see the pier. What time is it?"

He looked at his watch. "If I jog back I will make it with plenty of time. Are you alright here?"

"Yes. I am in paradise. Maybe I will meet one of these princes you are talking about, and he can take me back to his sand castle."

"Very funny. I should be done around 8 p.m. Meet me in the lobby. I know this seafood place with a deck and music. It is very french fries and flip flops casual."

"That sounds great. Text me if you have a better offer from a member of your female fan club."

"Not likely."

He was already on his feet jogging perfect strides in the distance with one hand securing the camera wrapped around his neck.

I decided to continue on my trek until I reached the pier, and then I would walk back. The waves were scattered with white caps as the wind kissed the bluish gray surface. I took in every sight I saw so I could attempt to bring what I was feeling onto the page. I wanted the readers of the foreword to actually feel like they are at the Outer Banks when they read my words.

When I returned to the resort I yearned for one of those outdoor showers we always had when my parents rented a cottage during the summer. I remember feeling the heat from the sun above as I took a cool shower after a long hot day at the beach. You could smell the wood as the water hit the sides of the shower which was basically four pieces of wood and a faucet.

There was a bathhouse area at the resort where you could wash away the sand so you did not leave a trail leading back to your room. I liked being able to stay at this fabulous resort, but I loved staying in the old cottages that symbolized the beach experience for me. Some of these older homes were included in Clark's photographs. The ones he took pictures of belonged to the families who had passed them down with each generation.

The cottages had survived many decades of hurricanes. Their weathered shingles wore the battle scars with the nor'easters and fierce winds of March. I imagined each of these places held an abundance of stories that were worthy of the pen.

I rinsed the sand off my feet under the showers, and I made my way back to the room hoping I still had enough time to get ready to meet Clark. I had taken my time on the beach not wanting to leave the ocean's side.

I stripped out of my bathing suit, sand falling to the bathroom floor and found no tan marks thanks to Clark's gift of suntan lotion. The cool shower was soothing to my heated skin. I doused myself in moisturizer from head to toe. I then proceeded to dry my hair with a towel and the warm beach air as I relaxed on a chair on the balcony.

I pulled a shift out of my suitcase. The pink and black geometric designs were both casual and stylish. I wore my sandals with chunky heels to give myself some height. I put on a dab of foundation, lipstick and a spray of perfume. I looked down at my watch and it was 8:30. I was late, but I checked my phone and there were no messages from Clark. He must have also been running late. I flipped on the television and sat down on the couch and waited. I had fallen asleep in the cool air-conditioned room when my phone's ringtone wrenched me from my slumber. It was a text.

"Sorry, I can't make it. The rehearsal dinner is running over. Have fun without me."

He sent a smiley face emoticon. Who was this guy? What man his age sends an emoticon to break a date or whatever it was that we were doing?

He was on a job. I was on a job. There was no reason for me to be upset at being stood up, but I was a little disappointed.

It was already late, and I was famished, so I headed downstairs to find a place to get a bite to eat.

I was reminded of my Grandmother's words, "Don't go looking for trouble, or it will find you."

I wasn't looking for trouble, but it found me anyway.

As I was getting off the elevator, I glanced down the hallway towards the entrance to the dining area where the rehearsal dinner was being held and Clark was talking to a very tall woman with fiery red hair. She was waving her arms dramatically at him. I could see from her profile that she was very beautiful even though her clownish hair was somewhat odd. He was attempting to placate her, but she continued to be distressed. He placed his hand on her lower back and led her back to the party. I noticed there was not a camera around his neck, so his professional responsibilities had ended.

Why didn't he just say he met up with a friend? I would have been disappointed, but I am not his date. He did not have to lie to me. I thought about telling him those exact words if he even returned to our suite tonight. However, I wanted this job more than I wanted to be right so I concluded that I should keep my thoughts to myself.

I drove to my favorite drive-in on the beach. There was still a line to purchase the famous burger at the decades old structure. It used to be one of the few places to get a sandwich and milkshake on the barrier island during my parents' youth. Now every other business was a food establishment or a souvenir shop. You can't stop progress, but I am fond of the memories.

I munched on a hamburger and a strawberry milkshake knowing that I would get up early for another long walk on the beach so the food guilt would not take over, and I could enjoy all the calories I was consuming.

"Hey, Lennon," said a voice from the crowd as I sat at a wooden picnic table.

I looked up and it was one of the mommy mob with her three adolescent children. Her husband was standing to the side scanning his phone. These devices are going to ruin the state of marriage. Piper was one of the nicest of the group, which was saying she would bite but not kill with her words.

"What are you doing here by yourself?"

I pointed to my junk food buffet. I was glad I did not order the giant onion rings, too.

She looked down at my food as if a roach were crawling across the picnic table.

"I wish I could eat anything without caring about my figure. Didn't you have some kind of stomach trouble?" she asked in a tone that was more of an accusation than question.

"I brought the boys and their father to get milkshakes, and then we are going back to the cottage."

"They are good. You should get one," I said, taking a sip from my straw.

She looked disgusted at my ingestion of pure flavorful joy.

"Tara said you were off with that Clark Vincent this weekend. Is he here?"

Her eyes searched the group of people around us.

"No. Just me," I said.

I made her day. Piper had gotten the scoop and would be texting the group as soon as she stopped talking.

"I better get back to my husband. He doesn't like to share me with anyone when we are at the beach."

I almost choked on my milkshake.

I took another big bite of my delicious greasy hamburger, so I would not reply with, "But evidently you don't mind sharing, because he has been texting away with someone else while you have been talking with me."

We both looked at her husband, and she seemed to read my mind.

"He's a dedicated surgeon. He always has to send messages and read emails the hospital sends him."

No one is that dedicated to their job, or gets that special secretive look on their face when they read an email about a gallbladder.

I waved at Frank, and Piper was by his side in seconds.

20 PINK IN THE CLOUDS

I came back to an empty room.

The rehearsal dinner had finished according to the clerk downstairs. He said it looked like the older crowd had retired to their rooms while the couple's younger friends had ventured to sample the nightlife. He said he called a shuttle service for the party to make their bar rounds.

Clark was certainly not photographing shots of the bride's cousins with the groom's fraternity brothers. Obviously, he had not retired for bed and he was not working, or he would have texted me.

I deducted with my Sherlock reasoning there was only one place he could be.

I looked at the empty rooms, and wished I had taken the nice one with the balcony since Clark was not even going to use it. However, the other room had a large window that I opened to feel the ocean breeze. There was no better sound to fall asleep to than the ocean.

I undressed and pulled out of my suitcase the silk pajama set that Quinn made me pack thinking I was going to have some romantic rendezvous with Clark.

I retrieved my phone from my handbag and texted Quinn.

"I did not need the dress or the silk pajamas."

Maybe it was the sugar from the milkshake, but I wasn't tired. I threw on my yoga pants and a T-shirt that I knew I would be using that Quinn scoffed at, daring me to pack.

I slipped on my flip flops and headed to the beach.

This was perhaps even less wise than the night I biked downtown to watch the stars hover over the river.

The beach was lit from the enormous moon illuminating the sand and waves with a radiant glow.

The cottages which I have to refer to as mini beach mansions that lined the Corolla oceanfront were full of activity. Music was booming, and kids without bedtimes were playing while the adults lingered on darkened porches drinking and sharing stories of the times when they were younger. I remembered our parents talking with their friends who had come to spend a couple of days with us at the cottage, while Quinn and I would play. Everyone felt so comfortable and at ease in the coastal setting.

It was weird that now as adults we had not continued the tradition. I tried going with her down to the beach once after she was married and staying at Jack's family cottage. She was so nervous the entire time, cleaning and constantly sweeping up sand. She even lifted up an enormous rug in the living room and got down on her hands and knees to make sure there was not a single speck of sand on any surface.

I asked her why she was so compelled to clean the entire time.

She did not answer me, but I knew Jack's sister was coming down the following week. He also had some cousins that alternated weeks at the cottage. She was cleaning for them.

It made me furious to see how they treated my smart, talented and caring sister. I did not go back for another vacation with her at the cottage. I don't think she ever did again either except when Jack asked her to go specifically for a certain family or work event at the beach.

When she talked about her discussions with Drew and her memories of the beach it was like she had found her love again for the sea.

My phone ringed with a text from Quinn.

"What happened?"

"Spent a lovely day at the beach," I replied.

"Why won't you need the dress?"

"He is with a friend."

"Why didn't he bring her then?"

"I guess she can't write his foreword."

"You will wear the dress someday for someone."

I ended the text conversation with a "ty."

I could not be mad at Clark. He had asked me on a professional outing, so I was not expecting what Quinn had concluded from his invitation. However, I did not like the fact that he had not been honest with me.

It was around 11:30 p.m. before I walked back up the pathway to the resort, having satisfied myself that I had burned a fraction of the calories I consumed earlier at the drive-in. I did not bother to rinse off the sand. After a while it becomes a part of you.

The lobby was pretty dead at night in comparison to hours earlier when I arrived amidst the hustle and bustle of the wedding's guests.

The same desk clerk smiled and waved.

"I get off in an hour," he said with a wink.

Yuck. Do I look like Ms. Desperation?

"My friend is waiting for me in his room."

Well, it was sort of true, except for the part that I knew Clark was definitely in someone else's room, and I really would not classify him as a friend at this point.

I flipped on the light switch in the suite, and once again I felt lucky to be spending a weekend at the beach. This was certainly a luxury I would never be able to afford unless I won the lottery. I opened my door to climb into bed, and the first thing I noticed was the breeze had picked up sending the curtains floating in the air like a ghost's dress.

The second thing I noticed was a half-naked man passed out on his stomach in my bed. The profile of his face in the moonlight was like a Roman statue. His shoulders were strong and contoured with a sheet just barely covering his lower back.

I stood frozen unable to move. If I moved an inch he would wake up and think I was insane staring at his admittedly fabulous form. Slowly walk away I convinced myself. I eyed my luggage that was still by the dresser. I would definitely not be moving that out of here.

I somehow backed out of the room and closed the door without rousing him from his sleep.

He had given me the best room. Was it because he felt guilty for standing me up twice in one day, or did he not even open the other bedroom door to see the incredible view from its balcony?

A less pessimistic person would say he was just a nice guy offering me the better room.

I closed my door and opened the balcony doors. I could feel the breeze, and the curtains began to float softly in my room as they did in Clark's room. I peeled off my yoga pants and climbed under the covers letting the softness envelope me like a much needed hug. I could hear the ocean in the distance, and it was miraculous.

As I began to drift off to sleep I thought it would have been nice if Clark had not messed things up by seeing that woman tonight. He would have probably enjoyed the breeze from this bed. My fingertips traced his jaw line followed by my lips. He awakened at my touch and pulled me close. I opened my eyes and shook my head waking up from my visions. Why was it that I suddenly had a dream about Clark once I knew he was not interested in me and was with someone else? Attraction to the unavailable and unattainable was my standard.

I closed my eyes and pinched my thoughts in my brain. Crushing on Clark was not an option. He had given me an incredible opportunity to write the introduction to his book, and I was not going to destroy it for any physical relationship with him that would end with us both shattering our professional wellbeing.

My eyes were heavy but my thoughts were heavier, keeping me awake until the sea finally sung me a lullaby that rested my thoughts.

When I awoke the next morning there was a note left for me on the table in the sitting area with a disposable coffee cup with a lid and a covered dish. It was nice to see a handwritten note in a world of electronic communication.

Lennon,

We are going to find the right time. Tomorrow everyone from the wedding will be gone, and we can finally concentrate on the book. Please attend the reception tonight at 7 p.m. I told them you will be coming.

Your sister said this is your favorite.

Clark

I stared at the note. Why would he want me to come

to the reception?

I held the cup, smelled the heavenly hot chocolate and smiled. When I uncovered the room service dish there was a bagel with cream cheese in the middle of the plate with a strawberry garnish on the side.

I sent him a simple text.

"Ty."

There was no need for me to hold grudges.

He texted back. "So I will see you tonight?"

"Sure. Unless I get a better offer."

The next text I sent to Quinn.

"When did you talk with Clark about me? This morning he left a note saying you told him about my favorite breakfast foods."

"I was making it for you on the day of the photo shoot at the house, and I told him it was your favorite."

That was so weird. Why would he have remembered that about me? Usually guys are not good with the details. It took my dad a month to realize my mom had dyed her hair another color, and that was after she finally exploded with, "Notice anything different?" pointing to her hair one night at the dinner table when we were in high school. He stared clueless for a while, but guessed correctly. Mom shrugged and we all laughed knowing they still loved each other despite the small hiccups in marriage.

"Cinderella is gonna wear her dress," I texted.

"Fantastic! Where?"

"Wedding reception."

There was not an immediate response, and she was probably thinking the same thing as me. Was he using me to deter the woman who was flailing last night? Did he realize his hook up with her needed a buffer in the form of a fake girlfriend—me? Here I go again, thinking too much. He was being nice by offering me an invitation, and that was all.

"Sorry for the pause. I had to help Ralphie with his breakfast. Have fun tonight," she texted.

Quinn was not overthinking anything either. Why did I assume the worst in every situation?

Clark clearly was never going to have the time to show me the locations of his photo shoots, so I decided to visit them on my own.

The breeze was almost nonexistent today with the ocean gently lapping against the shore fooling newcomers into thinking she was a giant salt water pool. They took their rafts and boogie boards, purchased spontaneously from souvenir shops, and attempted to ride the minimal waves that had been ironed out like a wrinkled dress.

I decided to drive south towards Jockey's Ridge where Clark must have taken to the sky to photograph the large sand dune. The sun beat down on my skin which was layered with three coats of sunscreen. I began to climb the dune like I did when I was younger, digging my feet into the sand while pulling myself up as if I was climbing a mountain. There were easier ways to battle the incline, but this brought back memories of school field trips full of glee and the laughter of my friends as we climbed up the sides of the dune. I took a deep breath, wiped the sweat off my forehead and wished I still had some of that same level of energy and spunk that I did when I was younger. When I finally reached the highest point, I took a minute to absorb the beautiful view. I was at peace at the top, with the sound on one side and the Atlantic Ocean on the other, it was if I had found a balance that was often difficult for people to locate in their daily lives.

I texted a photo of the dune to my father and mother who hopefully had their cell phones turned on. I captioned it with the words:

"Memories of my dad, the Wright Brothers' long lost

relative, as he took to the sky to fulfill a promise he made to his girls."

I laughed remembering my father telling Quinn and I when we were little if we made it to the top of the dune he would hang glide down. He was joking of course, but when we made it to the top we never let him hear the end of it. On the final day of our beach vacation that year he drove us down to Jockey's Ridge to get an ice cream, and then he surprised us by hang gliding off the enormous dune. We stared up at the clouds and waved and shouted at our father with my mother by our side nervously laughing at her husband.

He had never disappointed us. He was always there providing support even when we did not know he was present. I knew I was lucky. Many of my friends growing up would spend every other weekend with their dads as the divorce bug seemed to follow our parents' generation like an epidemic. However, some of my friends' parents who did not divorce would sit at the dinner table without speaking a word. Gruff and short conversation was a bitter side dish of their normality.

As adults we are often consumed in our own entanglements. I wondered what I would have thought if I had walked into Quinn and Jack's house as a child. Before the Drew situation they always seemed to be happy, laughing and talking. It was a warm environment, and I hoped that one day they would be able to go back to the same relationship as before. I knew going back was not possible without some fraying ends, but maybe they could make their relationship even better for Ralphie and for themselves.

I stopped by the same little ice cream shop that still seemed to be popular amidst all the competition that surrounded the small concrete building, and I purchased a mint chocolate waffle cone. I thought about texting that pic, but it would only remind Dad of the food he cannot enjoy anymore.

I did however, snap a shot of a hang glider in the sky over the dune, and I sent it to Clark. He replied within seconds.

"Awesome shot! I am glad you are able to visit some of the settings in my photographs today."

My next stop was a fishing pier I remember my grandfather and grandmother taking me to during summer vacation when Quinn was in art camp. The wooden walkway hovered over the waves extending into the sea. On a calm day like today you could hang your head over the railing and see a glimpse of floating jellyfish. As I reeled in my first fish with the guidance of my grandfather, a small little finned creature was on the hook and a crab was hanging on to his tail. Grandfather unhooked both and we walked under the pier sending them back into the sea in a grand ceremony. My grandfather was a pretty quiet man so whenever he spoke I knew there was a reason.

"You have the sea in your blood, Lennon. Respect her, fear her and most importantly love her."

Now as I walked under the pier, the waves lightly breaking against the long wooden pilings, I thought about my grandparents and missed them dearly.

Clark's photograph under the pier was unlike today. The waves were crashing fiercely against the strong wooden pilings in a tunnel of foam and gray black sea illuminated by dark storm clouds. It was haunting and beautiful. I took out my phone and looked at the image again. Everything was dark except for an abandoned plastic yellow pail in the corner. It was the kind used to form sand castles, collect shells and tiny sea creatures. The white plastic handle on the pail was broken. There had to be some significance to Clark having included this in the image. I jotted down the note on my phone so I could ask him later.

I examined the photographs again and was suddenly taken by an image of a couple walking along the shore. It was full of bright colors from the sea to the sky to the man's red baseball hat and the woman's bright yellow daisy swimsuit. For some reason it felt as if it was not from this decade. The cut of the woman's bathing suit and hair seemed more like the late 1970s early 1980s.

I began to wish that we had been able to ride to the beach together yesterday, so I would have been able to ask him all of these questions. On the other hand, it might be better to discover their meaning on my own, my imagination going in every direction towards any possibility.

I rolled down the windows with my long hair blowing in the wind as I drove towards my next destination. Gaillardias in bloom along the beach road gathered among the sea oats and mounds of sand by cottages. My grandmother told me they were brought to the Barrier Islands years ago by a man who had a broken heart. The flowers reminded him of his lost love. Even at a young age I questioned that logic. Why would you want to remember someone who broke your heart? Either if they did it maliciously, or if it was not within their power as in death or extreme circumstances, I would not want to be reminded of that love which I could not have ever again.

The flowers were beautiful and simple. That is the way love should be.

I stopped my car by one of the many beach access parking areas and snapped a photo of a gathering of the tragic flowers.

I came to the beach often, but looking at the Outer Banks through Clark's lens had me reminiscing about things I had long forgotten and taken for granted.

License plates from different states were on the cars I passed in the parking lot. We were so lucky to live only a short distance away from a paradise people had driven across the country to experience.

I looked at my phone. Quinn was texting me.

"Cinderella, don't be late for the ball."

She knew me well. I would have driven around the beach until the reception was almost over in a daze from the hypnotic salt air.

"Ty, my fairy godmother."

The thought of going to a large party by myself where I knew only one person who would be working the event and unavailable to talk to me would be terrifying for some people, but I saw it as an opportunity for character development for future short stories. The man sipping a vodka tonic and ignoring his wife could actually be the first love of the bride regretting ever having let her go. The woman who sat by herself at a table in a basic black dress may have just learned she had two weeks to live and she was pondering whether to spend any more minutes wasting her life at a reception for a marriage that would hardly last longer than her much abbreviated life.

Another bonus of being a stranger at a reception is not having to answer the question I always receive at receptions where I am known.

"Lennon, when are you going to get married?"

Another favorite, "Are you seeing anyone special?"

After I quit my job and moved back in with my parents the questions have dissipated and been replaced with a general statement.

"I bet your parents are glad to have you home."

In their eyes they saw what they used to say a century ago, a spinster.

Sometimes I would hear them say when they thought I could not hear, "But she is so pretty."

Then the reasons for my old maid status would perpetuate like an incapacitating virus, and I would move on to the buffet to sample some rubbery shrimp and cream cheese crab dip with cocktail sauce.

Tonight would be different. These people had no idea if I was one of the bride's sorority sisters married with children, a French fashion designer who made her wedding dress, an aide from her father's D.C. office or the groom's cousin who came home from a mission trip to South America just for the wedding. I could truly be anyone.

Usually I would never even think of soaking in a hotel tub, but this one was spotless and actually had a view of the ocean. I poured the entire sample size container of bubble bath into the steaming hot bath and slid slowly under the water until my muscles began to relax from the long walks yesterday and the trek on Jockey's Ridge today.

I wondered if Clark's Angel would hang on to Clark as he attempted to take photographs during the reception. The plastic fake tan ladies I met by the pool may even point me out to her, and then my character study under the guise of no identity girl would be ruined.

I looked down at my arms and lifted my legs out of the bubbles to inspect for lobster red sunburn lines, but I was all clear thankfully protected by my sunscreen.

I polished my nails with a blood red paint on my fingers and toes as my hair air dried. I stepped out onto the balcony in my thick fluffy robe and looked out at the ocean which had still remained calm in the evening hours.

There was pink in the clouds which my grandfather always said meant there would be a storm with perilous wind, but the ocean showed no signs of an impending weather change.

The dress fell over my skin like liquid silk. The nude color was so near to my skin tone that it looked as if I was wearing only a shimmering of glistening sequins and diamond dust. The powder on my face created a porcelain finish and the blood red lipstick matched my nail polish perfectly. I upswept my hair into a lazy French twist. Quinn's necklace was cool against my back. Lastly, I slipped on some strappy nude high heels.

I looked in the mirror and was stunned at my reflection. It somehow came all together, and I knew who would be happy to see me.

I snapped a quick shot of myself in the mirror, so she could get the entire view and texted Quinn my photo.

"Ty, Fairy Godmother."

She immediately replied, "You look gorgeous. Don't forget to stand up straight."

I stuck my tongue out at the phone and laughed.

"My pumpkin awaits," I said to myself.

The wedding had been on the beach, and the reception was at a restaurant where the couple first met according to the summary in the itinerary that was given to all guests during check-in.

I had been to the restaurant before. It was not a formal culinary dining experience, but I could see where a couple could have easily fallen in love while sitting on the deck and enjoying those initial questions you ask each other when you meet a person for the first time.

I wondered if my dress was too fanciful for the occasion, but when I walked through the doors of the older beach restaurant I knew I would be fine. The casual beach experience had been overturned by a wedding planner with an endless budget and a bride with an obvious affinity for a certain color. It was if an interior decorator had blasted everything with purple. There was no sign of the restaurant I knew. The tables had been covered in purple linen tablecloths and white chairs had evidently been rented and placed around each table. Candles floated in glass containers half way full of shells. As I stared about the room at the various floral arrangements mixed with wild flowers I could not say it was elegant or tacky. It was just fun. When I looked up I saw a few men in tuxedos gaping at me and women in all sorts of formal wear glancing my way. I suddenly felt very peculiar. I slicked my tongue over my teeth to make sure my red lipstick had not bled, and I glanced down to make sure everything from shoes to dress was in place.

I felt a hand on my elbow.

"They are staring because you are beautiful, young lady," said a grandmotherly type wearing pearls and a purple dress.

I looked at her and smiled.

"Thank you."

I walked over towards the table overflowing with food and stabbed a piece of pineapple with a toothpick and popped it into my mouth.

"You stand out like a sore thumb," said a gruff cigarette smoker voice beside me.

He had a pile of shrimp on his plate and had already managed to drop some kind of sauce on his lapel.

"Excuse me?"

"There is no one like you here. Even Angel with that red hair does not stand a chance against the likes of you."

"Hmmm. Thank you for the flattery. You have made my day."

"Not as much as you have made mine. I am talking to the prettiest lady in the room."

I stabbed a strawberry and nibbled at it this time.

"You should be wary of that group over there," he nodded towards the group of women I had talked to at the pool.

"They look like a nice group of ladies."

"Don't be deceived by their smiles. They have been talking about you since you walked in. They claim they are friends of Angel, who happens to be my sister, but in all truth none of them would turn down Mr. Clark Vincent."

I listened and offered no reply. This was my standard for not showing my cards while all the other players laid them right on the table.

"They were actually supposed to get married this summer, but something happened and it was a big to-do. Angel would never say what was the cause so I am pretty sure she was the guilty party, because if it was Clark she would have posted his sins on every social media app available as well as running an ad in the local newspaper."

He gobbled up a few more shrimp.

"I can't wait to see her face when she sees you."

This weekend trip was beginning to make more sense. Clark brought me to make his ex-girlfriend jealous. Stop right there I told my overthinker self. If he had wanted to make her jealous he could have called up a swimsuit model. He only asked me to the reception because he felt bad for standing me up. Besides I don't think Clark is a revenge type."

"This fruit is delicious. You should really try some," I said, and moved gracefully away from Mr. Gloom.

It was not long before one of the plastics clattered over to me in stilettos. I had to refrain from asking if she was in the same reptile family as Tara.

"Have you seen Clark?"

I looked around and shook my head no dismissively. I thought this reception would be more fun. I had not been able to play the character game at all in my head. I looked at the woman beside me. Now was a good time to start as I zoned out her words. I gave her the name Cleo and she was an extremely smart Rhodes Scholar who had fallen in love with a man from afar. She abandoned her glasses and mousy hair for a trip to the plastic surgeon, spray tan and extensions. She sought out the man in question and married him. He thought she was just a secretary, but an evil Bond villain scientist mind is behind all that makeup. I almost smiled at my silly character invention.

Her last words jolted me from my daze.

"Angel wanted to make up with him last night, but he would not hear anything about it."

My thoughts went immediately to the vision of Clark on the bed in the crumpled bed sheets. I had incorrectly assumed he had been with Angel before falling into that deep sleep.

I instinctively put my fingers to my mouth surprised at what I was hearing.

The woman lifted her eyebrows.

"Obviously he has his eyes on someone else. Men are always looking for a new toy."

I could not take her snide remarks any longer.

"Excuse me. I promised someone I would not have a miserable time tonight."

I walked onto the deck which continued the purple theme. I decided this must be the new style of gaudy slash rustic.

The breeze stirred the soft curls of hair that had escaped from my French twist. A rather decent band played a song as people flowed in and out from the deck finding a dance floor in the center of the dining room.

I heard a click, and I turned to see Clark holding a camera to his face and snapping away at me.

He released the camera from his hand and let it hang on his chest. He was dressed in a black suit and black shirt. I remembered him saying he dressed in dark colors to fade into the background at shoots, but it was impossible for Clark not to stand out with his blue eyes, thick black hair and sharp angled face perfect for the big screen.

"Hey," he said, softly.

"Did I break your camera?"

"You look amazing," he said without a smile.

"So do you," I said with a little laugh meant to ease the tense moment.

At that moment the bride started to talk loudly about cake, and Clark was off shooting the next spectacle.

I was interested to see if they were going to bring out a sheet cake from the grocery store to tie in with the unusual theme, but instead some ornate massive fondant layered sculpture of a cake that I am sure cost more than my vehicle was carried to a table in the middle of the room by four enormous men in chef's coats.

Everyone started to clap, and I found myself doing the same as I was able to appreciate the minute details as I inched closer to the cake.

I felt a presence beside me nudge my arm slightly.

I looked down and the woman beside me had inadvertently hit my arm with her elbow. I thought it was a mistake until I glanced back up and saw her red hair.

This was really not turning out to be Cinderella's ball. There were way too many evil stepsisters. I hoped she would not push me into the cake like we were characters in some bad Romcom movie.

She looked like she was at least half a foot taller than me with dangerously painful spiked heels and a tight purple spandex dress that left nothing to the imagination.

"I hate weddings," said the woman, who I assumed was Angel.

I decided it was best again to ignore the monster in heels. I had never been so aloof at a wedding before.

"You are Clark's new flavor of the month," she said, smiling at me.

This dialogue was straight from a bad soap opera. I laughed and glared up at the giant freckled mannequin.

"You must know he will never be happy with you.

He will never be happy with anyone."

"Why is that?"

Either she had sparked my curiosity, or I was bored with playing the mute card.

"The same reason we are all screwed up—our parents," she said, flatly.

I looked up into her eyes and realized she was wearing purple contacts to match her dress.

"He thought by publishing this book it would help him get over his demons, but taking a few shots of the beach isn't going to erase any memories," she said.

I looked around for Clark hoping to see his face.

"If you are looking for him, he's taking photos on the deck."

She took a sip from her champagne flute, and did a double take coughing on the fizz.

"You didn't know. Unbelievable. He really is a brick wall when it comes to sharing his emotions."

I continued to search the crowd for a camera, blue eyes or a man dressed in black. If I could capture a glimpse of him I would know if this was the truth. I needed to see his face.

"Don't feel special. I would have never known about his screwed up life either, but a girl's got to do what a girl's got to do."

I had not consumed any alcohol, but my mind was dizzy with her words.

"What do you mean?"

"I thought he was cheating on me like all men usually do. He would be so far away when I was talking to him or doing anything with him, not that I was complaining about that part. I do miss that part. He was so attentive and loving. He was the best lover I have ever had, and I have lived in Europe."

I thought I was going to be sick. Why was this woman spilling her life to me as if I was her paid therapist? I attempted to mentally not hear the words she was saying.

"I read his journals one weekend when he was on assignment taking photographs in Mexico. I assumed I would find a list of all his trysts, but it was something totally different. His parents really did a number on him when he was young."

I doubted if it was even true, but there was something significant about what she was saying. It was in his photographs. The sadness, the yellow pail and the couple walking down the beach were all images that had grasped my heart.

"That is exactly why I am never having kids. Adultery, fighting and divorce all end up hurting the kid more than it ever hurts us. We just keep on going, but they hold it forever."

My stomach actually grumbled, but for some reason my legs would not move away from this annoying demon who continued to pour out intimate details of her relationship with Clark.

Finally, Angel was interrupted by a man asking her to dance. His forehead came up to her chest and the idea of the two on the dance floor made me laugh out of my stunned zone.

I made my way over to the buffet and thought about some rumaki and mushroom caps, but my stomach was still grumbling from Angel's revelations about Clark. I took a tiny snippet of chocolate wedding cake, and my brain began to reboot with the taste of the decadent raspberry chocolate.

A few men asked me to dance. One reeked of garlic from too many helpings of the shrimp scampi as seen on his white dress shirt, one was doused in an aroma of smoke and the other propositioned me for more than a dance with his room number written on a cocktail napkin. I wondered if Cinderella had such a miserable time at the ball before Prince Charming showed his face.

"Hey, there. I heard you have been turning guys down all night," Clark said with a grin.

"Well, George Clooney had too much garlic for my taste, Brad Pitt wanted more than a dance and Johnny Depp was smokin'," I said, nodding towards the men.

"It's a good thing you said no to Johnny and Brad. They both are married to the women who you talked to earlier," he said.

"Those plastic women would have thrown me over the pier for shark food. I can honestly say my picky taste saved my life tonight."

"Who could blame them? You are the best looking woman here."

"I noticed you said woman. Are you trying to tell me something, Clark?"

He laughed and said, "I'm sorry, but my buddy, Samuel, over there has you beat for best looking by a mile."

Samuel was a tiny man in his eighties with a cute red bow tie and tuxedo that I had greeted earlier.

"I have to agree. Samuel was one of the highlights tonight. What happened to your generation? Why can't you all be more like Samuel?"

"I'm not Samuel, but would you make my night and dance with me?"

"I thought you were working," I said.

"I think I can take off my camera for a few minutes. They are all into the champagne now, and airbrushing and computer magic can't even hide a certain level of runny makeup and red ruddy faced inebriation."

"You are surprisingly graceful," I said above the band.

"You are so blunt, Tyler," he said. "Besides why are you surprised?"

"I've been surprised about a lot tonight," I said in

almost a whisper.

"Oh, really. What did you find so surprising?"

I hesitated. "Angel sought me out, and she told me her life story."

He pulled me closer as the fast song turned into a slow cover of a Lenny Kravitz song.

"What else did she tell you?"

"She told me you were the best lover she has ever had, and she described some move?"

"Ok. Ok. I get the picture. You don't want to tell me."

"Now why wouldn't you believe my last statement? I have to say there are a multitude of women who dream about you all the time. Look at them staring right now. They would be so disappointed if you are telling me what I think you are telling me."

"Ha ha. A real man doesn't kiss and tell, or so they say."

We looked over and indeed the women were glaring as if they could wrestle me to the ground and take Clark as their prize.

"I think I may need a body guard pretty soon."

"Lennon, I know you are good at avoiding conversations, but you can be honest with me. What did Angel tell you?" he said, talking close to my ear.

I pulled away from him. "She told me about the photography book."

He pulled me back closer to him as we danced.

"She told me about reading your journals."

He broke away this time. "Angel thinks she knows everything, and she knows nothing."

His face formed an angry frown that I did not even realize was possible.

"Please don't be upset, Clark."

The music stopped as the couple took the microphone.

"I think I need to start shooting again."

"Clark, I won't mention it again. It was none of my business. I am sorry."

"It is none of your business."

I was taken aback by his tone.

"Listen, Angel had no right to tell you anything. I rather not talk about it here," he said in a softer tone and touched my arm.

I sat down at a small table to enjoy a plate of chocolate covered cashews, pineapple and carrots. It was late and I was definitely out of my diet time zone, but I needed nourishment before I fainted from all the uproar during the evening. I pulled my phone out of my clutch and noticed there were several messages from Quinn, my mother and even Jack.

I went to the entryway of the restaurant so I could hear the messages away from the noise of the party and the band. This was not good. I hope Quinn had not decided to leave Jack, but from the numerous messages that is what I had concurred. I cursed Drew and his stupid emails.

When I heard the first message from Quinn, the phone slipped from my hand and dropped to the floor. I don't remember what I did next, but somehow I managed to collect my phone and run out the door in my heels to my vehicle without killing myself in the sand.

I refused to turn on the radio. The day my grandfather passed away when I was in high school I got into my car and drove over to meet my family 30 minutes away in another town. A Smashing Pumpkins CD was playing in my car. I have never been able to hear their music since that day without remembering how alone and sad I felt gripping the steering wheel knowing I would never see my grandfather again.

I did not want any music on that would remind me of this night. Everything was a dark blur with various passing headlights as I sped down the road. I think I could hear my heart beating in my ears as I tried to catch my breath that seemed to linger in my throat. A thousand bugs hit my windshield as I passed through one county after another until I crossed the final bridge home.

This could not be happening. Life could not be this cruel.

21 THERE ARE ALWAYS RISKS

As soon as the sliding glass doors opened and I walked through the entrance to the hospital, I immediately inhaled the smell of antiseptic and death. The last time I entered the building I was rushed in from the ambulance into the emergency room. I was more terrified tonight than I had been when the doctor told me I probably had cancer. I made my way through the chilled hallways, my heels clicking on the sterile shiny floors towards the emergency room entrance.

"How is he?"

Jack was scanning his phone, standing outside of the waiting room.

"Your mother and sister are in with him in the ER room. They are waiting to move him to another floor once a bed opens up."

"He's fine then. It was probably those green peppers on pizza he loves to eat but give him indigestion."

Jack looked at me with that expression parents use with their children when they want to explain bad news.

I looked away from my brother-in-law. He did not know anything about medicine. I needed to talk to a doctor. I wanted to see my father.

A nurse told me I had to wait, because only two people were allowed at a time in the room. I was about to enter the room anyway when my sister and mother came out of the door. We all embraced in a big hug, clinging to each other for some kind of stability.

"Can I go in?"

"The nurse is doing something right now. You can see your father in a couple of minutes."

The thought of them prodding and poking my father made me feel utterly useless in that I was unable to help him while having to depend on strangers to give him the best care possible. I wanted them to know he was a good man. I closed my eyes and willed them to treat him well. Don't give up on him, I silently pleaded through the walls.

"It's just indigestion I am sure," I said.

"I don't know. We have to wait for his test results to come back."

"Mom, let's go sit down in the waiting room until they finish. I am sure you are exhausted," said Quinn.

"No, I want to wait right here. The nurse said it would only be a couple of minutes, and then I can go back in."

"Are you sure? You can get some crackers from a machine and a drink to give you some energy."

"I'm not leaving him," said Mom, adamantly.

"What happened?" I asked.

"We went out to eat with some friends at that new restaurant down on the waterfront. Your dad ordered chicken fajitas, and I had the broiled flounder that was on special."

"Peppers. I knew it. Dad can't eat peppers. He has indigestion. Did someone give him an antacid?"

They both looked at me with the same look that Jack gave me. They thought I was totally in denial, but I knew I was right. There was nothing wrong with my father.

"I drove home, because he said his stomach was hurting. We watched some television and got ready to go to bed."

Quinn had obviously already heard the story and left in search of a snack and a ginger ale. I saw her crying in Jack's arms at the end of the hallway.

"I was already in bed, and he was brushing his teeth when he said he had a sudden pain in his chest and could not breathe."

She paused and looked at the door in anticipation that the nurse would soon finish.

"Well, I guess you made him come here. There was probably no need."

"He told me to call 9-1-1, Lennon."

Those were the only words I needed to hear. My optimism about his health suddenly vanished. I knew what that meant. I did not need laboratory test results or a man in scrubs reiterating what I already now knew. My father never admitted to any sickness, so for him to be the one to ask for help something was definitely wrong.

The nurse finally opened the door and said we could come in.

"When will he get a room?"

"They are still waiting for orders from his doctor after he receives his test results."

I peered around the corner, not wanting to open my eyes afraid of what I might see. It was not as if he had been maimed in a gory accident, but as I relaxed my lids and saw him lying on the bed in one of those horrible gowns my own body became weak.

"Hey, Dad," I said and went over and kissed him on the forehead.

"Mom told me about the fajitas. You know you can't handle salsa, peppers and onions."

"You look beautiful, Lennon," he said.

A small smile appeared on his face.

I had forgotten I was wearing my Cinderella dress, and as I looked down I realized I looked somewhat out of place in the hospital.

"She does, doesn't she, Patrick?" said Mom. "We made a beautiful daughter, two beautiful daughters."

"The best thing I ever did in my life," he said.

My father was fine. He could not be sick. They were talking just like usual. He was even watching sports news on the TV hanging in the corner of the room.

A man whom I assumed was his doctor came through the door with a tablet in his hand.

"Mr. Tyler, I have reviewed your results, and I think the best course of action at this time is surgery."

I felt my mom tense up beside me. "When?" she said.

"I think it is best if we do it soon. Our cardiologist can schedule it tomorrow morning which happens to be in a few hours," he said, checking his watch.

My dad was motionless and speechless in his bed.

"Are there any risks?" my mother continued, the only one of us able to talk.

"With any surgery there are risks," he said. "As I told you before you had the tests this is, in my opinion, your best course of action. Of course, it is ultimately your decision."

My father finally spoke. "I am having the surgery."

The parking lot was dark except for the few lights on tall metal poles floating their grayish green cast over the cement. Bugs congregated around the lights as if worshiping an idol of electricity. Just like the masses that hit my windshield earlier in the night the winged creatures seemed drawn to what was not good for them. The closest light to me flickered about to cease in existence leaving only darkness. My fingers searched my gold sequined clutch for my keys, but they were not there, probably left on a table beside an old magazine in the waiting room of the hospital. I leaned against the door, and I began to cry the first tears I had shed that night. I could not bear to walk back in there. The tears blurred my vision as I tried to squeeze my eyes shut to envision another hazy reality that did not have my father in a hospital bed waiting to have his chest carved open.

I heard steps approach, and my common sense was telling me an empty hospital parking lot in the middle of the night was not the safest place to be. My mind was so wrapped up in emotions that I swore to myself I could morph into Buffy the Vampire Slayer by kicking any loser down with my sheer determination and the void that was suffocating my heart.

I opened my eyes and prepared my hands and legs to produce a knee to the groin of my impending attacker.

"Lennon, are you alright?"

The familiar voice came from a tall figure approaching me.

My body tensed. I gripped my fingers into small fists and readied myself in a position I learned at the one kickboxing class I attended for an article I wrote for the newspaper.

"It's just me. Don't knock me out, Ali," he said.

I could see his wide smile even in the black of night.

My lips wanted to return his smile, but the tears continued to flow and were transforming into body shaking sobs.

"I'm sorry I scared you."

"I'll live, Dr. Kent."

"Dean," he insisted on me calling him by his first name.

"I saw your sister, Quinn, and she told me about your dad."

I started to sob again. He touched my elbow.

"Are you waiting for someone to drive you home?"

"No. I lost my keys and…and," I said, trying to gulp my tears down.

I had never been weak in my life, but there are certain times when you don't give a flip what people think about you.

"I can give you a ride somewhere."

Where did I want to go? I wanted to be with my father, but he needed to rest. My mother would not leave his side propped in an uncomfortable chair by his bed. Quinn had left with Jack to go home an hour before I did. I was all alone. Is this what my life was going to be like when my parents were no longer around? I began to choke on my tears at the disturbing thought.

I looked up into Dean's face and I could barely see his brown eyes, but I knew I was going to let him take me anywhere but here.

"Ok."

His vehicle was parked a few cars down and I remembered his SUV from the time I passed him on the road and the flirty email I had received from him when I neglected to wave. For two seconds I almost stopped crying.

He unlocked the car and opened the door for me.

His car smelled like peanuts, and I was reminded he had kids who had undoubtedly left the remains of peanut butter and jelly sandwiches in the crevices between the backseat. If I glanced down on the floor there would invariably be orange cheese doodle dust and a crayon or two.

I buckled in, he turned on the ignition and a CD started to play. I finally stopped sobbing and laughed. As a matter of fact I could not stop laughing. This man was listening to 80s pop music.

"I'm glad you find my music so amusing."

"No, I like it, but it was unexpected. I thought of you as a more hard rock or even a country fan."

"You made an assumption—an incorrect one."

He took his thick index finger and traced a tear that was falling down my cheek.

"At least I made you stop crying."

He put the car in reverse.

"Where am I taking you?"

"I live downtown in an apartment next to my parents' home."

"Do you have a key to get in?"

"I keep a spare with Bill."

He hesitated. "Bill isn't going to come after me with a shotgun for bringing you home in the middle of the night is he?"

I laughed again.

"I think you are safe. Bill is a toad."

"All men are toads, Lennon."

"Oh, really. Then why should I trust you giving me a ride home?"

"You shouldn't," he said without a smile. "Tell me more about this character, Bill."

"He is short, loveable, always there for me and is not the least bit condescending which is one of my pet peeves."

"He sounds like a good guy, so why do you think he is a toad?"

"Because, like I said before, he is one. Bill is my little amphibian friend that makes his summer home in a flower pot on my deck where I also keep my spare key."

He looked relieved for more than one reason.

"You are something special, Lennon. Not many people see the world the way you do."

He passed my street before I knew it, and we were already at the waterfront when he started to turn the car around.

Dean hit the breaks coming to a complete stop on the street where in the dead of night we seemed to be the only people driving around.

"Look at the moon shining on the river," he said. "It's incredible."

"Turn in here," I told him gesturing towards the waterfront.

He did so without asking why I suddenly wanted to park.

When he parked the car, I got out quickly as if in a trance. I walked towards the river's edge and leaned against the railing transfixed by the rippling surface as it moved beneath the moon's glow.

I heard the car door shut, and soon Dean stood behind me.

"You look like something out of a fairytale in the moonlight with that dress on."

I looked down at the glittering sparkles on the nude colored backless dress that had captured Dean's attention. It was hard to believe only hours ago I had been at a wedding reception at the beach discovering new things about Clark from his ex-fiancée. People often are not what they seem at first glance, and that was certainly true for Clark.

I could feel Dean's presence behind me. He picked up the star necklace dangling down my back between his fingers.

"Beautiful," he said, letting the chain slip from his fingertips, brushing against my skin.

"Have you ever noticed how the water, whether it is the river or the sea, just makes everything right? Even now, how I feel with my life falling apart around me, it is so calming."

He moved closer to me.

"I feel the same way. That is one of the reasons I moved here. Ever since I was a boy my family would take a trip to the Outer Banks every summer from our home in the Midwest. I fell in love with the ocean. Then

I did one of my surgical internships here, and later after I had moved away I ran into someone who offered me a job in his practice here. We found a home on the water, and it all fell into place."

"You were meant to be here."

"I think so. It is the only place my kids have known. We always thought we would go to the mountains and open up a clinic after we got older, but I don't know. Things change and people change. This is my home now."

"I don't think I could ever leave here either, but as far as my profession there is really no way to expand or climb a higher rung in the ladder."

"You could write a book."

I smiled. "Like you. You know your words are captivating. You really should continue to write, but you already know my opinion from my gazillion unanswered emails."

"I just don't have the time to write a book. Every day I think I will find time, but maybe I will have to wait to write when I retire."

"Don't ignore your gift, Dr. Kent."

"Dean. And the same goes for you. Your words inspire me, even your emails."

"So, you do read them?"

"Every single one."

I glimpsed behind me, looked into his eyes and searched for the B.S. signal. It is a certain glare of the eyes that all men get when they are full of flattery and evil intentions. That look was not apparent.

"You really did read my emails."

"You sound surprised."

"I thought you did not care, or you were busy. I assumed they all ended up in your trash."

"No. I cared too much for my own good."

"What do you mean?"

"Lennon, you know exactly what I mean."

I could feel his breath on my neck as he spoke the words, and a shimmer went through my body as I anticipated his touch on my soft skin.

"Are you cold?"

"No. Not at all," I said, turning around to look up into his eyes.

"I have told you this before, but you saved my life in more ways than you know," I said, turning away from him again and back to the river.

"I was doing my job, nothing more, nothing less," he said.

"No, that is not true and you know it. I would have never picked up the pen again if you had not given me a second chance at life. I owe you my everything."

He did not reply. I stared at the water and the lights from the docks, businesses and homes along the river.

I took a step back knowing he would either accept me or take a step back letting the air between us be an unspoken barrier. It was his decision. I felt his choice as he pressed into my leaning body. I turned around and wrapped my arms around his neck and he enclosed his arms around my waist and pulled me towards him.

My body fit perfectly against his as I felt his warmth and heard his heart beating as I held my head against his chest. His fingertips tickled my bare back.

Nothing made sense about this moment. I was devastated about my father, and he was a married man with children who was also my physician. I was not supposed to feel this way. It was not supposed to be this perfect.

I lifted my head and stared into his intense eyes. His smile had disappeared and was replaced by a smoldering gaze.

He leaned close to my face, and I saw his soft lips part before closing my eyes and feeling the faint intoxication of his nearness. Wet droplets hit my face and body, hanging on my eyelashes before trailing down my cheek. I opened my eyes and saw he had pulled away looking up at the sky where rain had burst through its seams. He took my hand and we walked quickly to the car.

It was a sign. He knew it and I knew it, so it did not need to be reiterated with words.

We sat in the seats for a few minutes as the rain tumbled onto the car in large drops and sharp lightning streaks cracked open the clouds and shattered the sky. The thunder was a distant backup singer to my heart that was pounding out of my chest.

He reached behind the seat, his arm searching for something on the floor. He pulled out a flowered beach towel.

"It might be a bit sandy, but it's better than nothing," he said, handing the colorful towel to me.

I dabbed my neck, face and arms with the soft fabric. Dean stared at my body and then turned his face swiftly away towards the river that was mashing about as the rain and wind sent it into havoc.

I looked down at my chest and saw my dress was clinging to my body, and I immediately covered my arms across my body. I knew my face was red, but then an idea popped into my head and I started to laugh.

"What is so funny?"

A smile appeared on his face.

"I am sitting over here basically embarrassed because my wet dress is leaving nothing to the imagination, and then I realized you have seen it all before, several times actually."

He laughed. "Yeah, but that was different."

"Sure, whatever," I said, not believing his words and laughing still.

I took the towel and lightly hit him on the arm. He

ran his hand through his blond wet hair and stared out at the river once again. His jaw tightened as I dabbed the droplets of rain on his arm.

I handed him the towel.

The rain stopped suddenly, but Dean made no move to start the car.

I wondered what he was thinking. My own mind was in a spiral. I yearned to reach out to him, but if I did it would be something that we could never take away. There were too many variables.

He finally spoke breaking the silence. "I think it is time to turn on my favorite singer's CD who obviously has an affinity for a certain hue of rain. I wonder why he did not refer to it as lavender rain?"

"Or lilac rain?"

We both laughed at his silly joke, searching for a way to cut the silence. He turned up the volume, and we listened to the famous singer's greatest hits.

We were halfway through the CD when the sun started to break through the clouds in a spectacular array of colors.

I looked at the clock on his car radio, and it was only an hour before my father would begin prepping for surgery.

"My father will be prepping for surgery soon."

He looked at me and grabbed my hand squeezing it hard.

I was glad he did not give me a physician's standard pre-op speech.

I wanted to start crying again, but I had to be strong for my father, my family and myself.

The sunrise over the river signaled the start of a new day.

22 A RUDE AND SINFUL WORLD

Waiting is excruciating.

Every time a person walked by our door with the familiar shuffle of scrubs, we all turned our heads in unison for an answer.

I had not left my keys last night on the table by the dog-eared magazine that Quinn now browsed through for the tenth time this morning. They were at the bottom of my clutch the entire time. I found them after Dean dropped me off at my apartment, and Bill was waiting patiently for his morning hello with my spare key under his clay pot home.

If I had found them last night, I would have driven away before Dean saw me in the parking lot. It is strange how things occur in life. I am constantly divided between destiny and the choices we make as the guiding path in our lives. When one seems feasible and set in stone, the other scores a point bringing ambiguity into the equation.

My stomach churned and my head throbbed whenever my thoughts drifted to my father on the operating table. Images of a knife cutting into his skin and dark red blood spilling out over the sides and onto gloved hands reversed this morning's hot chocolate I got from the hospital cafeteria sending me gagging for air. In an effort to not break down into a nervous wreck before my family, I chose to concentrate on what happened last night.

I wondered if Dean was sitting at the breakfast table with his wife and kids enjoying a bowl of cereal before he went to work. They would talk about homework and soccer practice. After the bus picked up his kids he would tell his wife he gave a patient a ride home after she lost her keys and was in shambles over her sick father in the hospital. She would roll her eyes and joke that it was simply a woman faking having lost her keys in order to make a move attempting to be the next Mrs. Kent. She was accustomed to having women fawn over her husband.

"She can have the job," she would say, clicking off all the burdens she endured being a doctor's wife.

"I give her a week especially after she finds out we do not have a money tree growing in our backyard, our whale of a mortgage payment, college loans and taxes."

She would frown as she realized her own sad reality and he would gather her into his arms, pulling her into his lap for a familiar hug and kiss.

The other scenario that played in my head had him telling his wife about his long all night surgery never mentioning the rain or the woman who he held in his arms. I thought I was special to him. Even if I was not special and only a mere number out of the 500 women he chose to flirt with on a regular basis, he was with me last night. Neither he nor I would tell a soul about my sobbing theatrics or our near kiss. It was a moment that belonged to us and no other.

There was also that other scenario that crept into my mind like a pessimistic fever that would not break in a chalk board nails voice exclaiming over and over in my head.

"You idiot. You would have given him your everything last night. You are nothing to him but flesh, an easy target, a disposable tissue to be used once and thrown in the garbage. Why would you abandon your moral code, your values that have been at your core for your entire existence for someone who would take advantage of you at your weakest moment?"

I felt ashamed of this possible scenario. I made excuses for him and for me. We were both good people. This could not be a valid determination of the events that occurred. It was not our reality, but maybe that was the point. We were both dreamers searching for some meaning, and for some unknown reason destiny put us into each other's path.

Quinn moved beside me to a pleather orange chair that looked like something from the 1970s. Jack had his earphones plugged into his phone and was playing a video game. Mom had walked down the hall to use the bathroom and grab a coffee. Quinn and I both asked if we could go with her to get a coffee, but she said she needed some time by herself.

"Are you ready to talk?"

"What do you mean?"

I had no idea what she was talking about.

"Why did you show up in a cab to the hospital this morning?"

"Oh."

"Yes, I did see you. What's going on?"

I wanted to share everything with Quinn. She told me everything about Drew, or had she? Last night was something I would not share with anyone. Maybe she had her own secrets, too.

"Nothing's going on, Quinn. I was upset, and I could not drive home last night."

It was not exactly a lie.

"Were you with Clark last night? Is that why you left your car here? How did it go at the beach?"

"No, I was not with Clark. I assume he is still at the beach. His ex-fiancée threw several whoppers at me about his life."

"Was she telling the truth?"

"I doubted her simply for the fact that I could not understand why she would be sharing all of his personal demons with me, as well as, his prowess in the bedroom which I really did not care to hear."

"She was probably trying to scare you off, but then why would she brag about him? That is totally weird."

"Absolutely. And then I saw him later, and I had to tell him what she told me. I don't like to keep secrets, and I knew she would probably tell him we talked. I did not want him to think I was holding something back."

"How did he react?"

"It was strange. I know now that he is trying to overcome some issues with this book. I just hope he still wants me to write the foreword. It is an opportunity I may never have again."

"Don't say that Lennon. You will write your own book one day."

She touched my shoulder and we both were suddenly jolted by a child's loud voice approaching us with great speed.

"Aunt Lennon, Mom, look what I made for Grandpa."

Ralphie ran into the room with a coloring sheet of Superman. I took the sheet and saw that he had made the S into a G for Grandpa and it said, "Get Well." A tear popped into the corner of my eye, but I refused to let the moist weakness of emotion drop down my cheek.

"Jack, Jack!" I heard my sister yell at her husband.

When he heard her shouting he slipped the ear

phones out of his ears. He saw she was holding her hands up beside her in a frustrated stance, and his son was now standing directly in front of him with the coloring sheet.

"Where is your mother Jack? She was supposed to take care of Ralphie."

As if waiting for the right entrance, Olivia glided into the room with a silk scarf flowing behind her, letting her expensive handbag drop into a chair before acknowledging everyone in the room.

"Glad to know I am on your mind with all that is going on. Ralphie and I came to visit his grandfather."

Jack had instinctively given Ralphie his earphones and phone to watch a cartoon on the screen with a storm of words about to rain down.

"Olivia, we did not want Ralphie to see his grandfather in the hospital. He was supposed to stay with you at home."

"Well, that is just plain ridiculous. That is precisely what is wrong with our youth. You want to pamper them, protect them from life, keep them sealed in a plastic bag from all the bad in the world. It is not going to happen, because the world is tough. You should not hide him from what is real."

"He is our child, Olivia," Quinn said in a tone that she had probably never used with Olivia.

"And he is my grandchild, daughter-in-law. He knew something was wrong with his grandfather. He heard you two talking. I am bringing him here, so he can see his grandfather and you. Ralphie needs his parents right now, and there is no doubt in my mind you need him, too."

Quinn looked as if she would scream, but then she saw Ralphie and she gathered him in her arms, and he laughed showing her the cartoon on the screen.

Olivia edged closer to me landing in a thud on the

pleather chair vacated by Quinn.

"I am glad you brought Ralphie," I said.

Honestly, I really was happy to see my nephew, and I knew my father would be overjoyed to see him when he wakes up from surgery.

"Of course you are," she said in her smug voice.

"Mother, how did you get here?"

Olivia has not operated a car since she had hip and knee surgeries a year ago, but that has not stopped her from getting around town.

"Since my family was not available to give me a ride, my friend Camille, the one who has a son who married a doctor and had two wonderful children, gave me a ride here."

"Is she going to give you a ride home?"

"No, son, I was thinking my family might be able to take some time to do that, or was I wrong?"

"No, mother, I will take you home."

"Is Patrick still in surgery?" she directed this towards me.

"Yes."

"What is taking so long? Have y'all contacted the doctor?"

"He is in surgery right now with Daddy."

"I know that, but they can still update the family if something has gone astray."

"Nothing has gone astray," I said, and I hoped it was the truth.

My neck felt heavy. I had been looking at my phone for at least two hours since Olivia arrived with Ralphie. I was not sure what I wanted to see as the second hand on my clock spun around and around the tiny circle on my phone. The hypnotic movement of the tiny red line eating away the seconds of my life was comforting and helped me ignore Olivia's incessant talk and imperative tone.

I started to text Quinn who was sitting on the other side of the room, but after the first few humorous texts between sisters complaining about a certain in-law we had to stop. The in-law found the ringing noise of our texts irritating. I thought about turning down my volume, but the whole mood was ruined with her sour speech about people constantly using phones.

According to Olivia phones would bring about a rude, sinful world.

I knew what I was giving Olivia for Christmas this year.

I glanced at my phone for the hundredth time hoping there might be a text or an email from him. Either of the two "hims" that had been on my mind the last 24 hours would work. I was thankful for anything to get my mind off my father's surgery.

I sent Clark a text when I was at the hospital last night telling him of the circumstances that caused me to leave the reception and thanking him for my wonderful stay at the beach.

I had not received a reply.

I regretted telling him what Angel had shared with me, but I wanted to know if it was the truth. After looking at the photographs, her information about his parents seemed like the key to interpreting the inspiration for his book. If he wanted me to write the foreword he should have been upfront with me, but maybe that is what he was going to talk with me about today.

I thought about sending Dean a message. I tried to compose a humorous email that would let him know I did not expect anything and would not share the details of our night with anyone. Really, nothing happened. It is what I kept reassuring myself to stay in good humor with my soul.

The familiar sound of scrubs walking past the door

jarred me from my thoughts.

"It's not him," Quinn said before I could even look in the direction of the door.

It was not my father's doctor. The figure hesitated for a few seconds and continued moving. He was wearing a tight surgical cap with his favorite team's logo that did not seem to fit over his thick blond hair. Undoubtedly a patient made it for him. I knew I was just one in a thousand of his fans.

I waved, but he did not stop, nod or even smile. He just looked right through me as if he did not even recognize me and kept moving.

My feet were urging me to get up and follow him down the hallway so I could say something, anything that would make sense of what happened last night.

However, I could not move, and when I finally was able to stand I knew he was already gone.

I felt ridiculous, and this man continued to keep me on a twirl-a-whirl ride of emotions. I glanced at my family and wondered if they noticed the heat on my face before I collapsed back onto the pleather chair which made an unfortunate sucking noise that even Ralphie heard with his headphones on. He began to laugh so hard that we all started laughing. It was just what we needed to cut the tension.

Like a ghost bringing daunting news, we did not hear him approach. We all lifted our heads toward my father's doctor as he cleared his throat.

My mother's face was fixed in a frantic pose as she brought her hands together in prayer. Jack moved over to Quinn and put his arm around her shoulder. I was the deer unable to move as an impending car came barreling towards me.

"The surgery," he cleared his throat again. "I am sorry, allergies."

"The surgery went well."

I jumped up from my seat into the air and began to hug everyone. It was the same reaction my mother had in the doctor's office when Dean told us I did not have cancer.

"Can we see him?"

"He is in recovery now. The nurse will let you know when he is ready."

After my mom visited with my dad for a few minutes alone, Quinn and I joined her in the room. He looked weaker than I had ever seen him in his life. For the first time I really saw him as a 60-year-old man and not the youthful man who would gather me in his arms when I was little and put me on his shoulders.

I did not know what to say to him, so I said what I felt, "I love you, Daddy."

I gave him a kiss on his cheek, and Quinn let Ralphie bring him the coloring sheet for just a minute before we left him to rest.

"Mom, come out to eat with us," said Quinn.

"No, I want to stay here with your father."

"Are you sure Mom? You are going to need your strength for when he comes home."

I reminded her of the obvious.

"Girls, don't worry about me. There is a grilled chicken sandwich calling my name in the cafeteria downstairs."

"Well, we will be back tomorrow morning, and if you need anything tonight you have your cell to call us."

"I'm fine. Your father is going to be well, and that is all that matters right now."

As we walked back down the hall, Quinn asked me to join them for supper.

"I've got to get home. Someone will have to drive me," said Olivia in a loud voice talking to her son.

"Mother, why don't you join us for supper? You love the salmon at the restaurant we are going to, and the desserts are fantastic."

"I need to go home, Jack. Are you going to take me, or do I need to call some ramshackle taxi? My friend, Jordan, who never had any children had to take the taxi everywhere when she broke her arm. I never thought I would be like poor Jordan."

"I will take you home, Mother. Quinn, I will meet y'all at the restaurant."

"I have a few errands before we go home, Son. I need to stop and get some milk, and I need to mail this letter," she said, pulling an envelope out of her handbag.

Quinn and Ralphie needed Jack right now, so I sacrificed myself for the good.

I whispered to Quinn, "I am falling on the sword tonight. We have good news about Dad. You all need to go have a nice family dinner."

"Olivia, I need some milk, too," I said, winking at Jack who was relieved. "I will take you to the grocery store, the post office and maybe we can stop at a drive-thru before I take you home."

"Heavens no, there is too much sodium in that cheap food. Takeout from the Catch of the Day seafood restaurant is healthier, and if there is anything we have learned today, it is that we need to take care of our health."

I pressed my lips together. It was supposed to be a nice comment, but the way she said it made me want to slam a door as if I was an angst filled teenager.

We all hugged goodbye, and Jack quietly said so only I could hear, "You are the best sister-in-law in the world, Lennon Tyler."

"I know," I said and laughed.

After I drove Olivia to complete all her errands we picked up her seafood dinner that was undoubtedly better than the fish prepared at the restaurant where Quinn, Jack and Ralphie were now. When I heard the cashier at Catch of the Day repeat back her order as he handed her the white boxes, I had to refrain from making a sassy comment about what she thought was healthy food. Her fried fish dinner included deep fried hush puppies, mayonnaise covered slaw, a heaping of greasy french fries and a fried apple pie which was certainly not a heart healthy meal.

I helped her carry in her food and groceries to her home, and instead of dismissing me from her presence, Olivia asked me to join her.

"Lennon, I can't eat all of this food by myself. Please have some. There is also some chicken salad in the refrigerator."

My thoughts immediately searched the database in my mind for her motive for asking me to stay. Olivia always had a reason behind her actions.

It must be about Quinn and Jack. She has found out something, and she wants me to tell her about the state of their marriage.

I glanced over at the older woman who was sitting at the table, having removed her food from its containers placing it onto fine china and using polished silverware and a linen napkin.

This spider was not going to trap me in her net. Besides, I really did not know the present state of Quinn and Jack's marriage.

"Have a seat, Lennon. It's rude to make someone eat alone."

I was thankful for my father's outcome today, so I felt like I should repay karma by doing a good deed. It would not be nice to leave her eating all by herself. I could dodge her questions after having practiced the technique all weekend long at the beach. It had only been two days since I first arrived at the resort, but it seemed like it was ages ago.

"Pour us some iced tea. The glasses are in the cabinet

above the oven," she instructed.

I got the glasses down and added crushed ice and a squeeze of fresh lemon, following Olivia's exact instructions before sitting down at the table beside her.

"I am so glad your father is doing well, Lennon," she said.

"Thank you."

"Jack told me that Quinn had to call you home from the beach."

"Yes."

I kept waiting for her to ask about Quinn and Jack, but that was not the direction the conversation was taking.

"Were you writing an article for the newspaper?"

"No, I am actually writing the foreword for a photography book about the Outer Banks."

She dabbed her mouth with the napkin.

"That sounds interesting. What does that pay?"

"Nothing right now, but it will be my first publication in a book so it is a very good opportunity."

"Hmmm."

"It is Clark's book, the photographer that took the pictures of Quinn and Jack's house."

"Oh, yes that is right."

She put down her fork and looked at her empty dinner plate as I continued to talk about Clark and his book.

When she finished her apple pie dessert, I helped her clean up and washed her dishes for her. I was adding up the good deeds, but I did not think anything I did today could repay life for giving me back my father.

I was feeling good about myself and even had some kind feelings for Olivia. It would not last long.

"I saw you today," she said.

Her mood had changed and I saw the glint in her eyes of deviousness that often accompanied her conversations with Quinn sending my sister into a shell to hide from the evil.

"And I am right here now," I said, laughing and trying to dodge whatever was coming next.

"I saw you when that doctor came by the waiting room. He stared at you when you were looking at your awful cell phone, but by the time you saw him he had already left."

My heart leapt out of my chest. Evidently Dean did not ignore me like I had previously thought.

"I don't know what you mean, Olivia. What doctor are you referring to?" I said, trying once again to dodge not just a ball, but a bullet.

"The tall, blond doctor, whom you obviously know," she said. "Your face is as red as a fire engine."

I touched my hand to my face and felt the warmth on my cheeks. I would not be a good poker player.

"Oh, that was just my doctor who performed my appendectomy."

"So, that is Dr. Dean Kent?"

"Yes. He probably recognized me but forgot my name so he moved on."

"That is plain absurd. He knew your name, Lennon."

What was the end goal of this conversation for Olivia? Did she want to embarrass me?

"Are you dating him? I know physicians are not supposed to date their patients, so is this why you are keeping it a secret?"

I shook my head and said, "No. I am not dating my doctor."

"Oh, don't worry. I will not tell anyone."

"I don't know what you mean. There is nothing to tell, Olivia."

"I know what I saw."

"Olivia, you did not see anything. He is a married man with children."

"Do you think you are the only woman on Earth who has fallen for a married man? You young girls act like no one ever lived before you."

I was beginning to wonder if Olivia had missed a pill or taken too many today. She was sounding not like herself at all.

She began to crumble crying on her sofa. It was a terrifying sight. The queen of evil was not supposed to weep or crack her Teflon exterior.

I grabbed my cell phone and thought about calling Quinn for backup, but I did not want to ruin her night with Jack and Ralphie. They looked like a real happy family tonight. In the midst of a life changing couple of days theirs had gotten better.

I would not dodge the bullet again, but I would take it square in the head for my sister.

I sat down beside Olivia on the antique couch which I felt like my bottom would leave an imprint on. I patted her back, and attempted to soothe her nerves.

"I know I have a lot to learn in life, Olivia," I said.

I thought this may be a ruse by Olivia to get me to spill my guts about some sexy affair she thought I was having with Dean. I would console her, but I would not let down my own barrier. I knew how to handle the situation.

"I think I need to go to bed, Lennon. Please turn off the lights, and lock the door."

She got up off the sofa slowly from either exhaustion or arthritis or a combination of both.

I was shocked. She was not faking her emotional breakdown. She did not want to know any gossip about my supposed affair with the handsome married doctor to share with her book club.

"Sure, Olivia. Is there anything else I can do before I leave?"

"No, Lennon."

She stopped abruptly and turned around. Her silk blouse was wrinkled and tear-stained at the collar and her rouge was smeared on her cheeks. It was unlike her usual prim style.

"Yes. Yes, there is something you can do. If you want to be with that doctor, be with him. Life is so short. I know that now. Whatever you do, don't have any regrets. Live for yourself and not what others may think of you."

I did not know how to answer her without admitting my own feelings, so I opted to say nothing. Silence was best in this situation.

This was the second night in a row that life had disturbed my balance and knocked me off my feet.

23 BETTER THAN EXPECTED

It was dark by the time I came home from Olivia's house. I walked straight up the stairs without daring to even glimpse at my parents' house next door. If I went inside and closed my eyes I could at least forget in my sleep the fear I had about losing my father and the inevitability of being all alone in the future with no parents, husband or children.

If Quinn heard me she would have reprimanded me for my pity party. She did not know what it meant to be alone, or perhaps she did. It could be the reason why Jack is now giving her more attention than ever before, and her look of dissatisfaction has transformed.

Bill was waiting patiently for me by the clay pot full of red geraniums. I have told people he smiles, but they don't believe it until they see the photo I snapped of him one night as I was watering my flowers and he grinned at me beside his clay pot abode.

"Hello, Bill," I said, bending down to greet the little toad.

"You will always be here for me, won't you?"

He was motionless, and I knew that was his way of

telling me, "Yes, Lennon. Don't worry. I will always be here."

I stood up, searching for my keys and blew him a kiss.

"You are better than a prince, Bill."

As I opened the screen door something fell onto my foot, and I immediately hopped back yelling an unintelligible remark remembering the time a snake had found its way onto my porch.

This time, however, it was not a slithery reptile but a manila envelope.

I picked up the package that had no postmark or writing on the outside. I unlocked my door and went inside, locking it behind me.

I turned on the light and placed my purse on the kitchen counter.

The envelope contained something hard and oddly shaped. I held it up to my face and took a whiff, but there was only a paper smell. I shook it back and forth, but nothing seemed to move except the object.

It was not an advertisement or someone offering a service, because the business name would be emblazoned on the envelope begging for attention. Work, family and friends always sent texts or emails.

Could this be a fan of my newspaper column leaving a trinket of thanks? On the other hand, could it be from an infatuated stalker who does not like the way I overuse the word "enjoy" in my articles?

I decided to indulge in some ice cream before I opened up the envelope. If I was going to die from some mysterious mail then at least I was going to have a couple of spoonfuls of chocolate in my system.

I slowly lifted the tab and shook the envelope. It landed with a thud, spinning on the countertop before it came to a stop. I picked up the smooth white shell with purple and orange flecks.

I found the shell on the walk along the beach with Clark. The last place I left the shell was in our suite at the resort on the dresser beside my bed.

I thought it was the only item in the package, but a paper with a glossy finish could be seen from the envelope's edge. I pulled it out, and let out a gasp.

It was a woman in the sun. Her black sunglasses, red lipstick and ivory skin were a sharp contrast to the beach that surrounded her. I stared at it for some time before I could admit that the photograph was of me, and it was beautiful. Clark had evidently taken a photograph of the day I woke up on the beach startled to see him standing above me with a camera hanging around his neck.

I was surprised by Clark's gesture and assumed both were meant to bring a smile to my face which they did. I could not comprehend their meaning, but they were both very special to me.

I texted Clark, "beautiful, smiling now."

I awaited his reply, but I received none. I love the technology of the phone, all its apps and the ability to find information in seconds. What I did not love was waiting for a reply from people. It always keeps you guessing about their motives for not responding. Was he too busy to reply? Did the text get lost in his list? Does he not care? Also, the opposite is true when you find yourself replying to texts and emails as soon as possible so as not to offend any of your contacts.

Tired beyond reason, I let my clothes fall onto the floor in a wrinkled clump. I slipped under the covers, and sleep consumed me.

Isn't it grand when you wake up from a deep sleep, forgetting all your worries?

I rolled around under the covers until I discovered that cool untouched spot on the sheets that can only be found on a warm summer day. I did not want to open my eyes, pulling my pillow over my head.

Unfortunately, the cement truck of reality pulled up beside my bed, poured its mixture on me and I remembered everything.

Tears started to spill from my eyes until my pillowcase was damp with misery and there was no need to remain in bed. I attempted to continue to sleep to melt the pain away, but the dark thoughts began to come at me with unequivocal force.

I dragged myself out of bed and stood under a cold shower letting it whip all my senses to attention.

My phone was ringing with a notification.

Quinn's email said, "Don't read your social media."

I picked up the phone and called my sister. This was out of the ordinary. I did not check my social media accounts regularly, probably the only person on the planet not frequenting them.

"What's up with the email? You know I don't check my social media accounts often?"

"Hold on. What do you mean?"

"Look at your phone."

I waited a few seconds while she pulled up her email.

"I am so sorry, Lennon. I don't know how I forwarded Jack's message to you."

"Why wouldn't I want to see them? Is there something about one of my articles?"

"No."

"Then what is it?"

"Did you run into Piper at the beach?"

"Yes. Why?"

I remembered seeing Piper with her husband who seemed more enthusiastic about the phone in his hand than her.

"She posted some things on social media, but it is just trivial stuff. She will be talking about her divine pedicure tomorrow, and the entire thing will blow over."

"What exactly did she say?"

I could not think of one thing that would be bad from our conversation at the drive-in a couple of days ago.

"She made some remark about Clark Vincent. It is not even worth talking about. Are you going to see Dad today? I can't believe they are sending him home so fast."

Quinn was attempting to fire me up about this topic that we had already discussed to avoid talking about Piper's online actions.

"I looked into some home health care options to help Mom with him at first, and they always have us so they can manage."

"We are not health care professionals."

"You are right. I faint when I get a paper cut, so that is why I am looking into hiring some additional help."

"I think Jack's receptionist's mother, Ella, is a retired nurse. Maybe she can help."

"That would be awesome," I said.

Although, I cringed at the idea of Jack's receptionist getting any closer to his family even if it was through her mother.

"I will see you soon at the hospital. I have a deadline tomorrow, but I am going to finish writing the piece tonight after I visit with Dad."

After I hung up, I avoided my laptop. It was egging me on to hit the power button and open up a Pandora's box.

It did not take long before I was logging on to see what posts Piper had on her site. She did not even bother to limit them to her friends or followers. They were public and available for the entire world to view.

"Guess who I saw at the drive-in at the beach this weekend?"

That was not too bad.

"Stood up by Clark Vincent?"

It was a question that received many replies from

women I recognized as members of the mommy gang. Some of the women were friends I had known since high school. The things they were saying were hurtful, but I had a tough skin when it came to these comments.

I realized ever since I lost weight some of the women had felt unease like I was a new glittering toy that somehow may be a dangerous temptation around their husbands. I think it was also pure jealousy. Who could blame them? Clark Vincent was definitely the most handsome man in town, and they could not believe I was spending a weekend with him at the beach.

Their replies were vicious and ranged from me making up the entire weekend to him realizing he could do "soooo much better."

I brushed all the comments off, especially with the weekend I had survived. I was thankful for my life and my father's recovery. Nothing they could say would be more devastating than when I sat with my family in the waiting room desperate to hear if he had survived the surgery.

I was about to shut down the computer when I saw it. It must have been what Quinn did not want me to see.

It was a photo of me taking a big bite of my hamburger at the drive-in with ketchup and strawberry milkshake slipping down my chin and arms. My eyes were closed, and I looked insanely intense. Instead of having a fit or crying for hours like most women from the mommy mob would have undoubtedly done, I began to laugh.

I shut down the laptop, and decided the next time I saw Piper I would have to thank her for her excellent photography skills.

In the middle of the day when you are not awaiting terrifying news from people in scrubs, the hospital is quite tolerable. I did not notice the distinct odor as much, and I could not stop saying thank you to everyone who had helped my father as I walked down the long hallway to his room.

Mom was still by his side in a chair she had pulled up beside his bed. She actually looked more tired than Dad.

On the subject of marriage so many people often say, "I don't want to die old and alone."

Well, I hate to burst their bubbles, but unless there is a freak accident where you die on the same day as your spouse even if you have been married for half a century there is a great possibility you are going to die alone.

Mom was scared and vulnerable thinking for the first time there was nothing she could do to fix a bad situation. There was no solution she could produce that could help my father but prayer.

I stopped and bought her favorite candy bar and some of those home and travel magazines she loved to read from the gas station. I handed them to her when I came into the room.

Quinn was already in another plastic avocado chair on the opposite side of the room talking with someone on her phone.

From the conversation I could surmise that Tara had Ralphie today, and she was taking him to karate and swim practice. She was an angel, and I would bet my next paycheck that she had something to do with Piper's posts. The mommy gang does not move an inch without seeking permission from her first.

"How was your trip with Clark?"

Mom was eating her candy bar and sipping her soda. She had become alert once again with the caffeine.

"I met his ex-fiancée. It was an interesting encounter. The beach was extraordinary, and his photographs are breathtaking. I think I found his motivation for his book, and I actually have an idea of how I am going to write the foreword."

"We have always loved the beach haven't we,

Patrick?"

My father was dozing off and on, but he managed a nod.

"I think when your father is ready we will get a cottage and spend a week down there."

"The beach is always so healing. Remember when I was little and I would get a scrape at the beach you would tell me, 'go splash some of the saltwater on it, and it will heal right up, buttercup.' It always did heal," I said, closing my eyes and remembering the ocean splashing against my cut knee.

Quinn finally stopped talking on the phone and asked where her candy bar was, and I threw her one from my handbag.

"Since when do you eat chocolate?"

She did not reply, instead taking a large bite of the chocolate bar in her hand.

"I saw the photo."

Quinn had finished her snack and was rolling the wrapper in her palm into a neat ball.

"I thought you would be more upset," said Quinn.

"No, I actually think it is hilarious."

"What photograph is Quinn talking about, Lennon?"

I took out my phone and showed her, and she began to laugh as well.

"I know. So funny isn't it?"

Mom shook her head and continued to laugh. She and I both shared the same sense of lightheartedness.

"Well, I don't think Piper meant it to be funny, and I am going to tell her at our next book club," Quinn said in a matter of fact tone.

"Don't bother. I already sent her an email thanking her for the great photograph."

"Lennon, how could you do that?"

"I really don't care what she says. All of them are pretty much vipers including the head reptile, Tara, who you were talking to minutes ago. If they don't have anything better to do than to make up a soap opera fantasy about my life then let them. I think I could write a pretty decent romance novel from all of their lies."

"You have a better attitude than me about this entire thing," she said, throwing the balled up candy wrapper into the waste basket.

"Changing the subject, I did bring something that they would love to get a look at. Maybe you can bring this for your next show and tell at the book club, Quinn."

I pulled out the manila envelope with Clark's photograph inside and held it up for them to see.

"Who is that, dear?" said Mom.

Quinn looked clueless, as well.

"It's me."

"What? Let me see that."

Quinn was out of her seat, holding the photograph carefully by its edges in mere seconds.

"Let me see."

Mom stood beside her and looked at the photograph.

"Really, is it so unbelievable that could be me?"

"Honey, not that we are being mean, but you just showed us a photograph with ketchup all over your face," she said, laughing again.

It was so good to see my mother laugh.

"Who took the picture?" she asked.

"Clark, of course, Mom. What other photographer has Lennon spent time with lately?" said Quinn.

"Hmmm."

Mom was pondering something with her eyes focused on Quinn's face.

They both raised their eyebrows in unison and laughed again.

"What are you guys thinking?"

"It is so obvious," said Quinn.

"What is so obvious?"

"He likes you."

"No, he does not. We are just friends. Really not even friends, we are professional acquaintances."

They erupted into giggles.

"Ok, ok. Lennon. Whatever you say. Mom, do you think they will have a beach wedding?"

"You guys think you are so funny. I am going to raid the vending machine. I gave my chocolate bar to my sister who I thought loved me."

"Get me a bag of potato chips, please," said my father, who opened his eyes and then closed them again.

Mom shook her head at me like I was actually contemplating listening to my father's ludicrous request.

Dad would never consume another potato chip as long as my mother was by his side. She had already asked me to clean out the kitchen and all of his hiding places. It was like I was looking for an addict's stash after he got home from rehab, except I did not flush bags of potato chips down the toilet. I dropped off all the junk food goodies at the newspaper, and the guys had munched down almost all of the snacks when I was finished with my brief conversation with my editor.

I walked down the hospital hallway, thinking about what Mom and Quinn said. When I first saw the photograph it seemed personal. He had captured me through a particularly attractive lens. I immediately let those thoughts escape my mind. Clark was a nice guy. He did not want any relationship with me. He dated swimsuit models and beauty queens, I told myself over and over. What would he want with a small town writer? My life was not even half as exciting as the life he was accustomed to having with his list of prior girlfriends.

As I walked down the corridor trying to find another machine that a nurse promised had a better selection than the one on my father's floor, I heard a familiar voice around the corner.

I paused before I continued walking. The man was laughing, and a woman was giggling at his comment.

He really knew how to melt hearts. I felt like a fool for thinking his feelings were anything more for me than what they were for all the women he came into contact with everyday.

I looked at the sign on the wall, and I realized this was the hall where people were recovering from outpatient surgery.

Was I subconsciously seeking Dean out?

I tried to turn around and leave before he saw me but the door was locked. I was trapped. I waited until I thought he had gone into a room, and I approached the nurse's desk and poked my head in through the frosted privacy window.

I asked the nurse to unlock the door, but as soon as she was about to reply, Dean came back to the desk. He did not see me, and the nurse immediately turned to him before answering me, forgetting I was there.

I started to move discreetly out of the way, and I knocked over a plastic office filing stand on the desk in what had to be one of the most embarrassing moments of my life. A picture of me devouring a hamburger on social media was nothing compared with this awkward purgatory.

"Hey…hi."

He was having trouble forming a sentence and remembering my name.

"What are you doing here?"

He probably thought I was stalking him.

"I was just looking for a vending machine."

He looked at me blankly devoid of any emotion or recognition, and I smiled like an idiot and walked on. He did not say a word. I was mortified.

I walked back down the hall quickly and began to pull at the door hoping it had magically unlocked.

Someone came up behind me.

"You have to turn it the other way," said Dean.

I did not want to look into his eyes, because I knew he would see how I felt which was completely mortified and heartbroken that I meant so little to him.

"Thank you."

"How is your dad?"

A blushing smile appeared on my face even though that was not the normal reaction a person should have when they are talking about their sick father. I was elated that he did care about me and had sought me out down the hall to talk in private.

Before I could answer, the nurse came around the corner and said, "Dr. Kent, they need you in room 378."

He followed her quickly down the hall, but not before turning around once to look at me.

My heart catapulted into an unknown place that I was unfamiliar with in my life. How could this man have such a hold over me?

* * * * *

After I emailed my article to my editor I began to write the opening of the foreword for Clark's book. I put on some music, and the words started to flow as my hands danced over the keyboard.

All of his images of the beach were present in my thoughts. The discarded yellow pail of a child and the rushing waves between the pier pilings were in my mind as the text came to life. I closed my eyes and remembered the senses I felt as we walked along the beach together. The way the ocean's waves hit our legs as the breeze teased our skin in the afternoon sun was the image that I continued to reflect on as I wrote.

Before I knew it I was done. I read and reread my words over and over until I thought there was nothing more I could add.

I hit the send button, and I awaited his response.

Again I was waiting for a reply from a man on my dreaded cell phone device. I put it on mute. Then, I turned it back on. I changed the ringtone. I checked the weather app. I placed the phone in the kitchen charger. I put it on the sofa beside my head as I watched an old comedy on television. I thought I heard it ring. I checked to see if it was working by sending a test email and a text to Quinn. It worked.

Still there was no response from him.

I finally closed my eyes and went to sleep on the couch under the shopping channel lullaby for a discontent and obnoxiously insecure writer.

When I woke up I checked my phone, and there was still a blank screen. It was beyond frustrating. I could take no more.

I got in the shower. I put on a shift and sandals. I was going to go to the hospital, but there was one place I needed to stop at first.

I reviewed the words I would say in my head as I knocked on the giant door. I saw his car and knew he was here.

"Good morning."

It was early morning, and his hair was wet probably freshly showered from a morning run. Even in a T-shirt and jeans he looked like he just stepped out of GQ.

"Hey," I said, brushing past him and walking inside.

"Please come in," he said laughing. "By the way I have your luggage you left at the resort."

"I am sorry. Manners are not my priority this morning."

He walked towards the kitchen where he had bread on the grill.

"I have a feeling you have something on your mind. Go ahead and say it."

"You didn't like it."

"I didn't like what?" he said, flipping over the French toast with a spatula.

"The foreword. I can rewrite it. Just let me know what you want me to change."

"What are you talking about? Did you finish it?"

He dabbed his finger in a bowl of fresh whipped cream and tasted it.

"I sent it to you last night."

He wiped his hands on a dish towel, picked up his phone and scrolled down.

"Oh, I must have overlooked it. I have been so busy."

"Well?"

"I guess you want me to read it."

"Yes, please."

"I just made some French toast. Sit down and have a piece while I read."

"There are some fresh strawberries and whipped cream. I have syrup if you are that kind of girl," he smiled at his own private joke.

He took out a pair of glasses, and I almost snapped a quick pic of him for the mommy mob. He looked like one of those handsome professors that sent all the college girls swooning.

He sat down in a chair at the bar and began to read, and I could not help but stare. I studied him closely for any reaction, but there was none.

He finally pulled off his glasses with his blue eyes shining bright directly at me.

"Well? I am dying here. Say something, please."

He took out a plate, placed a piece of French toast in its center and then added a few berries and whipped cream.

The forkful of toast entered his mouth, and he closed his eyes and said, "Yummm."

"You really are a complete...."

"Hold on. Hold on. Don't finish that sentence," he said. "I can't have the author of my foreword bad mouthing me."

He was going to use it. The relief in my system almost resulted in an embarrassing hug, but somehow I was able to restrain myself from making any mistakes I would regret later.

"It is not what I expected."

I took a deep breath.

"It is even better. It is wonderful, Lennon."

I was in shock. I was going to be published. My insides were doing somersaults.

"You have some syrup on your mouth."

I brushed it off with my fingers and licked them unabashedly, still in an exuberant fog of elation that had somehow managed not to burst from my mouth.

"You are speechless. This must be the first time in your life."

I nodded.

"Can I ask you something? How did you know?"

I expected he would want to know.

"Your photograph told me. Sometimes you don't need words for a story."

"Said the writer," he said with a grin.

"Are they the reason you did the book?" I said, remembering Angel's words.

He looked as if he wanted to walk away, but he gripped the arms of his chair and looked forward.

"Yes and no."

I was not going to push him further. I knew when to pull back. It was his story, and if he wanted to share it he would have to feel comfortable.

"That summer my parents bought me my first camera for my eighth birthday. The photograph is the only memory I have of them being completely happy."

I waited for him to say more, but he did not.

I ended the silence. "This French toast is amazing."

"I finished taking my shots this weekend, and now that you have written the foreword, I will be able to send it to my editor."

My phone started to beep, and it was a message titled "Urgent" from Quinn.

"I'm sorry. I need to look at this," I said. "They are sending my dad home today from the hospital. I need to go."

"Sure. Please, go," he said.

He walked me to the door and stood on the steps as I got into my car. I rolled down the window.

"I loved the photograph. Thank you."

Clark blushed and waved goodbye.

Could this day get any better?

"Clark Vincent blushed."

"Are you serious?"

We waited in the familiar pleather chairs in the waiting room while my mother and father talked with his doctor.

"I could not believe it either. Maybe you were right. He does have a crush on me."

"What about you? Don't you like him?"

"He's handsome, but…"

How could I tell my sister that I could not consider dating the most eligible bachelor in town?

"He has issues. I have issues. It is not going to happen."

It really was not a lie, but it really was not entirely the truth.

"Every woman in town has been dreaming about this guy. Why don't you do them all a favor and at least have a coffee with him?"

"They would rip me to shreds. The social media hamburger episode would be a blip compared to what the mommy mob would do if they found out we were actually dating."

"Don't let them dictate who you date. Ask him out. Do it for me."

I could not tell Quinn the real reason I would not go out with Clark. I had fallen for an unavailable man who did not even remember my name most of the time.

"I just can't right now."

"Why?"

Mom came out of Dad's room with the doctor saving me from replying to my sister's insistent agenda for my love life.

"He's looking good," said the man, who was about our parents' age with tiny glasses and an ultra skinny body.

"Thank you so much for taking such good care of my husband," said my mom, and she embraced him in a hug.

Doctors were used to this kind of reaction. When you deal with life and death on a daily basis, you are the recipient of the ups and downs of human emotion.

I thought at first this was the reason I had become so infatuated with Dean. He had saved my life. However, whenever I thought of him now it was not as my doctor, but as the man who held me in his arms at the waterfront. He was the man who had written such poignant words about his childhood.

He was the thief of my most needed organ, and there was nothing Quinn could do to convince me that another man could just as easily steal it away.

I awoke in the middle of the night tossing and turning beneath my sheets in search of something that would bring me closer. I needed to make a connection.

I was half asleep as my hand searched for the phone in the dark that I left on the floor beside my bed. I hit the power button and began to type. The words were meaningless, but what I yearned for at that moment.

"Don't you love to feel the summer sun on your skin as it shines above you in an outdoor shower by the beach? If I ever publish a bestseller or win the lottery I am going to buy a small cottage by the sea with an outdoor shower and a porch swing where I can listen to the waves talk to me as I write."

I hit send, and then I collapsed back into a sound sleep under my covers.

When I awoke the next morning and was brushing my teeth by the sink, I remembered an odd dream from last night where I sent Dean an email about how much I loved the beach. I had the beach on my mind after writing the foreword for Clark's book.

My phone started ringing, and I looked down at the text notification and it said Dean. I scrolled down to my sent emails and realized it had not been a dream.

The toothpaste started to tingle on my tongue, and I almost swallowed the glob sending me into a coughing fit.

I scrutinized my red face in the mirror.

How many more times was I going to embarrass myself with him? He was definitely going to refer me to therapy for lovelorn pitiful crushes.

"How is your dad?" he texted.

They were the four words which told me everything.

This man cared about me. He did not refer to my silly comments about the beach which was a great relief.

The next couple of weeks flew by like a dandelion after a wish. We texted or emailed every other day. I was not sure what we were doing, but I looked forward to every message he sent.

They arrived in the morning, the afternoon and in the middle of the night. He wrote about the stresses of his job, and I sent him particularly entertaining excerpts from my articles. He sent me an email when his son scored the winning goal in a soccer game, and I told him about a particularly humorous comment Ralphie made out of the blue. I told him about my concerns for my father's health and he offered some suggestions for his rehabilitation. I teased him about his unusual music selections, and he quipped back with a history lesson on the greatness of 1980s music. We debated famous basketball players, the Heels and the Yankees. He admitted he liked Duke, and my reply button was silent for a while. Our correspondence was fun and always made me smile.

When it would take him a while to reply, I never doubted he would. He was a busy man with a busy life. My emails were only a fun distraction from his daily routine. I was one out of a hundred people he probably communicated with I kept telling myself over and over so I would not be distracted into thinking his messages were anything more than entertainment.

The only problem was that while it was nothing to him but another message on his screen, I had totally fallen for this intelligent, humorous and kind man.

I reflected again on how I could have been so dismissive about Quinn's feelings for Drew. At least they had once both shared some sort of relationship years ago. The feelings that I had for Dean were pure fiction based on email messages and not reality.

Karma was laughing at my folly that I could somehow avoid her pensive reckoning.

24 I WAITED ALL NIGHT

"Have you heard anything from him?"

Quinn was preparing a grilled chicken with mint and pine nut gremolata that smelled fabulous in our parents' kitchen while stirring up a bit of my love life.

"No."

"Honey, that chicken smells wonderful," said Mom, whose eyes were fixed on a laptop at the kitchen table.

"Thanks. I emailed you the recipe if you want to try to make it one night."

She was enrolling in an online course in art appreciation.

"It says at the end of the course we are taking a field trip to the National Gallery of Art in Washington. That is so exciting!"

"It sounds like fun, Mom. I am glad you decided to enroll in the course."

"I have always loved art. I never made the time before I retired."

After my father's surgery my mother had taken a literal carpe diem approach to life, similar to my own self awakening after my surgery.

I stuck my head into the living room where I spotted a scene that had become routine for my father.

"Mr. Patrick, it's time for your exercise," said my father's home health care worker, a woman in a cartoon character patterned nurse's scrubs top, pink pants and rubber clogs.

From the sound of my father's groan I knew she would struggle to motivate him to move from his recliner and remote. She and my mother had formed a tag team and had managed to keep him away from the junk food which was a miracle.

At least mom did not have to worry about him having a tryst with her. She did not exude the same flirtatious behavior that her daughter, Jack's receptionist, did with Jack.

"It looks like Dad is giving Mrs. Ella a fit again," I said.

"Taste this, and tell me if you think it needs anything," said Quinn, holding her hand beneath a spoon so it would not spill on the floor.

"Yummy. Delicious."

"We are still waiting," said Mom, who had closed her laptop.

"What do you mean?"

"Clark Vincent. The man you once described as a JFK Jr. slash Superman look-alike. What is going on with him?"

Mom was being so direct. Maybe this was part of her new transformation.

"I really don't know. He sent me an email that he was leaving town and was going on a photo shoot in New Zealand for two weeks."

"Maybe he doesn't have access to a phone or email," said Quinn.

"That is very doubtful. I think he is done with our town."

239

"If he did not care, why did he take that photograph of you while you were sleeping on the beach?" asked Quinn.

I had not told them about the shell. That would really send them into romance novel mode.

"I have not given it a second thought. The only thing I am anticipating is when his book will come out."

"Is lunch ready yet?" asked our impatient Dad. "That woman is going to send me to the hospital again."

"Ella is here to help you, Patrick."

"I know," he grumbled.

"Dad, it will be ready in a few minutes."

"It smells out of this world, Quinn."

"When the book comes out you should meet him for a drink," said Mom.

"Am I really so pathetic that you think I need someone to fulfill my life?"

"No, we want you to be happy, that's all."

"Leave her alone," Dad said. "If she does not want to date him something must be wrong with him, and I trust my daughter's judgment."

When Quinn and I were cleaning up, she took me to the side.

"If it is not Clark, it is someone."

I avoided her inquisition.

"It is no one. I am not seeing anyone."

The last statement was more or less true. I had not seen Dean face-to-face since my awkwardness at the hospital searching for a vending machine.

It was only words on a screen, but somehow all of those words had meant more to me than any physical relationship.

"You are not telling me the truth. Don't you think I can tell?"

"It is nothing."

"If you can't tell me his name he must be some kind

of freak, one of Dad's golf buddies or he is that bartender with those awful orange denim pants."

I laughed. "My, how your good opinion of me grows with each guess."

"He is married, isn't he?"

I would not look at her, and continued to put away the dishes.

"That's it. Oh, Lennon, how could you let this happen?"

Her voice was sad and disappointed. She grabbed my arm. "You have to end it. Nothing good ever comes out of it. I should know."

I did not want to reply, sharply reminding her of her own dalliances with Drew and how I had always been somewhat supportive of her choices.

"Promise me."

I did not answer her, and she threw her dish towel in the sink and walked away.

As I slid under the covers that night, I could not help but hear the words of my sister echoing in my ears.

We were not doing anything that was wrong, I kept saying to myself. I had fallen for him, but he never said anything of the sort back to me. If anyone read our correspondence it could have easily been described as words between friends.

I closed my eyes justified in my thoughts and fell into a slumber. The image of him holding me in his arms by the river played in my dreams. There was no rain and instead of pulling away from me his lips met mine. We were falling through the sky.

I awoke from the dream, grasping my sheets in fistfuls. The dream left me panicked for some clarity. I knew I wanted it to be more. For once in my life I was not going to weigh the consequences. Olivia had been right. Life is short.

I took out my phone, and I texted Dean.

I slipped on my favorite jeans that fit my form perfectly, a lace camisole top the color of rose pink and my silver hoop earrings. I sprayed a whiff of Chanel on my wrists and neck, a smudge of blood red lipstick across my plump lips and ran my fingers through my tousled long hair.

I knew he would have read the message. He was on constant alert for texts and email messages with his occupation.

I stepped out of my car into the cooler air of the last summer nights. The stars were cast over a dark sky. Everything was still except for the few cars that drove by and the stop lights intermittently changing from green to yellow to red.

I waited on a bench by the waterfront.

I clutched my keys making red indentations in my palm as I saw a figure in the distance walking the long journey home from a downtown bar drifting from side to side. I was not scared of the people that may linger on a dark night with adrenaline running through my veins like a drug.

I thought about returning home to my comfortable bed, but I would always wonder if he came so I remained.

If I stilled my thoughts I could hear the music we listened to in his car that night in the distance. I could see the lightning in the sky, the rain pour over the windshield and his breath on my neck.

Every time I thought I heard a door slam or a car near the park, I hoped it was him.

I looked at my phone, waiting for a message or at least some sign that I had not made a big mistake. I knew our communication would end after this night. I had offered myself to him, and any person with an ounce of self-worth would never talk to him again if he denied his presence.

He did not appear by my side. I had not expected him to, but I was going to tempt our fate with the possibility of something more. It was not his fault. I wanted something that he was not ready to give. I knew it was over. I had been too greedy. I should have been satisfied with a friendship.

By the time the sunrise appeared the tears started to fall, and I realized I had been deceived by my own dream.

"Quinn," I said into my phone.

"What's wrong?"

"I am ready to talk."

"I'll be there."

That was the thing about the people who love you, they show up when you call.

As she rushed over to the park bench were I sat silently looking at the water, I wondered how I could ever tell her the truth.

She had managed to slip on one of Jack's old surf shop T-shirts, a pair of khakis and mismatched flip flops in her hurry to rescue me from my stupidity in the form of a crush on an unavailable man.

She held me in a tight hug as I cried. I did not cry for Dean. I cried for the one time in my life that I had let someone penetrate through my cement barrier surrounding my heart, and how it was dismissed like a flyer placed on the windshield of a car in a parking lot.

"I know this hurts now, but I am proud of you that you finally let someone in. I am not judging, but your past relationships have been pretty surface with you knowing they all had an expiration date."

She was right. I always knew there was an end date with all of my relationships, some having a longer shelf life than others.

"It was not a real relationship like the others, so I don't know why this is affecting me so hard. He did not know until tonight that I even had feelings for him."

"Well, you are a writer. It did not have to be physical for you to fall for him. Words mean so much to you, so it was probably his words that captured your attention."

I did not tell Quinn about us meeting here at the park the night Dad went into the hospital. If I looked at it from a third party's perspective, he was not exactly blind to the emotions between us both. However, I felt if anyone was at fault it was me for continuing to email him from the very beginning. If I had never sent that first message I would not be sitting here right now crying on my sister's shoulder.

"I don't know what it was, but I am a wreck. Please tell me how to stop thinking about him. I wake up at night like I did last night, and all I want is to be with him."

"The first thing you need to do is delete him from your contacts, but you can't block him now or you will drive yourself crazy wondering if he is still sending you messages that you can no longer see in your inbox. On the other hand, if he does not send you a message then you are constantly questioning the reasoning. The most difficult thing is not replying to his messages, but you must ignore them. If you even reply to just one the cycle begins again. It is like an alcoholic taking just one sip of vodka. It can't happen."

"It sounds like you have experience."

"It is over with Drew. I don't know why I was so tangled up with him, but I decided to end it one morning after Dad's surgery. I woke up and saw Jack with Ralphie in the kitchen eating their cereal in bowls both with milk dripping off their chins, laughing and talking. It was like my eyes were open for the first time. I did not want a life where I could not walk into my kitchen and see the two most important people in my universe. I would be an empty shell of a human being."

"I am so happy for you."

I began to cry jubilant tears, relieved that my sister had found happiness again with her family.

An image of Ralphie's smiling face flashed as I remembered how thankful I was for everything in my life. I was incredibly selfish to think I could ask a man with his own family to sacrifice that which means so much to him for a fling that would probably have lasted for a few weeks or months at the most. I thought if we met it would just be fun, a rendezvous that would make us both feel good, but I had not thought of the consequences. I was not that kind of woman. There were plenty of women who would throw caution to the wind to be with him, and I almost was one of them.

"I feel like a hypocrite now. I refused to let myself understand your relationship with Drew, and now it is like I am reliving another version of it in my own life."

"No one knows what it feels like until you are in the middle of the mud. There is nothing you can do to make it anymore than what it is—an affair. Just be happy he ended it before you were unable to clean up the mess. At this point you could still be friends or even passing acquaintances who say hello in the grocery store. If he met you tonight, I don't know what would have happened, but it would not end well. It never does except in the occasional romance novel or soap opera."

Quinn was right about everything, but I did not know how I would have the strength never to email him again. I thought seriously about throwing my phone towards the river and letting it skip over the ripples in the brown water, but all I had to do was open my email from any computer in the world so that was really not an optimal solution.

As I held my phone in my hand, the ringtone jolted me from my thoughts.

"Are you going to read it?"

"I agree with everything you have said, and the practical part of me is listening."

"But?"

"Honestly, I don't know."

25 OLIVIA'S STORY

"What in the world does she want with me?"

It was not exactly the most mannerly reply to my sister, but the last thing I wanted to do right now was spend an afternoon with Olivia.

I had an overwhelming fear she would do something that would expose my non-existent relationship with Dean. I always imagined the worst scenarios, so I could prepare myself for the actuality of an unpleasant situation.

It was weird how she encouraged me to have a relationship with Dean the night I took her home after Dad's surgery, but she was a tricky individual. She had acted completely vulnerable and open that night. Still I did not trust her with the biggest secret of my life.

"She said she has a possible story for you."

"What is the story? She could tell me over the phone."

"I don't know, Lennon. You will have to ask her. You could ignore her, but she will drive me crazy, so please go visit her if you get a chance."

My stomach started to growl, and my hands began to

sweat on the steering wheel as I pulled into her driveway.

I rang the doorbell, but there was no answer. I thought about leaving, but then I would have to return another day sending me into a stress spiral worrying about her intentions.

I knocked loudly, and I finally heard her voice say, "Come in, come in."

"Olivia, I was about to leave. Did you hear the doorbell?"

"Oh, that horrible thing hasn't worked since Jack's father was alive. It broke the day after he passed, and I never fixed it. I was glad I never had to hear its irritating ring again."

Wonderful, she is in a cheery mood today, I thought to myself. Most intelligent people would make a run for it, but I was going to take it head on.

She sipped a Bloody Mary with a freshly cut celery stick languishing in the red liquid in a crystal glass, placed it down on a coaster on the table and sank back into the cushion of her sofa with a paper plate of saltines, a jar of peanut butter and a knife appropriately pointed in my direction as she spoke to me.

"Have a seat," she said, gesturing the knife toward a nearby chair.

There were many things wrong about this scene. It was like one of those puzzles in the back of a magazine that asks you to circle the objects that don't belong in a photograph. First of all, Olivia never ate food in her living room area. Second, she was eating on a paper plate, something she declared "only feeble minded poor trash use" to Quinn when she served Ralphie's cake on his favorite cartoon character paper plates for his third birthday. Quinn had cried the entire night after the party from exhaustion of trying to make everything perfect and being publicly reprimanded for her paper plate offense in front of all her friends and family.

The third thing wrong in the picture was that Olivia was grinning. She never grinned or smiled. She did, however, sneer often.

"Have a cracker, Lennon. You look pale," she said, the crumbs landing on the floor as she extended a saltine towards me.

"No thank you, but thank you anyway," I said, politely hoping for some normality to appear during this extremely odd visit.

She munched away for a while, and took a gulp of her Bloody Mary. Then, she belched loudly and cackled in her witch's laugh.

I almost fainted. She must be inebriated.

"I should come back when you feel better."

"I feel fine. I am not drunk if that is what you think. I have been nursing this same watered down drink for the last hour while I waited for you to arrive."

"I had to turn in an article before I came. I am sorry I was a little late."

"You are not sorry. I doubt you wanted to even come."

I nervously straightened and pulled at the hem of my black shift.

"Don't worry. I have not told a soul about you and your doctor friend."

"Thank you. There is really nothing to tell."

"You are a terrible liar, but that is not why I asked you here."

I let out the breath I had been holding since I stepped inside the door, and my stomach started to settle down its grumbling.

"I wanted to tell you about Mr. Vincent."

The way this odd exchange was going she would probably be asking me for his phone number.

"What did you want to tell me about Clark?"

"You young people don't listen," she said, hastily slamming down the crystal glass on the table with a few sprinkles of red Bloody Mary landing on her hand.

She licked them off. I had to pinch myself, because I was definitely in an alternate reality. If I had been fast enough I would have filmed it on my camera phone. Quinn would never believe me when I tell her the events of this meeting.

"I am talking about Clark's father, Mr. Vincent."

"Did you know him?"

"Shhh. I am not one of your silly people you interview for the paper. Be quiet, listen and you may learn something."

"Mr. Vincent and I grew up together. Our parents were friends. They used to have the most amazing parties in that grand old home they lived in. You saw it. It's the one Clark stayed at while he was here. Mr. Vincent and I would sneak away from the woman who was supposed to be looking after us children, and we would watch the grownups mingle and dance."

"Our parents spent vacations at the beach together in his family's cottage. He was a year ahead of me in school, but we always seemed to find each other as we got older at school functions, ball games and birthday parties."

"I had no idea you knew Clark's father."

"When we were in high school he called me and asked me if I thought my best friend would go with him to the school dance. Well, you can imagine. It was like someone had shot me in the heart."

"I asked her if she would, and she said yes. I never doubted that she would not say yes. Every girl our age had a crush on him. If you think Clark is a good looking man his father, Michael, was even more handsome."

"I filled punch glasses the entire night while they danced on the floor. It was the most pain I have ever experienced in my life."

I wanted to say to her that this sounded just like one of those 1980s Molly Ringwald movies, but I was fairly certain she would not get the reference.

"Their relationship did not last, and he had many other girlfriends when he went off to college the next year. We both worked at the beach that summer before I went off to Peace. I saw him at the Casino, a place we all used to go to after work, and he asked me to dance. I could not believe he finally felt something more than friendship for me. I was in love and I thought he was, too. We spent the entire summer together. It was the best time in my life."

"We wrote to each other every week. He went to school at UVA so there was a great distance between us. The letters from him started to come less and less and by Thanksgiving when we were supposed to meet each other back home they had stopped completely."

"I was startled by the news from his parents."

"They sat down with me and my parents. Lennon, I thought he had died. I thought they were going to tell me he was in a car accident or something. What they told me was much worse."

I was sitting on the edge of my seat. I had never pictured Olivia as someone who actually experienced this kind of romance filled tormented young love that you see on the screens and novels.

"He had eloped. The girl was pregnant, and I knew I would die. I seriously thought I would die. I did not come out of my bedroom, and I could not even make it back to Peace that semester. I never did return. My world had been torn apart, but I did not know what pain and being alone was until much later."

"What happened?"

"I met Jack's father at a soda shoppe downtown. He was a grown man, an attorney who had just moved to town. He was wealthy and many women had eyes for him, but he asked me to marry him and I accepted his proposal. I did not care about the money. I just did not want to be alone."

"Jack's father was a cold man. I did not know what alone meant until I was married. He never talked to me, and he would often go to social gatherings leaving me at home. My babies are the only things that kept me from running away."

"He always enjoyed a drink when he came home, but then it started to be more and he was not a good man to me, Lennon."

A tear showed in her eye.

"About nine years after I last saw Michael he appeared on my doorstep. Jack's father was at work, and we had a long conversation about our lives. Michael told me he was unhappy in his marriage. His wife constantly wanted material things and had committed adultery with a man where they lived in Virginia who was an extremely rich and well-known farmer and politician. She asked him for a divorce, and he was granting one. He told me all he could think of was me, and he asked me for a second chance."

"I loved my children more than anything. Sharing custody with Jack's father seemed like an intolerable proposition, so even though I knew I still loved Michael it was not something I could agree to immediately. I wished I had said yes when he first asked me."

"He told me he was returning home to Virginia that Sunday, and he would be back the following weekend for my answer."

"He never came. I was broken hearted once again. I found out later his wife had confronted the wealthy politician and told him she was pregnant and he would have to divorce his wife and marry her. He told her no, offered her money to terminate the pregnancy or raise it with Michael as their own child. She left enraged and was in a car accident which ended the baby's life and left her paralyzed from the waist down."

"They sent Clark to live with his grandparents that year while she recuperated. Michael never left her after that, and I received one letter from him that I have kept my entire life telling me he had always loved me, but he made a promise that he had to keep."

"Michael died when he was 50 from a heart attack and his wife soon after."

The tears had fallen from my own eyes, and I had not even noticed the wetness on my cheeks as I was so enthralled by her story.

"I wanted to share my story with you, because I see that same torment in your eyes that I felt."

She paused and took another sip of her Bloody Mary.

"Do you love the doctor?"

"I don't know," I said, and that was the truth.

"If you do, let him know how you feel. There are no second chances."

I took a peanut butter cracker she offered, and we sat for a few minutes in silence as I digested the cracker and her story.

"I did tell all of this to your friend, Clark, before he left. I called him over here to talk. He did not even know I knew his father."

"How did he react?"

"He told me he had always assumed it was his father who was at fault. He never knew about his mother's affair."

I left Olivia's house that afternoon with my thoughts reeling over how Clark must feel now. He was looking for answers with his book, and invariably he had found them on his journey. I wanted more than anything to talk with him. I hoped I would get a chance, but he would probably never return here now that he had found out

such tormenting news about his family.
He had no reason to return.

26 BIG NEWS

The golden autumn leaves were falling from the trees as I rocked in the porch swing listening to music while I waited for my parents to come home.

Mom called early this morning asking me to come over tonight for dinner.

"We have some big news," she said, excitedly.

I could not imagine what they wanted to share with me. I hoped they were finally taking a cruise, or Dad was buying a new recliner for Christmas.

Quinn, Jack and Ralphie unloaded from their minivan and came up the steps with Jack holding a large dish.

"What is it?"

"I made a pumpkin pie," Quinn said.

"Oh, my favorite."

"I know. That is why I made it."

She and Jack exchanged a worried look. I hoped they were not on the outs again.

He squeezed her shoulder and gave her a soft kiss on her cheek as they walked into the house. Scratch that theory. I was contemplating what their worried exchange meant when Ralphie ran back onto the porch and plopped on the other side of the swing holding a book.

"Read to me, Aunt Lennon."

I picked up the book that he had located on my parents' bookshelf.

"This is one of my favorites. It is about a pig and his best friend who is a spider."

"How can a pig and a spider be friends?"

"I don't know, bud. Sometimes life just happens that way."

It was not a logical answer, but I of all people did not understand relationships even between fictional animals.

I began to read to him as the swing lulled us into a tranquil space.

It was not long before I saw my parents' car pull into the driveway. Mom was holding a folder as my father got out of the car carrying a bag of takeout food. He was almost back to regular speed since his surgery, and he had a celebration the day Mrs. Ella's services were no longer needed.

"Hey, my honey bunnies," she said, grinning at us in the swing. "Come on in. Let's go have a seat in the living room."

"This must be real big news," I whispered to Quinn, who was sitting beside me on the sofa. "I think Dad is going to get that new flat screen that he keeps talking about."

Quinn flinched and looked the other way.

Ralphie was on the floor playing with a puzzle he had pulled down from the toy shelf Mom had created for him from our old toys, and Jack was sitting in an armchair staring straight ahead.

Mom and Dad stood at the front of the room as if there was an invisible podium. I thought she might flick an imaginary microphone testing it for sound quality, but instead Dad began to clear his throat.

"Your mother and I have decided it is time for a

change."

I looked over at Quinn, but she was avoiding my every nudge and attempt to get her attention.

"It is something we have not taken lightly. We have weighed all aspects of this decision," said Mom.

"We are moving to the beach," said Dad.

I swallowed heavily. I looked at my sister and her husband. They both had known.

"You knew and did not tell me," I said, looking at Quinn.

"Jack is preparing the closing, so yes, we did know," said Quinn.

"Don't be upset, Lennon. We asked them not to tell. It is our surprise to you."

"What do you mean? I am confused."

"We talked it over with your sister, and we would like to give you the house."

"What? How can you pay for a condo at the beach without selling the house?"

"We have some money in our savings, and Jack got us a real good deal. The condo is part of a retirement community."

"But how could you leave?"

"It is what would make us happy right now," she said.

I got up and wrapped my arms around both of them giving them big kisses on their cheeks.

"I am so happy for you, but I will be lost without you. Thank you so much. You are the best parents in the world."

"It is only a few hours away. We have two extra bedrooms, so you can all come live with us if you want," she said.

"Can I? Can I?" asked Ralphie.

We all laughed. I wanted my parents to be happy, but I would miss them dearly.

"You are all welcome to move back with me, too," I said.

Quinn came up beside me.

"I felt so terrible keeping this from you, but they said if I said anything you would probably not let them give you the house."

"They were right. I would not have let them. It is not fair to you. This is your house, too."

"Lennon, I own at least half of my dream house by the river. It would not be fair for me to ask for half of yours."

It was true. I had always loved the house we had grown up in.

"Thank you, Quinn. You know I love you, right."

"I kind of had an idea," she said, giving me a hug.

The kitchen table was littered with Chinese takeout boxes, paper plates and abandoned chopsticks except for the two in my hand which I used to capture a piece of broccoli out of one of the boxes.

Everyone was talking and relaxed when Jack stood up and reached for Quinn's hand who was sitting beside him.

"We are so happy for Patrick and Rachael. We are coming to visit y'all often. Lennon, you are the best. You deserve this house. Just don't paint every room Carolina blue."

"Well, some of them will be purple, my second favorite color," I said, laughing.

"We did not want you guys to have all the fun today, so we are sharing our own fantastic news," he said unable to cease grinning as he spoke. "Quinn, why don't you tell them?"

"I'm pregnant."

Everyone gasped and began wishing them congratulations at once. I gave Ralphie an enormous hug, swinging him in the air.

"I'm gonna be the best big brother."

"There is no doubt in my mind, Ralphie."

"Was this a surprise?" I whispered to Quinn.

"It was a meant to be surprise. I think it happened during our shower escapade," she said, blushing.

"Well, that is something you both will never forget."

I hesitated before asking, "Was this the reason you were so ready to give up your email?"

"No, I ended that before I even found out. I went to the doctor a couple of days ago. When he told me I was in shock, but a happy shock."

"It will be a spring baby. I already said this, but I really am happy, Lennon."

I looked around the room at the smiling faces.

"I think we are all happy."

* * * * *

I held a tiny silver locket in my hand in the shape of a sand dollar.

"I think I will take it. I would like to have it wrapped," I said.

"That is a wonderful choice," said the woman, who was not frowning for the first time since I arrived in the shop.

I glanced at the woman again unable to understand how the women thought she was the mistress of the town. I still wondered if that had been her jogging with Dean after the women had talked about her having an affair with a married physician, but the entire scene could only have been a figment of my imagination.

She showed me a variety of boxes and gift wrap when the door opened with the sound of chiming bells.

I looked up and saw a tall man with blond hair entering through the doorway. At first sight I thought it was Dean. As he came closer I realized it was a familiar face, but it did not belong to my doctor. It was another doctor.

"Excuse me," the woman said to me as she walked swiftly to meet the man.

I could not hear what they were saying, but I could tell from their gestures he was not buying a gift. I continued to look through the store at the gifts, attempting to be invisible and feeling as though I was witnessing something that should not be seen.

He walked back out the door, the bells chiming to single his departure.

"I think this is the one," I said, pointing to a purple paper with ladybugs. "Ladybugs are good luck."

"Great."

"This will be the perfect gift for my sister at her baby shower."

"I think I am going to order a similar locket for my little one," she said, rubbing her belly.

I was stunned. The woman had to be in her mid to late 40s. The shock must have been apparent on my face.

She laughed, "I know. It was a big surprise. I did not even think I could have a child at my age."

I did not know why she was opening up to me, but maybe she had seen the social media milkshake hamburger photographs and knew I was not a fan of the mommy mob.

I left the shop with mixed emotions. After witnessing the scene between the two people, I was overjoyed that it had not been Dean jogging with her on the road. On the other hand, why should I be so elated? I did not want to be in the shop owner's position, a mistress pregnant by a married man.

I looked at my phone. I had erased Dean from my contacts, but it had been a day by day struggle not to contact him.

I had tried to stay focused on my writing, helping my

parents move and getting ready for a niece.

* * * * *

Everything was yellow at the baby shower. The linens, the flowers, the plates, the food and the attire of everyone at the party except for me were a bright yellow hue. I stood out like a black cloud amongst the sunshine in Tara's large Florida room overlooking the river.

"I guess you did not get the invitation," said one of the women, snickering at my basic black dress and heels, my safety outfit for every slightly less than formal occasion.

"No, I did," I said, a fib that was needed to not let the mommy gang get the best of me.

Another woman behind me guffawed at my comment, and I turned and had to bite my tongue at the reply I so desired to direct at Piper.

Instead I said, "Hello, Piper."

I grabbed a cheese straw and popped it into my mouth.

I wanted to say something sassy about snapping a picture while my mouth was full, but I felt like karma had already repaid that debt.

The mommies had already begun to talk behind her back, and soon she would find her invitations to parties would fade.

"Psst, did you hear about Piper's husband? He got that woman who owns the jewelry store pregnant."

I did not know the woman who was whispering to me, but I assumed she was one of the hangers on. She saw a position soon to be vacated from the mommy mob, and she was pouncing on the opportunity. I felt like telling her that I was the last person she needed to be talking to if she wanted to become part of the group.

"It happens," I said, moving on from the cloud of

gossip afraid that it would linger like a bad luck stain on my sister's special day.

Tara came up beside me.

"Piper is having a real hard time. She will not even admit what is going on. She keeps referring to her husband as if the whole town doesn't know he impregnated the town harlot. I didn't believe a woman that old was still fertile, but maybe she just looks old. My mama always told me certain women get that used up look early in life if they say yes to every man that asks."

I took a sip of the flavored crushed pineapple punch.

"You could give Piper some advice on how to live by yourself without a man," Tara said, smiling.

I could swear I saw her fangs appear.

"It's really easy especially when the alternative is living with a complete idiot," I responded.

"I am so lucky I have Steve," she said, putting an emphasis on the "I" evidently still afraid that I was out to steal her horrible husband.

I decided to play her game.

"You are so lucky to have Steve. I saw him at the gym the other day, and I could tell he is really working out."

She pouted up. I had a feeling Tara would be accompanying Steve to the gym for at least the next couple of weeks.

When Quinn arrived Tara presented her with a bouquet of a dozen yellow roses.

Quinn looked so happy among her friends, so I attempted to put on a smiling face for the rest of the afternoon.

The shower was a success I had to admit. The food was scrumptious, and everything was a beautiful yellow from a distance.

"Thanks for coming, Sis. I know my friends aren't

your favorite people, but they do have their good qualities once you get to know them."

I rolled my eyes and kept my mouth shut as she returned to her group of friends.

I picked up a carrot, and there was a loud snap when I bit into it.

"Lennon, we can fix you a plate to take home. You sound like you are hungry," Tara said, knowing how to issue a mannerly offer while stabbing a person in the stomach.

"Actually, do you have some crackers? My stomach is feeling a little woozy."

"There is a basket of crackers at the end of the table with various cheeses and spreads."

"I think I will leave off the spreads, but a plain cracker may do the trick."

"What trick?" asked Quinn, approaching us in between her baby shower games.

"You know my stomach. I just need a cracker. Go back to your games and have fun."

Quinn returned to the group who were busily playing a name game.

I walked back and forth, but the pain in my stomach grew. I looked at my phone and checked when I was supposed to get my period, but it was a week away. It could not be cramps. Maybe I had eaten something that did not agree with me.

The pain began to be severe in my abdomen, but I was determined to make it through the shower. Maybe it was something resulting from my appendectomy. I leaned against a door frame unable to join the group, because if I moved I may have screamed out in pain. If I could just stand still and breathe I knew it would go away. My clenched fists were wet. Beads of perspiration began to fall from my neck and slide down my back. The pain increased, but I did not move. A fake smile was plastered on my face, and I would shake my head occasionally whenever someone would begin to talk to me. Although, by this time I was so far gone in my zombie like pain daze that I did not hear a word they said.

Quinn was laughing, and then she turned to look at me and said something.

I nodded again, still smiling, but not hearing a word she said, focused on surviving this pain.

She got up and moved towards me.

"Lennon, Lennon."

She took her hand and felt my forehead.

She was moving her hands, and all the women gathered round.

Everything went black, and I felt my back sliding against the door frame. I landed somehow with my bottom on the floor without killing myself.

"You fainted," said Quinn.

Tara brought me a cold compress which Quinn held on my head.

"Are you allergic to something?" said a woman beside me.

"No."

"Is she pregnant?" asked Tara.

I laughed. "That would be a miracle."

"I think it is her…ulcers," said Quinn.

Quinn had not said the word cancer, but she was probably thinking it. When you have one brush with that villain you are constantly on the lookout for the Evil C's return.

I looked down, and I was unaware that I had been holding my stomach.

"Oh, no. It can't be," I said.

Quinn had her phone out and walked into another room.

"Can you walk Lennon, or do I need to call an

ambulance?"

"I can walk I think."

Tara helped me to my feet.

"We can take my van," she said.

"Where are you all taking me?"

"To the hospital."

"No, absolutely not. I am fine, besides I just finished paying for my surgery. I don't need to rack up another set of bills."

"Don't be foolish. Get in the car," said Quinn, following behind me.

Tara drove us as if she was at Daytona to the hospital. I was seeing an entirely new side of the mommy mob. Maybe Quinn had been right about her friends.

When Tara drove up in the semicircle carport to the emergency room entrance, she quickly exited the car and found a nurse who brought out a wheel chair.

Seeing Quinn, the nurse immediately thought she was the person in need.

"No, it's my sister," she said, gesturing to me as I half slid out of the seat onto the pavement before plummeting into the wheelchair.

I wondered if everyone who entered the hospital saw their lives change as dramatically as mine did every time that I crossed through the sliding glass doors.

The first time I entered by way of an ambulance I had my appendix removed, changed careers and moved next door to my parents. The second time I visited my father who made his own life changing decision to pick up and move after his surgery, and I found myself in the arms of a married man.

"What's going to happen to me today?" I asked aloud.

The nurse shook her head. "I don't know. The doctor will be with you shortly."

She and another nurse managed to help me onto a bed and check my vitals while I formed a small ball hugging my knees to my chest. I could not cry, because I was in such pain that it hurt to breathe.

Quinn walked into the room, and stared at me with a shocked look.

"The doctor will be here soon. It will be alright."

I moaned.

"What can I do?"

She got up, panicked at the sight of my pain.

"He will be here soon. I had trouble getting past his receptionist, but Tara took over and he was on the phone in seconds."

"Tell her thank you," I said.

Tara had really shown her true colors today, and I was astounded to find out she had a heart.

Quinn kept looking at her phone and the clock on the wall.

"He said he would be here soon."

"Dr. Whitley's office is across town. He is probably in some afternoon traffic."

She shook her head with a confused look on her face.

"I did not call your primary physician," she said.

I was not thinking clearly. Who would she have called?

The door opened and there he was in a yellow short sleeve button up shirt and khakis.

"Hey, there."

I wanted to pull the sheet over my head, but I did not feel like lifting it.

"What seems to be the problem, Lennon?"

I looked at him with my slanted eyes, "Really? You have to ask? I am in pain!" I said louder than I expected.

He smiled and looked at my sister who shook her head and threw her hands up as if to say, "I don't know what's wrong with her."

"When was the date of your last period?" he said, looking at his clipboard.

"I'm not pregnant."

"Let me get a nurse, so I can examine you."

"Whatever."

He left the room. "What's wrong, Lennon? Why are you acting so rude to Dr. Kent?"

I rubbed my stomach and abdomen as if it would stop the pain.

"Ask him."

I did not realize how angry I was with Dean until I saw his face. I understood why he chose not to meet me at park that night, but I still was hurt that he did not even address it with me and offer an explanation in an email, phone call or text. He had continued to email me and I had given in, not following Quinn's advice, and the pattern started all over again. I don't know if I was in love, but I was deeply infatuated with the idea of being with him. I tried every day to stop emailing him, but it was a struggle.

The town's own medical Adonis returned with a petite nurse with extremely short black hair and an annoying giggle at every word he spoke.

"Can you give us a minute?" he asked Quinn.

After Quinn left the room, the nurse asked me to sit up. Dean washed his hands and then dried them off before slipping on latex gloves.

He began to touch my stomach, and I let out some groans of discomfort.

"We need to do a CT scan immediately," he said to the nurse.

She left the room, and I looked into his eyes.

"Don't worry, Lennon. I promise I am going to take care of you."

He squeezed my hand and the door shut behind him.

After the CT scan, the nurse said the doctor would

return with the results. I was surprised when a very short bald man entered the room, and under his name tag were the letters OB/GYN.

He reached out his hand and shook mine.

"I am Dr. Gogh. Has anyone ever told you that you have endometriosis?"

Within five minutes I learned that my pain had not been ulcers but the result of my severe case of endometriosis. He was going to operate to hopefully alleviate the pain.

When I awoke from my surgery and was wheeled back to my room in a fog, Quinn, Mom and Dad were waiting while a dancing reality show played on the television in the background.

"Hey, honey," Mom said.

"You are going to be fine. The doctor said the surgery was a success. Dr. Gogh will check on you tomorrow morning, and then you may be able to go home."

"Did they...will I still be able to have children?"

The thought sent me into a terrified state of never even being able to consider having a baby in the future with my reproductive system in shambles.

"Of course, Lennon. Why would you think otherwise?" she asked.

I breathed a sigh of relief as Quinn told me Dr. Gogh had to remove a cyst, but he did not find anything that he thought could be cancer.

My family eventually left me to rest, which was hardly the case with nurses coming in and out of the room to take blood and monitor me the entire night.

I heard a knock at my door in the middle of the night, and I looked up and saw Dean. He smiled that amazing smile that made me catch my breath.

"I just finished a surgery, and I wanted to check on you."

The fog from my anesthesia had lifted, and I was able to concentrate on his words while being quite mellow from the pain killers.

"Thank you. Dr. Gogh said you immediately knew what was wrong and called him. If it had not been for your diagnosis in the ER, the cyst may have continued to grow."

"I was just doing my job."

"No, you say that, but that isn't true. You know what you have done for me, what you mean to me."

He pulled up a chair and sat beside my bed. I could smell the familiar detergent from his clothes.

"How do you feel?"

I ignored the obvious response, and I don't know if it was the pain killers or his nearness to me, but I decided to cut right to the matter.

"I don't know why I feel the way I do, maybe it is because you have always been so nice to me or saved my life, but you know the way I feel."

He turned and stared at an object on the wall.

"I have put my book on the back burner. It will be a good project for me when I retire."

"That is at least 15 years from now," I said, adding up the years in my dazed state.

"I know."

"Why didn't you meet me at the waterfront?"

He did not answer me.

"It's not like I was asking you to marry me."

"I am married, Lennon."

I wanted to say I was obviously joking and respond with a joke, but I could see he was not in a humorous mood.

What I really should have asked was, "Why did you continue to play with my emotions by emailing me when you knew how I felt about you?"

Instead, I turned into a tongue-tied mess and told him

thank you again before he left.

Thank goodness for the pain killers that lulled me back to sleep, or I would have died of sheer embarrassment.

It was a month before I would see Dean again. I felt someone tap me on the shoulder in line at the coffee shop one night, and he motioned for me to have a seat at a table after we placed our beverage orders.

He mentioned the soccer team he was coaching and something in the news.

He paused and looked down at his feet.

"I've been doing some home improvements."

"Really."

"I built an outdoor shower."

He was unable to look me in the eye as he described how he enrolled in an online home improvement class and learned how to install the appropriate plumbing and use the right tools.

Maybe it was a coincidence and I was overthinking things as usual, but I knew it was not. When I emailed him about my dream home at the beach I had talked extensively about an outdoor shower and the way the sunshine felt on my bare skin as the cool water and breeze from the ocean cascaded over my body.

I did not know what he wanted me to say. We finished our beverages with the remainder of the conversation about trivial things I would not remember the next day.

"Thank you for everything," I said, as he walked me to my car.

He wrapped his arms around me in a friendly hug that I knew he gave to most of his patients like 85-year-old Vera. But I could not stand to just be another patient any longer.

I pulled him close and laid my head against he chest.

I stared into his brown eyes and then felt my arms

gently pushing him away. As he walked towards his car, I whispered in a voice that he was unable to hear, "I would have given you my everything."

If he did hear my words, he never turned around.

I knew that would be the last time I would let myself feel anything for him. It hurt too much to be around a man that could steal my soul with a mere look or gesture.

I sent him an email.

From: Lennon Tyler
To: Dr. Dean Kent

A person once said to me you never have to write the words "the end." It is obvious when a good story ends.

27 I DISCOVERED MY SPINE

"This photograph is amazing," said my editor.

"Clark Vincent shot it on the Outer Banks last summer," I said, fondly remembering the day when we walked along the beach.

"I can't believe it's you," he said. "You look so relaxed."

"He works magic with his lens. Underneath those sunglasses I was fast asleep, so I was pretty relaxed."

Clark and I had begun to email shortly after my surgery. You would have thought I had canceled my account after my escapades with Dean, but actually Clark and I had developed a nice friendship with him emailing me photographs of his travels. There was nothing ever serious discussed or deeply meaningful. It was just how's it going kind of frivolous stuff. I did not panic when I did not receive a reply or message from him like I did with Dean. We were just friends, and I was content with being alone. Besides, as far as I knew, he never planned on returning to this area.

My home was full of people for my house warming

get together. I had much rather turned on my speakers and listened to music while I read a good book on my comfy purple sofa. A party was the last thing I had wanted, but Quinn and my parents had been persuading me to open myself up to new possibilities.

"You have done some lovely things here," said Sophia, my mother's sassy friend who brought her latest boyfriend, a man close to her age which was unusual.

"Here's my card. I helped her with the design and style. Lennon would have filled the entire place with thrift store relics if it had not been for me," said Tara.

I laughed good naturedly at Tara. Amazingly we had become friends over the past year, and she had helped Quinn decorate her new nursery and my new home. We encouraged her to use her abandoned design degree to open up a freelancing business which had taken off rapidly.

She was still Tara with her bitter comments, but I had learned she was a good friend.

"I think I will take one of those, Tara," said Olivia, who was dressed to the nines in a Chanel suit and sipping a glass of champagne. "I want to liven up my sunroom with some color."

Quinn was in the kitchen with Ralphie, and Jack had little Sanderling in his arms. She was wearing the silver sand dollar locket I had given Quinn at the baby shower.

"We have a special present for you. Ralphie do the honors," said Quinn.

Ralphie picked up a large present the size of a square basketball wrapped in a glistening purple foil wrap with a Carolina blue bow.

"Thank you little man," I said, bending down to give him a hug.

I placed it on the kitchen island and opened it carefully so I would not rip the paper. I lifted the lid of the box and pulled out our grandparent's pottery bowl that had been in Quinn's home.

"It was meant to be yours," said Quinn. "It was just waiting for you to find your home."

My parents walked in through the back door at the second I held the bowl in my hands.

"Wonderful. You have Mama's bowl. You know it meant so much to her. One day I will sit down and tell you girls the story," Mom said.

"Maybe that's what Lennon's next book should be about," said Quinn.

"You come from a long line of storytellers. It is only natural that Lennon has the gift," said Dad.

My parents both looked so happy as they talked. They had the air of beach people, those fortunate enough to wake up to the sound of the ocean.

I placed the bowl on the mantel above the fireplace where the flicker of the fire would catch the deep colors in the finish of the curve of the bowl.

"It looks absolutely splendid. I don't even recognize it as the same home, and that is the way it should be. You made it your own," said Mom.

"You and Dad are welcome to come back at any time," I said.

"No, this is your home. We are truly happy at the beach. I never thought I would be able to say that at my age and it be the truth, but it is and I am so grateful for every day."

"I know what you mean. I have never been so content in my life."

"That man over there is rather handsome. What is his name?"

I laughed aloud.

"No, Mom. I am afraid you won't be playing match maker with him. He is the new pastor at Quinn's church. I interviewed him last week for the paper. I invited him over to welcome him into the community, and if you notice he has a very nice wife standing right beside him."

"Oh, well. There is this attractive man who is living next door to your dad and me. He is going through a divorce, but I will try to get his name and see if I can connect with him on a social networking website so you can check him out."

I gave my mother a hug.

"Really Mom, I am very content with being alone right now. Besides with my writing night owl hours no one would want to be around me."

She looked up at me since I was several inches taller and stared.

"Are you alright, Mom?"

"Yes. I think you are, too. I think I am finally realizing that now as I see you in your home and I read your wonderful words. I am glad you have made your life about you. So many women lose themselves in a marriage and then end up hating their spouses later. If you find someone I know you will be happy, but if you don't I still know you will be happy."

She grabbed my hand and kissed it. Then her friend, Sophia, came up behind her and lightened the mood by introducing Mom to her new boyfriend.

I stood back from the group of people, and I felt a warm feeling in the pit of my soul. It was nice to be around so many people that I knew and cared about, their voices mingling like a song of life that I would always remember.

The next afternoon while I was sitting at my desk writing my story for the newspaper clicking away at the keyboard, I heard a knock and then a loud truck shortly pull away. Usually I wrote with music playing in the background, but for some reason I wanted a quiet, tranquil environment today. It was like I knew something was going to happen and it did. I opened the door, and a delivery was on the porch.

My hands trembled as I read the return address.

I ran my fingertips over the package, and I felt a lump in my throat. I did not know whether I was going to cry, dance or faint from the unreal fever that seeped through my veins as I realized what I had longed for more than anything was in my hands.

I felt like I needed to fully appreciate its significance, so I placed the package on my dining room table. I went over to the kitchen to make myself my favorite hot chocolate with a handful of marshmallows.

I turned on some music and began to dance around the room feeling the excitement course through my muscles. As I spun around the room doing my perfect imitation of Wonder Woman circles, I stopped suddenly when a mirror caught my reflection.

The image of the person in the mirror was one of a self-confident extremely optimistic person who just reached her lifelong goal.

I ripped open the package and held the bound book in my hands. I smelled the pages of freshly printed ink as my thumb slid across the smooth spine.

I laughed to myself. "I finally have a spine."

I looked at my bookshelf where Clark's book of photographs had a home, and now my own book would be placed by its side. I hoped to one day fill the shelf with my stories.

During the last year, whenever someone would ask me what my book was about I felt as if I could not answer. For some reason I thought it would break the flow of my words or cause me to lose control of the characters by inviting comments and distracting opinions.

The truth was the story began to unfold in my mind the day Olivia told me the story of her life. I added the details which were pure fiction to a love that could never be. I asked Olivia if she was comfortable with me using her story as an inspiration for my novel during one of Quinn's Sunday family brunches, and she stopped drinking her Mimosa.

"The character must say yes, before he returns home and his wife is in the life altering accident, she must say yes," said Olivia, with a tear in her eye. "I have always wanted to know what would have happened if she said yes."

When I began to write I started with the characters in their own time period, and that was unfamiliar to me, so I set them in the present day amidst social media.

It was not unfamiliar territory.

I flipped through the pages of the book in my hands, elated that my dream had been achieved.

It was exactly five minutes before I texted Quinn, and I am pretty sure I heard her shouts of joy across the river.

28 YOU REMEMBERED

The sidewalks and streets were icy after a snow melted and refroze during the night. I decided I would walk downtown to my interview in lieu of playing winter bumper cars with another vehicle.

I wrapped up in a pair of tights, corduroys, a turtleneck, sweater, scarf, coat and hat with earflaps. My boots came up to my knees and my gloves made any kind of hand movement non-existent, so I plunged them into the pockets of my coat.

A few people waved to me, but I found it difficult to remove my hands from my pockets so I nodded hello.

From a distance the icy surface of the river with snow covered knobs from tree roots and branches along its edges had the faint qualities of a root beer float.

As I crossed the road and lifted my foot onto the curb I felt the heel of my boot start to give, and I landed flat on my rear shouting out for everyone to hear.

I made several attempts to get back onto my feet, but it was quite impossible with all my layers. I was about to give up and start calling out for help when an arm was extended before me.

The person lifted me to my feet in one quick precise motion.

"Lennon, I have never known anyone who could make me smile the way you do."

The voice was muffled beneath my earflaps, and my hat had fallen over my eyes so I could not see.

The hat was pulled back off my face by his strong fingers, and I do not recall another feeling in my life that was equivalent.

He peeled off his own glove, and opened his hand.

In his palm was a shell.

"You remembered."

ABOUT THE AUTHOR

Anna Goodwin McCarthy is a freelance writer in Elizabeth City, N.C. She earned a bachelor's degree in journalism and mass communication from the University of North Carolina at Chapel Hill and a master's degree in library science from East Carolina University. McCarthy believes true happiness is reading a book while listening to the sound of the ocean's waves.